Evie

By E.P. Stuart

For all of those who want to have their cake... and eat it too.

SBN (Trade Paperback): 978-1-0670204-0-8
ISBN (ebook): 978-1-0670204-1-5

Evie. First published in 2024

Evie is a work of fiction. Names, characters, places and incidents are either the product of the author's imagination or are used fictitiously. Any resemblance to actual persons, living or dead, businesses, companies, events or locales is entirely coincidental.

Cover art and photography © Bianca Worboys

This edition published by arrangement with E.P Stuart.

Dedications

To my dearest husband, thank you for your unwavering love and support. Without you, I would never have dreamed I could keep a husband and indulge in writing this story. Words can't express how much you mean to me; you are my soul mate and the love of my life.

To Drew and Trish, thanks for cheering me on and encouraging me to finish this book. Your guidance, industry knowledge and friendship are invaluable.

To the many women in my life who inadvertently and innocently brushed against me, thank you for the many starting points in which I could indulge my imagination.

And last, but by no means least, to the girl that lit a fire inside me all those years ago. My life is richer for having known you and you will always be the only woman I have ever loved. You're always in my heart, even though we are no longer in each other's lives.

Content Warning

Dear Reader,

While the following romance is a saucy tale, designed to excite and evoke emotion, there are scenes that some readers may find disturbing.

This story is ultimately a love story, but one that touches on dark themes. A list of trigger warnings has been included at the back of this book for sensitive readers. My hope is that the themes I have touched on are handled appropriately within the context, bringing emotions of drama rather than trauma.

I've done my best to handle the above with nuance and compassion. Please take care of yourself while reading.

With love,
E.P. Stuart

One

Evie

My name is Evie and I have a secret.

It's not something you bring up in everyday conversation. So, I keep my thoughts to myself. The conversations I have these days are about my children. What they're doing, what their school is fundraising for.

I am, actually, no longer, known as Evie. I'm Jackson and Hannah's mum. I'll admit I only know the other mums based on who their children are too. It's a bit sad to lose your identity and it feels *very* anonymous.

In the school circle I keep friendships cordial and functional. Just because we aren't the one's attending school doesn't mean that we aren't still part of the grapevine.

Gossip is currency.

So, I hold my secret close.

They just wouldn't understand. It's not my fault if I notice the nape of a female friend's neck or a sparkle in their eye. They wouldn't feel an internal quiver when a hand accidentally brushes against you during a hug at the school drop off.

You see, the thing is, I *like* women.

That's my *secret*.

I'm happily married, with kids, but I can't help noticing beautiful women around me. Now don't get me wrong, I don't like *all* women. But sometimes, someone just walks into your life and takes your breath away.

The first moment I saw her, I knew I was in trouble.

It was the first day of school for the year. The warm sun cast dappled light through the branches of the tall oaks lining the school entrance. I said goodbye to Hannah at the gate and I paused to watch her run over to a little girl I'd never seen before. The little girl was being embraced affectionately by a woman with soft, curly brown hair. Her whole face emanated love, from the smile on her lips to the crinkles at the corners of her closed eyes. As she let go, she watched her daughter embrace mine. Somehow our eyes met across the path despite all the chaos of the adults and kids in the school drop off zone. She smiled at me warmly, enjoying a mum-to-mum proud moment.

There was something else in her eyes… a flicker… no, a spark?

Well, whatever it was, it was fleeting because another parent walked between our gaze and broke the connection. By the time I caught sight of her again, she had turned and was walking back to her car.

Nice bum.

I sigh. Another gorgeous woman I'll never touch.

"Hey Evie, don't forget about the committee meeting tomorrow night!" Sandra, a fellow mum and member of the school parents committee, breaks into my thoughts.

"Sure thing, Sandra! It's in my calendar." I call back over the heads of children dashing to their classes. Glancing at my watch, I realise I need to get to work. Thank goodness the meet the teacher and orientation was yesterday and my husband, Steve was able to show Hannah to her new classroom then.

I head to the boutique insurance call centre I work for with my own music blaring loudly from my speakers. I'm not exactly old at 34, but I miss the freedom to have complete control over my car audio system. The bright chartreuse building front of my workplace springs into view as I pull into the staff parking area. Their branding is bold with lotus flowers drawn daintily on the side. At Lotus Business and Family Insurance (LBFI), we cater mainly to families and small businesses and offer a range of bespoke insurance packages.

I put my handbag on my desk then carry my lunch to the staffroom and make myself a coffee. The grind and whirr of the real coffee machine is loud, but it calms me. Abigail, the owner, spared no expense in making her staff feel appreciated. Coffee in hand I return to my desk and pick up my headset.

"Nice of you to finally join us, Evie." Greg snidely remarks over the sound barrier between our desks.

"You know I work part time, Greg." I roll my eyes. I'm not getting into this with him, again. The phone switchboard is flashing, indicating a waiting caller. I click on it, grateful for the excuse to not talk to Greg.

"Welcome to LBFI, Evie speaking. How may I help you?"

Greg scowls at me and returns to his own work screen. I roll my eyes at my computer and happily type away as I listen to the gentleman on the phone. He has a small plumbing business and is thinking of changing insurance companies. I'm in my element as different packages that will suit his needs spring to mind. Fifteen minutes later I've signed him up to our deluxe plan and he's decided to bring his private health, car and contents insurance to us too. Pulling up the new business spreadsheet I proudly enter the new details. Another new client gets me closer to earning a monthly bonus.

Two more this month and I'll be the top salesperson again.

At lunch I mention Greg's sarcasm to my supervisor, Josie, but she laughs it off.

"Don't worry about Greg, the sour-puss. Abigail and I know that you close more claims and secure new business in your 20 hours than he does in his 40! Well done by the way, that new plumbing business will really help us reach our targets for the month."

"Thanks Josie."

I'm so lucky to have two female bosses. Abigail is hands on and a mum herself. She runs a tight ship, but she is fair and understanding. Josie, her second in command, is more of a friend than a supervisor and I praise my good fortune in finding this role when Jackson turned three. I've been here over a year now and it has brought back part of my sanity.

Becoming a mum is one of my greatest achievements but I was under prepared for the round the clock hours. Now I'm not complaining, being in a position where we could afford for me to be a stay-at-home mum for five years is a privilege and I know many parents do not have the same luxury. But boy, is parenthood tough. Hannah didn't sleep through the night until she started school at five and Jackson still wakes at least once or twice a night. I lost myself those first five years. I was a milk-making, nappy changing, toilet training, cooking, cleaning, appeasing, argument-mediating machine.

Thankfully, I now have the respite of working 20 hours a week, with half of them in a clean office, the other half from home. It feels so good to use the brain I was given and indulge in adult-to-adult conversations again.

Having some child-free space in my day has also re-ignited my sex life with Steve. It's amazing what a bit of distance from the kids, a little financial independence and a gym membership can do for the body and soul.

Finishing my lunch, my mind is pulled back to the task at hand. My afternoon flies by in a whir of phone calls, emails and closing of claims. Before I know it the *beep-beep* of my alarm sounds and it's time to pick up the kids. I shut down my computer and wave to my colleagues as I dash out the door. I chuckle to myself as I catch a last glower from Greg who won't finish until five. I already know I've beaten him with the number of claims I've logged for the day.

The office is less than fifteen minutes away from the kids' school and I arrive to get one of the last three carparks before the bell rings. Walking briskly up to the main entrance to wait for Hannah, I spot my friend Rachael standing at the gate. We embrace and banter about the chaos of the last few days before returning to school. Lily, another mum joins us. It's so nice that our children are all in the same year at school. Rachael gabbers on about her son, Archie, refusing to wear the outfit she'd set out for him that morning and Lily chimes in with her recollection of her daughter, Willow, screaming as she tried to brush her hair before school. I do my best to be engaged in the conversation. However, I've just glimpsed the woman from this morning over Rachael's shoulder. As she approaches the gate, I can't help but notice she's wearing a mid-thigh sundress, showing off her toned legs. It's very *distracting*.

"Excuse me ladies, there's a woman over there I haven't met but I think our daughters are friends. I might just go say hello. Rachael, catch up for a coffee over the weekend?"

"Yeah sure! I'll message you later." Rachael opens her phone and I know she's setting an event in her calendar. Lily looks disappointed that I didn't invite her, but I don't know her that well. Rachael starts yammering on to Lily about something else Archie got up to over the holidays and I'm relieved to see the disappointment lessen on her face.

I must make more of an effort to get to know that woman.

I take a breath and make my way over to introduce myself. She's wearing sunglasses, but as I approach she pushes them up to the top of her head so I can see her eyes. They're an earthy dark brown and they sparkle warmly at me.

"Hi, I'm Evie. We haven't met." I beam welcomely. "I'm Hannah's mum. I believe our daughters are friends."

"Hi, I'm Simone, Katie's mum." Her smile reaches all the way to her eyes and my stomach does a small flip.

Wow. She's beautiful.

My appraising thoughts are abruptly interrupted as I am ploughed by an excited six-year-old with a heavy backpack.

"Mummy! Can I have a playdate with Katie? Please!" She bounces up and down with little Katie beside her. Simone and I laugh at their excitement and even though we have literally just met, we exchange small nods.

"Yes, that can be arranged. Are you busy this Saturday Simone?" I ask while the girls' tremble with anticipation.

"I'm sorry, we're busy this Saturday." Simone says regretfully. The girls bottom lips fall and Simone and I exchange an 'awww' look with our eyes. "But we're not doing anything right now if you'd like to visit for an hour?"

The girls burst into a fit of giggles and 'yes's' as they hug and jump up and down at the same time.

"Is that OK with you?" Simone asks. "It's very last minute."

I look at how happy the girls are. "Well, how could I say no to that! It looks like we're coming to yours. I just need to get my four-year-old, Jackson, first. Is it alright if he comes too?"

"Of course." She smiles.

We exchange numbers and addresses and within ten minutes I arrive at her beautiful cottage and set the kids loose in her back yard.

She makes me a cup of tea and we sit on the deck watching the kids play. The conversation flows easily, as if we've been friends long before this moment. I learn that Simone is not your average mum. She's *cool*. She is busy most weekends with friends doing outdoorsy stuff. She leads a clean, green, organic existence but doesn't rub it in your face. She's humble. The more we chat I'm amazed that she finds the time to do things that are just for her. As we sit here in the afternoon sun, her eyes dancing as she shares details of her life, I can't help but feel a forbidden crush brew inside me.

I am *very* attracted to her.

But I'm an adult.

A happily *married* adult... and so is *she.*

Just because you find someone attractive doesn't necessarily mean anything.

With this thought I glance at my watch. I need to get these kids fed and into bed, so I say my thanks and round up the kids. Naturally they do not want to leave, but with the promise of another play date they drag their feet to the car and allow me to strap them in.

"Thanks for the tea, I had a wonderful afternoon." I stand poised with one leg inside the car, my arms resting over the top of the open car door.

"Likewise. We should do this again." She beams. A warmth flickers from her eyes to mine and I feel a butterfly flapping inside my stomach. I hold her gaze for just a second more before I climb into my car and drive away, my heart hammering in my chest.

Two

Evie and the Committee Meeting

As an involved mum, I decided to join the school committee. Little did I know there would be so many boring committee meetings. I understand they are a *necessary evil.* We are ensuring that the future world is run by, hopefully, literate and intelligent beings. For that to eventuate, the school needs financial support to buy specialised equipment that the standard ministry of education funding won't cover.

Steve dutifully comes home from work early on the nights that I am required to attend these meetings. The kids love it as he makes them their favourite meals for dinner, and they always end up staying up until I get home.

Tonight, being the first Thursday of term one, marks the first scheduled meeting of the year. The hall echoes with my footsteps as I cross the room and pull up a chair. I'm glad to see so many familiar faces and I gravitate to those I already know, sitting down next to Sandra and Jennifer. Four rickety old rectangular trestle tables have been laid out in a rectangle with a hole in the centre. There must be roughly sixteen of us tonight.

Stacey, the chair, hushes our pre-meeting gabble with a clap of her hands, as if we are all children. It grates me and I struggle to suppress an eye roll. She runs through the agenda and calls for any last-minute additions. The meeting runs like monotone clockwork until she announces the main agenda item.

"We need fundraising ideas for new electronic devices for our classrooms".

In my head my thoughts drift to my own electronic devices sitting in the bottom drawer of my bedside table and I let out a small giggle. Rachael, sitting across the table from me meets my eyes and emits a stifled snort. She knows *exactly* what I was thinking about.

"Something funny Evie?" Stacey's green eyes flash angrily. She's a natural auburn redhead which used to be *my type* before I met Steve, but this woman really rubs me the wrong way.

"Right, who has event ideas?" Stacey opens the floor for discussion and despite my loathing of her, I actually have a few ideas to contribute. Stacey shuts down every concept I offer. She may be hot, but she's such a bitch. I glare across the table at her as I argue my point, but she shoots me down and kills my suggestion. I can feel myself getting hot around my collar.

Rachael, ever the peacemaker, comes to my rescue. "Why don't we call for a vote?"

I send her an appreciative glance and mouth the words 'thank you'.

After a few more deliberations and tallies of hands we have fixed the event calendar for the year. The biggest event is always the Agriculture Day in Spring but I'm looking forward to the pop-rock themed summer disco booked for the second to last Friday of term one. I'll definitely sign up to chaperone that event.

With nothing further to action, the meeting is adjourned. We are free to mingle over home-baked biscuits paired with nasty, cheap tea and coffee. I spy Rachael chatting with Sandra and Jennifer and make a beeline to her.

"Thanks for the save in there."

Rachael looks over my shoulder and judging by the awkward look on her face I sense it's Stacey. I slowly turn to face her.

"Yes, aren't you lucky Rachael came in to save the day." She throws at me, scathingly.

"Oh, give it a rest Stacey." I retort. Ughh I hate how she gets under my skin.

"I suppose you think I'm jealous when really I'm realistic and some of your ideas were rubbish." She glowers at me. The tension in the circle of parents can be cut with a knife and the mums cast each other furtive, nervous glances. I put down my cup of tea. I don't have time for this drama.

"Thank you, ladies, it's always a

pleasure…." I beam at my fellow mums. "Stacey…" I glare at her. "I'm going home."

Turning to Rachael, I give her a quick hug goodnight. "See you Saturday." I say into her hair.

I can feel Stacey's resting bitchface burning into my back as I confidently depart with my head held high. I mean who does she think she is? This isn't a totalitarian organisation. We're a volunteer committee which runs off the smell of an oily rag for the benefit of our kids. Scowling to myself I get in my car and drive home.

As I climb into bed with Steve that night, I complain to him.

"Honestly Steve, she's a nightmare. I wish I could wipe that sneer off her face."

Steve laughs at me. "My little fighter, Evie. I'm sure she's not that bad."

"You weren't there." I pout.

"OK, she's an evil cow and needs to be put in her place." He grins at me for a moment before pulling me to him, kissing the anger from my lips.

He always knows how to make me feel better.

Meeting Steve was like winning the jackpot. At 24 I'd had my fill of late nights and broken hearts. He just appeared in front of me one afternoon when I was browsing books at the corner bookstore. Nonchalantly, he struck up a conversation with me. He was so calm and confident, clearly older and wiser than I. It was easy falling in love with him. He had no *baggage*. No emotional dramas ensued after any of our dates. He had a good job as a junior architect at a large firm and had his own apartment. Steve was respectful and didn't push to sleep with me too soon… and I was pleasantly surprised that he was worth the wait. He was a *dynamo* in the bedroom. I found the more time I spent with Steve, kissing girls in bars became a thing of my past, fading memories to be locked away in the archives of my life.

Three

Evie and the Secret Crush

It's no secret to me, that I've noticed women over the years. Women are just so magical. They have soft, beautiful figures that I'd love to spend my empty afternoons sketching on a sketchpad… but my artist days are over. The only art I get up to these days is colouring in unicorns with Hannah, or outlining dinosaurs for Jackson to colour in.

Under normal circumstances I admire someone for just a moment, then carry on with my day. It never *lingers.*

The morning birds rouse me from my dreams, but I wish they hadn't. I'd been dreaming of Simone and my mind frantically tries to claw back the details. Steve rolls over and kisses me with his morning breath. I pinch my lips closed, trying not to inhale. He laughs, knowing I hate being kissed first thing in the morning.

"Alright, alright. I'll make coffee." He climbs out of bed, and I admire his muscled body. He sleeps in jocks now that we have kids but I miss the days when he always slept *naked*.

I try and remember the dream, but it's fading fast. Butterflies swirl in my tummy as I remember that first shared glance at the school drop off.

Get a grip Evie. Let it go.

Steve returns with coffee and the aroma relaxes me. I'm so glad it's Saturday. Steve has agreed to watch the kids so I can have coffee with Rachael. I lean into him and he kisses my forehead as we look out the open window. The green grass glistens with dew and the air is already warm with the promise of another beautiful day.

We sit in comfortable silence until our tranquil moment is upended as the kids jump onto our bed. Bracing ourselves, we do everything in our power to not spill our coffees.

As the morning wears on, I help Steve as best I can by ensuring that the kids have been fed, dressed and brushed their teeth before I leave. Really all this prep is in *my* best interest. The easier I make it, the more Steve is likely to offer to do this again for me. Once everyone is ready, I kiss each member of my family as I happily head out the door.

Rachael and I meet at our favourite café near the beach and sit at a table outside. It's so nice to breathe in the salty air.

"I'm so glad Mum could have the boys today. I *so* needed some space." Rachael sips her coffee, then tilts her face to the sun.

"I honestly don't know how you do it Rachael. Two boys, alone. I take my hat off to you." I pause wondering if I should even ask, but curiosity gets the better fof me. "Has Sean been in touch?"

"Yeah right. Tosser. He still owes child support for the past three months. He hasn't once asked after the boys or offered to have them over the summer."

"What a cock." I sigh. We both know what he's been up to this summer. His new, hot young flame has been posted all over social media and Rachael has had the hard job of explaining to the boys that their daddy is too "busy" to see them. Rachael walked in on him with another woman in their marital bed when she was six months pregnant with their second son. She'd just popped up the road to her routine midwife appointment, but on arrival found her midwife had been called into the delivery room, so Rachael went home again. Sean was clearly not expecting her back so soon. Rachael took Archie, her then, three-year-old and moved back in with her Mum. Which is a blessing and a curse.

That was three years ago now and Sean is still behaving like a teenager with no responsibilities. Rachael's Mum is still ropable about it. At his every mention, she mutters 'he is a good-for-nothing-waste-of-space' along with 'what were you thinking Rachael? I told you he wasn't good enough for you'. Being regularly reminded that her mother 'was right' makes for a strained living situation.

"Any hot dates lately?" I change the subject.

"I met one guy for a drink last week. Nice enough. Good job... but just no *spark*. I want to find someone that makes me want to jump their bones. You know. Where's the lust?"

"You'll find someone. I bet Mr Right is just around the corner and when you meet him, there'll be fireworks."

"Yeah... well until Mr Fireworks comes along, I'm in need of a new toy... a silent one that my Mum can't hear!"

I laugh loudly. "Well, let's not waste our morning. Let's go shopping!"

Rachael is awesome. I love having a friend I can buy sex toys with and share saucy... yet *heterosexual* stories with. There's no way I could tell her about my life before Steve.

Hell, even Steve doesn't know about my life before Steve.

In honesty, I'd love to tell Rachael about noticing other women. If only she wasn't so... *straight.*

Two hours later I arrive home with a *discreet* shopping bag and quickly hide it in my bedside table. Luckily the kids were outside with Steve, so no one knew I'd done shopping of any kind. Hannah, in particular, can sniff out when I've been shopping. She always expects there to be a gift for her. So now I need to hide bags until she is in bed, or smuggle them inside before she sees and rifles through them. I don't know what I'd say if she actually discovered a sex toy instead of a pretty new dress.

Alone in my room, my thoughts stray to Simone. Thinking back to that Wednesday afternoon, her magnetic energy floods my mind. I picture her, sitting on the edge of her deck. The warm breeze sending wisps of her hair around her face. Bare tanned and toned legs from the outdoor pursuits she mentioned, bounce over the wooden lip. Brown, expressive eyes lighting up as she talked.

I couldn't help but notice these things about her, and I know nothing will happen. Resolutely I vow to keep this crush *a secret*. Confessing any of these feelings to a straight, married woman is bound to kill any blossoming friendship.

The sound of Steve and the kids coming up the stairs drags me from my thoughts.

I'd better start making lunch.

The weekend as always, disappears so quickly. With Hannah back in school, the days fall into a steady rhythm and routine. In the back of my mind, I find myself waiting in anticipation for Hannah to demand a playdate with Katie. When she finally mentions it over a week after the first one, I feel relieved that I can legitimately message Simone.

'Hey Simone, fancy getting together for a bike ride and coffee with the girls?'

I watch the dots cycle and I'm relieved when she responds.

'Yes, sounds great. Saturday morning? Beach track?'

Air escapes my lungs in a whoosh, I didn't realise I'd been holding it in. I punch out my reply.

'Perfect, will see you there. 9:30am?'

'Perfect.'

I relay my weekend plans to Steve as we head to bed, feeling slightly giddy with excitement.

"It's nice to see you making new friends." Steve smiles tenderly at me.

Dismissing the queasiness growing in my stomach I agree with my husband. "Yes, it is nice."

If only a world existed where Simone and I could be more.

Four

Evie and the Bike Ride

Saturday morning is finally here! I rush around the house getting ready. Hannah can't think what to wear and neither can I. Steve observes the two of us with a smirk as he sips his coffee.

"See Jackson, us boys don't have to worry. No matter what we wear, we'll always look good." Jackson is playing with his cars on the floor near the kitchen. He glances up confused.

"What Dad?"

"Never mind, son." Steve winks at me as I march Hannah into her room again to help her find an outfit.

Fifteen minutes later, Hannah is ready and so am I. I've gone for the casual but nice look. Yoga pants, baggy T-shirt and just a flick of mascara for a morning coffee and walk. At 34 I can still get away without a full face of makeup. Steve wolf-whistles at me as I brush past him, grabbing my keys off the kitchen bench. My hair is swept up in a ponytail so I can wear a baseball cap and Hannah's is the same. She's my little mini-me and I love it. I kiss Steve and he pats my behind as I leave. I give him a cheeky grin over my shoulder as I wiggle my bum at him before I head out the door.

It doesn't take long to get to the beach. One great thing of living where we are is that we are inland enough to be country and close enough to the local beaches to enjoy them regularly. I park up and make our way to the café. On opening the door, I'm hit with the busy café sound storm. The hiss of the milk frother, the grinding of beans, the many conversations and cutlery scraping on plates. The sweet smell of coffee wafts over my nostrils and I sigh contentedly. I start searching for a table when I hear:

"Evie! Hannah! Over here!" Simone calls and beckons us over to a booth near the far wall.

We make our way around the tables to join them. Hannah and Katie hug and even though I don't know Simone that well, she rises to hug me too. It's the briefest of embraces, her chest bumps against mine and my face ends up in her hair as I hug her one armed. Her hair smells nice, floral, like cherry blossoms and as we pull apart, I feel a zap of electricity fizz between us.

"Oh wow, did you feel that?" Simone looks at me, surprised.

I nod and cast my eyes over the bench seat she rose from. "Must have been a static charge from the couch." I laugh, trying to attribute the spark we both felt, to something tangible.

"Can I have a hot chocolate Mummy?" Hannah looks up at me expectantly.

My eyes linger on the couch for just a second more before I answer, "sure darling. Katie? The same? Simone?"

Katie nods happily and I look at Simone expectantly.

"Flat white please."

I nod and make my way to the counter to place our order. I pretend to peruse the cakes in the cabinet while the electric hug plays over again in my mind.

It was the couch, Evie. I admonish myself. *Why am I even thinking about it?*

Once the drinks are ordered and paid for, I return to the table. The girls are colouring, and Simone and I start discussing which direction we'll head, after our drinks.

The coffees and hot chocolates arrive and the girls' eyes light up at the sight of marshmallows and a chocolate on the side of their plates. I search my plate to see if we've been given a treat with our coffees. I sigh.

Not today.

Simone chuckles as she observes the disappointment on my face.

"Looks like you should have ordered the hot chocolate." She says with a grin as she takes a sip of her flat white.

I blush in embarrassment. "No, it's ok... sometimes they surprise you, that's all."

Simone starts laughing in earnest. "If you really want a sweet, I'll get you one." She starts to stand but I wave her back down.

"No, no really!" I sip my coffee and pinch a marshmallow from Hannah's plate. "This is all I need." I pop it in my mouth before she can stop me.

"Hey!" Hannah protests.

"Mummy Tax." I say to Hannah, mid-chew, then wink at Simone.

"Mummy Tax... I like the sound of that one." Simone grins and takes a marshmallow from Katie's plate.

"Hey! That was mine!" Katie bellows. Simone pops it in her mouth and Katie's jaw drops open in shock. Simone laughs heartily.

"You're right Evie, this coffee did need something sweet."

I watch as the girls quickly drop their remaining marshmallows into their cups, then encircle them with their hands protectively. I snort in mirth and almost spill my coffee.

The girls continue to colour while Simone and I make small talk as we finish our drinks. After another ten minutes everyone is done, and the girls are ready. We unload the bikes from our cars and help them with their helmets. As we step onto the winding path, Katie and Hannah zoom off ahead of us.

"Don't go past the playground!" I call after them. I hear a giggle then a "Yes Mum!"

from Hannah as she flies after Katie.

I sigh and look at Simone. "Do you think they will wait at the playground for us?"

"I'm sure they will. Otherwise, this will be the last bike ride for a while." She says with authority.

I look towards the sea and breathe in the salty air. The tide is out, and the wet sand is dotted with shells and seaweed. Seagulls fly overhead screeching their caws as they search for unsuspecting crabs and sandhoppers on the beach below. The wind blows and bends the long grasses and rabbit tails in the dunes. For a moment I'm so lost in the beauty of the scenery, that I don't notice the path has changed its' curve. My hand bumps against Simone and brushes her backside. Embarrassed, I pull my hand away quick, but not before I realised how pleasantly toned it felt.

"Copping a feel are ya?" Simone laughs as I stammer out my apology.

"Don't sweat it Evie, I know it was an accident." She chuckles and carries on as if nothing happened.

I laugh feebly and try and follow her unflappable example. We increase our pace as the girls disappear around a corner. I become hyper-focused on following the winding path. Cresting another bend allows us to see the girls again, so we fall back into a steady rhythm. As we walk, Simone's knuckles graze mine. I try my best to ignore it, assuming, that it's completely accidental. The conversation doesn't even pause so I know this is all in my head. I focus on enjoying the company, the scenery, and keeping my hands by my sides.

This is normal, human interaction between friends.

Simone's knuckles brush the back of my hand yet again, but this time I feel a small jolt of electricity.

There it is again.

I do my best to ignore it, but my heart is thrumming in my chest and heat is pooling inside my yoga pants. How can such a simple accidental touch cause such a *response* in me?

Luckily, we arrive at the playground to find that the girls have abandoned their bikes and are screaming for us to push them on the swings. I welcome the distraction and the opportunity to place some physical distance between us. The squeak of the swings and the peals of laughter from not just our kids, provides a soundscape of happiness and all things non-sexual. I relax back into the friendly banter about mum life and before I know it, an hour has passed and it's time to head back to the car.

The girls race ahead and again, we are left to speed walk after them along the winding beach path. I notice the tide has come in while we were at the playground. The water sparkles under the sun and the warm, sea breeze soothes me. We make it all the way back to the car without any accidental grazing of body parts. I'm not sure if I'm relieved or disappointed by that fact.

We load the bikes into the backs of our cars and the girls hug each other goodbye. I stand awkwardly near Simone, wondering if we will hug, or just get into our cars and go. Wondering if it's best to do the latter, I start moving away but suddenly Simone grabs my arm and pulls me into a chest-to-chest hug and unintentionally, my lips graze her cheek, just touching the corner of her mouth. As her bust rubs against mine and her floral shampoo wafts over me, a shiver of pleasure runs straight between my thighs. I intake a sharp breath and pull away.

I shouldn't be feeling this way.

I feel my face burn under her gaze as I stammer out another apology. She laughs heartily, seemingly enjoying my embarrassment. She kisses me on the cheek and with the most delicious sparkle in her eye, says "I'll see you next time." Then without a care in the world, she climbs into her car and toot-toots as she drives away.

Five

Evie the Heroine

I love Fridays. They're my one day I get to myself. No work, the kids are in school and I can take time out to breathe… and do the shopping. Today I'm heading to the gym first. Just the sight of Simone's lithe body has me wanting to keep myself in shape.

Driving along our country road, flashing hazard lights slow me down. As I approach, I spy Lily struggling to pull a spare tyre out of the boot of her car. I pull in behind her, putting my own hazards on as I park as far off the road as I can.

"Looks like you could use some help." I call as I step out of my car.

"Aren't you a sight for sore eyes." Lily beams gratefully as the tyre bounces onto the ground. "Three men drove straight past and never looked back."

"Bastards." I laugh. "Flat tyre, is it?"

Lily nods and scratches her head as she

looks at the tools sitting in her boot.

My Dad was a mechanic before he passed away. My teenage years were spent hanging out with him at his workshop and I'm glad he took the time to show me how to do a few basics. I lean in next to Lily to inspect what tools she has. Looking at the wrench and jack I can't help but inhale Lily's perfume. It's fruity and reminds me of the cocktails and nightclubs of my youth. I reach out to pick up the jack and Lily's fingers brush over mine as she tries to pick it up at the same time.

"Sorry." She stammers. "I actually have no idea what to do with that."

"I do. Let me have it. If you can direct any cars around me while I position it, I'd be grateful for not getting squished."

Kneeling on the tarmac I search under her car for the indented grooves, stone chips biting at my knees. Her tyre is well and truly flat. A protruding nail the obvious culprit. I find the designated spot and position the jack. I glance behind me to find Lily watching me curiously. Her eyes had been square on my backside.

Now for the hard part.

I stand and join Lily at her boot again. She hovers closely as I search for the wrench. It's moved deeper into the boot somehow, so I bend over, reaching further into the back. As I return to standing, I catch Lily unabashedly checking out my butt. Innocently she meets my gaze.

"Off to the gym, are you?" She motions to my yoga pants.

"Yeah, I'm a member at 'FitFrames' in town."

Lily nods as if she knows it and I take the wrench and head back to the tyre.

I hope these aren't too tight.

Positioning the wrench on the first nut I push down hard, but it doesn't budge. I lift my leg, placing my trainer on the wrench suspended in air and step up, hoping my weight will help with the first turn. It gives a half turn before the wrench dislodges and I stumble unceremoniously forward. Lily rushes to my side and holds my arm to steady me. Her hip presses into my side.

"Thanks." I murmur. She smiles and I reach down to pick up the fallen wrench. She holds on longer than necessary and I have to extricate myself so I can carry on with the task at hand.

"Sorry, I need a bit of room to do this." I explain. Lily nods and retreats a few feet and scans the road for traffic.

I lock onto the nut again, this time it turns easily and I'm relieved. The other four nuts don't give me nearly as much trouble.

"Lily, can you pass me that metal bar with a hook in the end?"

"Oh right."

She rummages in her boot and hands me the tool. I hook it into the loop and crank it up. Soon the car is off the ground, the ruined tyre hovering in mid-air.

The tyre is stiff and takes a few kicks to loosen it from the shaft. Finally it's loose enough and with one last heave I pull the damaged tyre from her car. Lily wheels the spare around to me and we lift it into place together. I screw the nuts back into place and tighten them as much as I can. I help Lily put the spare into her boot and release the jack.

"I've tightened those nuts as much as I can. But you need to pop into Gary's tyre shop, they can tighten them properly there with their impact wrench."

I place the jack in with the tyre and help her put the tray back over the spare bay.

"Thanks so much for stopping Evie. You're my hero!" She wraps her arms around my neck and places a kiss on my cheek. I'm taken aback at how affectionate she is. I hug her back, enjoying the smell of her perfume once more.

"You're very welcome." I say as I pull away. Lily's arms brush down the sides of my body as she releases me. It sends a delicious tremor all the way down to my toes. I can't look her in the eye, knowing she's just turned me on.

"Cam will be so grateful he didn't have to leave work to help me." I glance at Lily's left hand.

Of course she's married… and so am I.

I really need to get girls out of my head, it's making me imagine things that aren't there.

"Glad I could help. I'm going to head off now. You'll be alright? You will go to Gary's Tyres right now, won't you?"

"Yes Mam." She salutes.

"Good."

I climb into my car as Lily closes her boot. I pull away from the curb and Lily waves energetically at me.

"My hero!" She calls spiritedly through my open window.

I can't help but grin. She's sweet. I grip the wheel tighter trying hard not to imagine her exuberance in a different setting.

I focus my mind on the gym workout ahead of me. It's going to take a whole lot of pain to burn off this pent-up energy.

Six

Evie and the Beach Trip

Summer is cranking and our household is officially in water-saving-mode. We shower over a bucket so that there is water for the garden and the dishwasher is officially off-limits. The kids peel off their clothes as soon as they get inside, choosing to run around in just their underwear as they try to get cool.

Friday being my day off, I've been running around all day cleaning the house and prioritising clothes to be washed. I've just made it out into civilisation to complete the grocery shop. I'm relishing in the crisp breeze from the cool industrial air-conditioning when my phone emits a *ping.* After placing a large bag of potatoes into my trolley, I fish around in my handbag to see who it is. My heart skips a beat as I see Simone's name flash up on my screen. It was just the other weekend that we took the girls for a drink and a bike ride. I've been trying my best to push the memory of her hand brushing against mine far from my mind, but the reality is I can still feel it when I close my eyes. Eagerly, I unlock my phone screen and click open her message.

'My goodness it's hot Evie! I'm taking Katie to the beach this afternoon after school. Want to join with the kids?'

I wipe at a small bead of sweat forming on my forehead. A dip in the ocean would be amazing… and *oh…* I'll get to see Simone in a swimsuit. Glancing at my watch, it's 1:30pm. If I race through my shop I should be able to get home, unpack, pack a bag of togs and just make it in time to get the kids. It will be a rush, but it will be worth it.

'A swim sounds great! Our local beach?'

I can see Simone typing as I quickly grab a few more things off the shelf, checking my list.

'Yes, but far end by the inlet. I'll meet you there.'

'OK'

I suddenly wonder when the last time I tidied myself up was… I'd better hurry so I can check I don't have any unwanted hair to remove. Consulting my list again I push my trolley down the aisles like a rally driver. A few meandering old ladies block my way from needed goods and I try and manoeuvre my hands around them to grab what I need. I receive a few disapproving tuts and glares but it's all worth it as I make it to the check out in record speed.

Once home I hastily put things away before I rummage through the kids draws to find their swimsuits.

The kids will be so happy for a swim today.

I find my bikini then head into the bathroom to inspect the situation.

Not too bad.

I tidy a couple of stray hairs away then put my bikini on, so I just have to take off my T-shirt and shorts when I get to the beach. I like my bikini, I bought it at the beginning of summer, a treat for myself as I finally feel like I have my body to myself again. It's a racy shade of deep red. It was a bold decision for a mum to buy, but if I'm going to finally put my post-pregnancy one-piece aside, I might as well do it right.

I quickly chop up some fruit and throw some snacks into a lunchbox for us all. The bag I've prepared is suddenly bulging with beach paraphernalia. Who knew you had to think of *so* many things when taking your kids to the beach for an hour or two. Grabbing a second bag, I pack the drink bottles and snacks then awkwardly carry all the gear down the stairs.

I wait eagerly at the pick-up zone with Jackson, having signed him out before the bell rang. He wriggles beside me, trying to pull his hand free from mine, his eyes fixed on the school kids' playground. I hold his hand tighter, knowing that I can't have him run off if we want to get to the beach and make it home at a reasonable hour to make dinner. Hannah finally skips down with her class and her teacher, Mrs Fuller smiles warmly as she nods for Hannah to be dismissed into my care. Taking Hannah's hand I pull both kids in front of me.

"I have a surprise for you both."

Their faces light up in anticipation so I pause for just one more moment to add more excitement.

"We're going to the beach!"

Little happy gasps emit from their mouths as they look at each other.

"With Katie."

Hannah squeals in delight and Jackson jumps up and down shouting "Katie! Katie! Katie!"

I laugh and lead them to my car. I scan around for Simone and catch a glimpse of her racing up the ramp to the pick-up zone. She's obviously a few minutes late. I pack the kids into the car deciding I'll meet her there.

It's only fifteen minutes to the beach and I'm relieved there are a few carparks available. I'm guessing this is why Simone chose this end of the beach, the main carparks were all full along the way. I open the back doors and set my kids loose onto the grass verge while I collect the bags and picnic blanket. By the time I've set up a cosy spot and dressed my kids in their swimsuits I catch sight of Simone following Katie down the sandy beach path. A breeze toys with her curls, making them whip around her face. She's wearing a linen shirt over little shorts. Her tanned legs lead down to naked feet.

I know I'm staring.

Hoping the warmth in my cheeks isn't obvious, I stand to greet them, gesturing for them to join our little set up. Katie rushes to Hannah and Jackson, the three of them jump up and down shouting "Beach! Beach! Beach!"

Simone puts her bags down and embraces me with a hug. Her earthy-floral scent wafts over me and I can tell she's been in her garden today.

Awkwardly stepping back and looking for a distraction from the mild ache I'm now feeling below my navel, I focus on the kids.

"So who's ready for a swim?"

"Me!" "Me!" "Me!" They all chime.

Simone pulls her shirt up over her head and drops it to the floor.

"And me!" she exclaims as she drops her shorts to the sand. It takes all my willpower to not gawk at her. Sheepishly I remove my outer layers too.

Get a grip Evie. She'll never invite you to the beach again if she catches you checking her out.

The kids race to the water's edge and start splashing. Simone and I are in close pursuit, keeping our mother-hawk eyes on our offspring.

"So, how have you been?" Simone asks me as we stride into the water together.

"Yeah, good. Busy with work. You?"

"Alright."

But it doesn't sound like she's alright. She sounds a bit flat. I look into her eyes, searching for what she's not telling me. Suddenly both Jackson and Hannah tackle my waist and thighs, bringing me to my knees in the cool water. Laughing I try my best to keep their heads above the water before a new wave washes over us. It's not deep, but each wave brings the water level a little higher. Simone and Katie laugh as we all struggle to find our balance within the swirling water. I finally manage to stand and my kids start gleefully splashing Katie. I laugh along with the kids and move deeper into the water, setting the play zone between me and the shore. I crouch down, submerging my shoulders under the blissfully refreshing water. Simone joins me and for a while we bob side by side, enjoying our kids playing.

"I like your bikini." Simone smiles at me. Suddenly I feel her fingers slide under my bikini strap, straightening it over my shoulder. All I can do is look at her with my lips slightly parted, my skin searing under her touch. As her eyes meet mine, a scorching glint is evident for a split second, before she hastily pulls her hand away, darting her gaze back to the kids.

"Where did you get it?"

Thrown, I follow her gaze to the kids, trying to clear my mind… and suppress the tingles that are running amok within my body.

"Oh… umm the surf shop in the mall. I finally feel like I have my body back now that Jackson is four. Thought I'd retire my one piece so my pasty skin can see some sun again." I laugh and do my best to ignore the growing feeling that *perhaps* Simone might find me attractive too.

"Nice, this one is from before having Katie. So *super* old. I'm just glad it still fits." She glances down at her body and my eyes follow taking in her glistening lithe, curves and simple black bikini.

"You're doing well." I smile. "Who would have thought we'd have bikini bodies again after having kids!"

"Yeah, I thought I'd never fit my clothes again. I'm glad I didn't throw anything out."

"Me too. I actually had a colleague tell me that when I was pregnant with Hannah. They made the mistake of throwing out a bunch of clothes thinking that she would never be that size again. Our bodies are amazing elastic things."

Jackson starts splashing me and I chase him towards the shore as he laughs loudly, looking over his shoulder at me with the biggest grin. I scoop him up then stride back into the water, dropping to my knees when I'm almost waist deep, holding Jackson tight as the water engulfs him up to his chest. He squeals in delight, trying to wriggle free. Scared that I'll drop him, I take him back into the shallows, plopping him into the water with a splosh. Glancing up to see where Hannah is, I discover Simone's eyes on me. I smile my best happy-mum smile, shirking the growing heat I'm feeling under her gaze.

Behind Simone the sun is starting to dip and I know it's time to head home.

"Come on kids. It's time to go now." I call above their laughter which quickly turns into groans. The kids start running away from me as I try to round them up. Thankfully Simone joins the chase as we rally them back onto the sandy shore to get dry and dressed.

Finally, our pouting kids are strapped into their seats and it's just Simone and I lingering beside our cars, the setting sun casting a golden glow over us and our surroundings.

"I had a wonderful time this afternoon, Evie. Thanks for coming." Simone reaches out and squeezes my arm.

"Thanks for inviting us. It was definitely required after the heat of today!"

We stand opposite each other, momentarily lost for words. My mouth turns dry so I lick the sea salt from my lips. Simone's eyes dip to my mouth before focusing on pulling at an invisible loose thread on her shirt.

"Alright, I'd better get going. Got to get dinner on." I venture trying to fill the void.

Simone nods and tentatively takes a step closer, leaning in for a hug. I meet her halfway, our bodies bump against each other and I can feel Simone's nose at my neck. All of my senses are on high alert as I feel the pressure between us.

That's when I hear it.

The sound of Simone breathing in my

scent as her nose nuzzles just under my ear.

My whole body tenses, focused on the sensation of her breath on my neck. Then as quickly as it started, it stops as Simone hurriedly pulls away from me, a blush rising in her cheeks.

"OK, I'll see you later." Simone climbs into her car, buckling her seatbelt as I stand there, unable to move. She waves as she reverses out of her carpark, heading towards the main road. The golden scenery reflects off her rear windscreen as she disappears from view.

I shake my head.

She couldn't possibly *like* me.

Could She?

Seven

Evie and the Opportunity

It's been a few weeks since our beach trip. Simone and I have seen each other at the school drop-off zone but we're often in a rush, so greetings are often just a smile and a wave. Things don't feel awkward. So again, I question if I did truly feel her smelling my skin, or if it was just my wistful imagination. Pushing my meanderings down yet again, I focus on the present.

Now, I *love* me a themed party where I can dress up. Especially one where I can hit the opportunity shops. In preparation for our first school fundraiser, the kids pop-rock disco, I've been super organised. I've arranged for a group of us to have coffee in a nice café, then hit the local op shops for inspiration and cheap outfits.

Arriving at the café, I'm the first one there so I grab a table where we'll all fit together. Rachael, Sandra, Jennifer, Simone and Lily will join me shortly. I put my stuff down and head to the till. The cakes look so delicious, so I order a lemon cheesecake to go with my latte. A sweet looking young girl delivers my order and I murmur my thanks. Mindful eating is the latest trend, but to be perfectly honest, I've always taken my time to savour tastes and textures. I pick up the dainty cake fork and slice off a morsel. As it nears my mouth, I inhale the sticky lemony scent. My eyes close as I pop it in my mouth and let it roll around on my tongue. The citrus is tart, the base sweet, and the velvety white filling is a little taste explosion in my mouth. A gentle 'mmm' of pleasure escapes me.

A nearby snigger makes my eyes snap open, finding I have a bit of an audience. Rachael snorts as she puts her bag down next to me. I catch Lily staring at me with her lips slightly parted, until she catches my eye and closes her mouth. Simone is here too.

"Well. I think I'll have what you're having!" Simone's eyes are playful as she pulls her purse out of her bag.

I blush with embarrassment and stand to give each lady a hug. Rachael is brief and heads quickly to the counter to order much needed caffeine. Lily leans in a little closer than I expect, her fingertips gently trail down my bare arm, unexpectedly making my body stir.

Woah.

I pull away quickly, averting my eyes. Simone is next and after our trip to the beach, my skin is aching to be touched by her again.

She leans in and gives me a little peck on my cheek. Her soft breath just reaches my ear, sending a delicious throb between my legs. It takes everything I have to compose myself. Simone releases me and follows Rachael and Lily to the counter. Sitting back down my gaze drifts back to Simone and Lily. I wonder if they have any idea how they make me feel.

Jennifer and Sandra finally arrive to join the party. After quick hugs, we all sit down with drinks and slices and the mum-life banter ensues. I can't ignore that Lily *and* Simone have ordered the lemon cheesecake.

Food devoured, coffees drunk, we pack up and head to the op shops on the street. There are three in the same block which is perfect for bargain hunting.

We enter the first shop, dispersing quickly amongst the racks. Rachael dives in, pulling clothes out in a frenzy and holding them against herself. Like me, she loves a good dress up. In between the dresses I spy a pair of men's patent leather shorts with silver rings and zips. I can't help but pull them out and press them against me, calling to the others that I've found my outfit.

"Ha ha, yes Evie!" Rachael bellows. "But maybe take them home for Steve!"

"That's not a bad idea." I laugh and hand the shorts around the group for a closer inspection. It honestly amazes me what you'll find in an op shop these days. Soon each of us have a few outfits in hand and we each take turns trying things on. Sandra and Jennifer stay behind their curtains and come out when finished, discarding most items to the return rack. I'm disappointed they didn't show us what they tried on, but I can tell they're just shy. Rachael shows us every outfit, even the ones that really don't fit. Our laughter at the many fashion faux-pas rings throughout the store and my heart feels light.

Sandra and Jennifer head to the counter and purchase a couple of choice items, followed by Rachael with her stellar find of a leather jacket and studded belt. The three women having completed their purchases say their farewells. Lily decides to head to the store next door, and I call that I'll join her soon.

I don't know how it happened, but I find myself *alone* with Simone. Playing it cool I continue to search for outfits while Simone heads to the change room.

I browse the racks, but nothing is standing out as an obvious outfit. I'd really like to dress like Axel Rose from Guns n Roses.

"Hey Evie, can I get your opinion please?" Simone's head sticks out from behind the curtain and as I get closer, she reaches for my arm and pulls me into the small room with her.

"What do you think?"

Simone is wearing a black lacy sheer top that really should be lingerie. I can't help but notice the shape of her nipples pressed against the fabric. For a moment I'm speechless.

"Oh. You don't like it. I was thinking it

could be a Madonna type outfit. I was going to get a black tutu or something to go with it."

I blink, trying my best not to gawp at her.

"No, it's a really good idea… but… umm might not be appropriate with the kids. You might need a… a jacket or a slip top underneath."

I do my best to stop looking at her nipples, but they're just so *proud*. Our eyes meet and I know she saw me look. I swallow nervously.

"I'll a… let you try on something else." I feel my cheeks flame, clearly caught in the act. Hastily I leave the small changing room.

Fuck.

I frantically search for other outfit ideas but there really is nothing else in this shop. Simone is still behind the curtain, but I'm so embarrassed I don't think I can face her again.

"Hey Simone, I'm going to catch up with Lily. Will you be alright?"

"Yes Evie, I think I've found something. I'll see you at the disco."

I don't want to leave things as they are, but I don't know what else to say. Saying sorry for gawking at your nipples just sounds so *stupid.*

"OK, I'll see you there."

I leave chastising myself under my breath and head to the next store. Through the window I see Lily at the counter. Swallowing my awkwardness, I push through the door to the sound of a friendly chime. Joining Lily at the counter I take note of the gorgeous sequined dress she's purchasing.

"Great find Lily!" I beam at her.

"Oh, thanks. I was thinking of going as a pop princess. I think I may even have the perfect pair of heels at home to match." She says proudly.

"I'm going to look around, see what I can find." I leave her to complete her purchase and start perusing the racks.

I must find something. Everyone else already has their outfits.

A pair of ripped white jeans catch my eye and I can't believe it, but a black mesh top is next to it. The top isn't quite guns n roses, but it's definitely 80s pop rock.

If I can just find a studded belt…

Lily appears beside me, eyeing up my finds.

"Ohhh I saw the perfect belt to go with that. Go try it on and I'll pass it through to you." She saunters off and I spy the entrance to the changing rooms on the back wall.

Inside, I strip down to my knickers and bra, pulling on the jeans. What a find! They're a perfect fit. I know I have a black tank top at home to wear under the wide-mesh top, so I try it on over my lacy bra just to check the size. I appraise myself in the mirror.

I look good.

It's a shame this is a G rated party.

The curtain rustles and Lily slips in behind me. Her breath hitches as she sees my reflection in the mirror. I keep my back to her and hastily try and cover myself.

"Oh! I wasn't expecting you to come in. I have a top I'll wear under this at home. Definitely won't be this risqué at the kids disco." Self-consciously, I laugh loud.

Lily instantly composes herself. "It's OK, I have sexy underwear too you know. Now here. Turn around."

Lily puts her hands firmly on my hips and swivels me around so I'm facing her. She starts fumbling with the hoops in my jeans and I realise she's threading the belt around me. Our bodies are so close I can feel the heat between us. Lily pulls the belt through the buckle and tugs until she finds the right notch. Her knees bump against mine as she leans back to admire her work.

"There. Perfect."

"Thanks." I mumble as I spin to look in the mirror again. Lily leans against the wall watching me take in my reflection.

The belt truly completes the outfit.

"I'll take it." I smile at her.

She smiles sweetly, appraisingly.

"Umm I'll get changed now." I start unbuckling the belt but look at her quizzically before unbuttoning the jeans.

"Some privacy?" I ask.

"Oh right! Sorry!" She laughs and exits the room. The curtain billows behind her.

What was that?

I push the odd interaction from my mind. Clearly, she's just friendly. I pull my clothes on and take my finds to the counter to pay. Lily is waiting at the door.

"I had so much fun today. Thanks so much for inviting me." She leans in and gives me a hug, her bust pressing into mine.

"Sure thing Lily. I'm glad you could come along. I'll see you at the disco then."

"I look forward to it." Her happiness clearly etched across her face.

I watch her as she heads to her car.

Is it just me, or is she swaying her hips provocatively?

Eight

Evie and the Disco

"Owww" Hannah screams at me as I attempt to brush the knots out of her hair.

"I'm sorry Hannah. But if you just stopped wriggling, I could be gentler."

Hannah pouts and holds herself still while I finish brushing her hair. She wants to go as Taylor Swift. I style her hair with wispy strands around her face and help her into her sequined tutu-dress. It's actually just her party dress, but she believes she looks like Taylor from the latest music awards ceremony. She holds her plastic microphone proudly and belts out 'shake it off".

"OK Taylor, mummy needs to get ready now." I leave her to dance around in her room while I pull on my ripped jeans. I settle for a black crop top to wear under the mesh shirt. Those Friday gym sessions are really paying off and I feel confident to show a little bit of skin. As I thread the studded belt through the loops of my jeans, the memory of Lily's hands swivelling me around in that small changing room floods my mind. Followed by the image of Simone wearing that *lace top*.

If only I could…

What?

Ruin my marriage? Ruin theirs?

I shake the horniness from my body and place the piece de resistance Axel Rose bandana around my head. I nod to my reflection. This look *works for me.*

Steve is busy calming Jackson down in the lounge as I emerge from the bedroom. Jackson really wants to go to the disco too but it's for school kids only. Jackson runs to me and jumps into my arms, tears streaming down his face.

"I'm sorry Jackson. Next year OK. But you're going to have so much fun with Daddy. I hear he's going to make popcorn and play some board games with you."

Steve catches my eye with a raised eyebrow. This is news to him. I throw him a conspirational 'work with me' glance. I need Jackson calm so I can leave with my little Taylor Swift.

Jackson turns in my arms to look at Steve with watery blue eyes.

"Yes buddy. You can pick any game you want to play. Why don't you go choose one now… while I make popcorn." Steve jokingly glares at me.

"Thank you." I appreciatively nod to Steve as Jackson squirms out of my arms. Steve leans down and pecks me on the cheek. He pokes a finger through one of the large holes in my mesh top, tickling my tummy.

"Mmm I like this top." He growls.

I reach my hand behind him and give his bum a quick squeeze.

"Later" I whisper into his ear.

"Come on Hannah, let's go!"

Hannah emits a squeal of delight and proceeds to dance to the car. We listen to Taylor Swift all the way to school and I can't help but feel like tonight's going to be a fun night.

The hall is decorated with sparkly streamers and the mirror ball is sweeping little white lights around the room. The DJ (Mr Tate from year four) is dressed as MC Hammer. As if on cue, Hannah enters the hall to 'shake it off' by Taylor Swift and she shrieks hysterically as she runs to her group of friends that are already dancing in the middle of the room.

Stacey is at the back of the hall, so I check in to see where she wants me. Stacey is dressed in jeans, a plain black T and is wearing heavy eye make-up. I can't quite figure out who she's meant to be. She looks like herself, just with her hair down...and slightly heavier make up.

"I'm Shirley Manson from Garbage." She announces curtly before I can even ask.

"Nice Axel Rose."

I can't believe it. Stacey just gave me a *compliment.*

"Right. You're on drinks duty." Her tone clipped and business-like as she uses her clipboard to point me to the tables across the hall.

I nod and make my way over. The pricelist and instructions are laminated next to juice boxes and bottles of water. I inspect my cash box for something to do but it's not long before thirsty children approach with their gold coins.

The outfits are amazing. Most of the girls are dressed in sweet little dresses, not looking like any particular pop singer. The boys similarly non-descript. But I take note that I *think* one or two could be Bruno Mars or Ed Sheeran.

Rachael comes running up to me and slips behind the table giving me a big squeeze.

"Eeeee! Perfect Axel, Evie!"

Rachael is dressed like Mick Jagger with her black leather jacket over a white T with the famous image of the red mouth with the long tongue hanging out. Her son Archie nervously approaches the table for a drink. He's dressed in black with a large cross around his neck. Rachael has applied eyeliner to his eyes too.

"Nice Ozzy Osbourne Archie!" I exclaim.

He shudders.

"I don't know who he is!"

Rachael and I stifle a giggle. None of the

kids here will know who Rachael and I are dressed as either.

Archie glares at his mum, drink now in hand and joins his friends looking awkward.

"I take it you chose the outfit?" I shoot sideways at Rachael as we take in all the characters in the room. She nods then points excitedly at a little boy wearing the exact same outfit as her.

"My twin!" She squeals in delight.

It's still early and children continue to file in through the doors. Rachael and I have a ball playing 'guess the singer' until Stacey… a.k.a… Shirley Manson stands in front of us, glaring.

"Rachael, you're on bathrooms. They're due a check."

Rachael's smile instantly falters. She casts me a furtive glance and with shoulders hunched she heads dutifully to the toilets at the rear of the hall. Stacey shoots me a 'get back to work' scowl before striding over to the sign in area. Jennifer glances up from her clipboard, twitching nervously before she is engulfed in Stacey's formidable shadow.

Eyes still on the door to see what Stacey will do next, a vision catches my eye. Simone enters the hall holding Katie's hand. She's dressed as Madonna. Black elbow length lace gloves lead up to bare shoulders. She's wearing a strapless black top with a black tutu, long white and silver beads hang over her chest. Black lace tights cover her toned legs and she's wearing little black pumps to match. Her hair is piled messily on top of her head and curly tendrils graze her neck and face.

The outfit is so *tight.*

Simone glances around the room, clearly looking for a familiar face. Her eyes meet mine and I'm startled from my thoughts of running my hands *all* over her body.

I wave enthusiastically in greeting. A lame attempt to pretend I wasn't just checking her out.

Did I really just do that?

I cringe at myself for being so over the top. Lily has stopped to give Simone a hug and I'm left hanging with my hand in mid-air. I put it down awkwardly and scan the room in hope no one saw me.

Lily has brought it too. Her sequined dress sparkles under the lights. Diamante encrusted high heels support slender legs. The dress is actually rather *short.* As she bends slightly to hug Simone I can almost see her…

I need to stop staring.

Looking down, there's a ten-year-old boy dressed as Elvis wanting to buy a juice box. Grateful for the distraction I focus on my work. I give his juice box a shake.

"I'm all shook up, ahuh" I do my best Elvis impression with the lip curl and everything before I hand it to him.

He frowns, clearly not a fan of my impersonation.

"Who are you supposed to be?" He asks

rudely.

"Axel Rose."

Elvis gives me a blank stare.

Clearly his parents aren't into Guns n Roses.

Elvis turns to leave, but not before giving me a piteous look. Like I'm *tragic*. Shocked at his arrogance I call out to him:

"Maybe I'll get the DJ to play one of my songs *just* for you later. My *sweet child o' mine*!" I belt out the last few words in true Axel fashion.

Staring at me like I'm unhinged, he scarpers back to his friends. I chuckle to myself at my own joke.

"What was all that about?" I look up to find Simone across from me, wearing a quizzical smirk.

"Oh, you know, embarrassing children is my forté." I grin as I spy Elvis casting me a furtive glance.

"You look great Simone. Perfect Madonna."

Lily sidles up beside her, joining the conversation. She puts her arm around Simone's waist and gives her a squeeze.

"Yes! Doesn't she look amazing!"

Seeing Lily with her arm around Simone makes me feel strange. I'd like to push her hand away.

Jesus. I'm jealous.

Simone looks uncomfortable and shuffles slightly away from Lily's grip.

"I don't have a job to do, do you mind if

I hang out with you?" Simone's eyes are wide, hopeful.

My mouth runs dry. I'm not sure how to answer. Obviously, I want her close to me... but I also *don't* want her close to me in case I do something stupid.

Lily spies Jennifer and Sandra on the dance floor with a group of little pop princesses. Flashing us a big grin she sashays across the dancefloor.

Simone joins me behind the table.

"I like this." She touches my bandana, and her fingers stroke my face for the briefest of seconds before she retracts her hand.

"Thanks." I mumble. I'd like to compliment something specific about her costume too. But all I really want to do is rip it off her body.

The DJ turns up the volume and the lights dim. The doors have been closed and the disco is officially in full swing. Simone and I stand side by side watching everyone dance. My bare arm bumps against hers and I feel the back of her lace gloved hand press into the back of mine. I note her gloves are the kind where the fingers are bare.

I daren't breathe. I can't believe she is standing so *close* to me. The sounds of laughter and music become dull to my ears as my brain hyper-focuses on the sensation of our shoulders and hands connecting.

Standing stock-still, I'm scared to move.

I'm scared to look at her face to see what

she might be thinking.

I'm also scared that I'm reading *way too much* into this.

Subtly, I feel Simone's little finger snake it's way around mine.

My eyes close as I feel her finger gently dance across my skin. Desire floods my body and my heart hammers in my chest. I squeeze her finger in return, indicating that I like it. Suddenly, her finger is withdrawn. Startled, I open my eyes to little Willow, Lily's daughter.

"Can I have some water, Miss?" She innocently looks up at me.

Simone has inched away, and I feel like I can breathe again. I glance at her, noting her cheeks are flushed and there's a look of trepidation in her eyes.

"I'll leave you to it." Simone murmurs, then practically runs towards the group of mums and kids on the dance floor.

I sell Willow the water and watch her take it to her mum. Lily unscrews the cap and raises the bottle in a toast to me. A devilish grin on her lips.

Did she just?... No. Our hands were behind the table. There's no way she could have seen anything.

I watch the mums and children dancing for the rest of the evening from the safety of my drinks table. I do my best to focus on my job, but my hand still tingles where Simone touched me. Lily continues to catch my attention and wave at intervals as the night wears on. I do my best to laugh and wave back at the cheesy dance moves she's pulling with the kids.

My eyes keep flitting back to Simone, hoping to catch her attention. She's acting silly with the kids, dancing and singing along to the catchy songs. I'm not sure if it's on purpose, but she keeps positioning herself in the dance circle to have her back to me. A weight drops into the pit of my stomach.

She didn't mean to touch me.

Now I feel foolish for squeezing her fingers.

After two hours of dancing and frivolity, the night finally wraps up and I can take my tired little Taylor Swift home. I hug all the mums I know goodbye, but Lily and Simone are nowhere to be seen.

They must have left while I was counting up the drink takings.

Driving home the memory of Simone's skin on mine drives me slightly crazy. The image of her flushed cheeks flashes through my mind.

Was that embarrassment?

And that look in her eye was *fear*. Something tells me what happened tonight, won't happen again.

It's probably for the best.

Nine

Evie and the Sneak Peek

That moment with Simone at the disco plagued my dreams all night. I woke before the sunrise on Saturday morning in a cold sweat. Simone has invited Hannah for a playdate today. We booked it over a week ago but after last night I am nervous to see her again.

My squeeze of her hand clearly startled her. Maybe I misread the situation…

My mind spinning, I swing my legs over the bed and head to the kitchen. I make myself a coffee as quietly as possible. Opting for an instant to keep the noise down. With steaming cup in hand, I sit outside to await the sun from our veranda. It's nice to be alone at this time of morning. The birds are only just waking up and there are still a couple of stars in the sky. The pre-dawn air is crisp and fresh, and I breathe in the sweet country scent.

Why would I jeopardise this?

Resolutely I push Simone from my

thoughts.

It's not real. I assure myself.

What I have here is real. Steve and the kids.

I smile as the sky turns a glorious shade of orange as the sun crests over the hill.

A new day.

The kids and Steve sleep late. The sun is well and truly up and I've polished off two cups of coffee before they emerge from their bedrooms bleary eyed.

I purposefully don't rush our morning routine. I know I'm delaying the inevitable, but I want to be mindful with my family today. Hannah however, will not be slowed down. She knows she has a playdate so she races around, continually asking what time we will leave.

By 10am I can't delay her any longer, so I pile her and Jackson into the car. Even though I can feel the season on the verge of changing, it is turning into another balmy Saturday.

The drive to Simone's is short.

Too short.

I pull into her drive and open the rear door so Hannah can get out.

Still loving these child locks.

I leave Jackson firmly strapped in the car with the windows down. Firstly, to stop him running off and secondly, it's a good excuse not to stay. Hannah and I walk together, hand in hand, around to the back yard.

Climbing the stairs to Simone's deck, my eyes meet an unexpected sight. The image burns into my retinas with every step closer I take. Behind the sliding door, Simone is wearing a sheer white T-shirt. The dark shadow of her nipples clearly visible as they jut out and strain against the fabric. She pulls a lightweight jumper down over her chest, but not before her breasts are tattooed on my brain.

She is bra-*less*.

My breath catches in my throat. I have no idea if she knows I've seen her… or if she has any inkling of the fire stirring within.

"Katie! Hannah's here!" Simone calls behind her as she opens the door to us.

She leans out and gives me a peck on my cheek while I do my best to compose myself and push the image of her hard nipples from my mind.

"Staying for a cuppa?" She asks warmly, as if the moment from the night before never happened.

"I can't sorry. Jackson is in the car. I need to get some things at the shops."

I'm suddenly cursing myself for offering to bring Jackson with me. Then I wonder how I'd even segue the topic of her little finger entwined with mine into our conversation.

Simone's smile fades slightly. "No trouble, 3pm pick up alright? Or I can drop her to you later?"

Seizing the opportunity to not have to make another trip. "Yes, if you can drop her home that would be great."

I call bye to Hannah through the open door. She can be heard giggling from the depths of Katie's room. I don't bother waiting for a response. An understanding mum-smile passes between us.

"OK, I'll see you later then." I pause as I say it, torn between wanting to ask about last night and wanting to forget it happened.

"Muuum! Can we have popcorn?" Katie wails from the bedroom.

Simone rolls her eyes, duty has called.

"I'll see you later Evie."

I nod and walk back down the stairs.

I carry out my shopping with Jackson in a daze. The image of Simone's hard nipples playing on repeat inside my mind. I shouldn't indulge, but I let my imagination run wild.

She was braless.

I bet she would be the kind of free-spirited woman to lie naked on her private back lawn, basking in the warmth of the sun.

I revel in the delicious image for just a moment, then continue with my day.

Life goes on whether you've seen someone else's nipples or not.

Ten

Evie and the Summer Garden

The last week of term one has finally arrived. Hannah and Jackson are giddy with excitement for the holidays and Steve and I are just a little bit ratty and in much need of rest.

The days fly by in a whir of family life and sales deals at work. I'm relieved when Friday, the last day of term, finally arrives. By lunchtime I've finished all the household tasks and I'd love a bit of company. My thoughts stray to Simone and I wonder if she's free for a cuppa.

We're friends, a cuppa is normal.

I just need to not picture her naked while she drinks it.

I pull out my phone and type off a quick message.

'Hi Simone, are you busy? Was wondering if I could hang at yours until it's time to get the kids?'

Simone flicks a message back almost instantly.

'Yes, I'm home. Pop over for a cuppa.'

I drive the short distance and Simone walks out to meet me with a hot tea. We sit on the edge of the deck enjoying the late summer sun as it warms our faces.

"Any plans for the holidays?" Simone asks.

"Not too much, will probably do a few local activities. You?"

"We might go camping."

There's something slightly sad about the way she said '*we*'. I notice a stray lock of hair has fallen, obstructing one side of her face. Instinctively, I brush it aside and tuck it behind her ear. The sun kisses her skin and it looks like she's glowing.

"You're so stunning Simone" I whisper. Then hastily I add, "I bet your husband can't wait to get home to you."

She laughs.

Then sighs.

"We're separating".

"Oh no!" I reach out and embrace her in a hug. She smells wonderful, like sweet flowers, soap and rain on the earth.

"Whatever the reason, I'm sorry. If it's his fault, he's an idiot". I pull back and our eyes lock onto each other. There's a turbulent look in Simone's eyes, but her lips part as her eyes flick to my mouth. There's something *inviting* about the way she looks at me. I know I shouldn't, but before I can stop myself, I'm running my thumb across her bottom lip.

"When was the last time you were kissed Simone?" My voice is husky, a mix of lust and nervousness.

What am I doing?

She looks down shyly and says, "it's been a while." Her eyes dart back up to mine. Suddenly, we notice how close we are sitting and it feels *electric*. Simone's eyes sparkle with longing, her body inches towards me, the gap between us, heavily charged.

One kiss couldn't hurt... right?

Against my better judgement, I lean in, closing the gap as I brush my lips against hers. I pull back slightly, hovering inches from her, my eyes trying to read her beautiful face.

Simone suddenly looks ravenous. She pulls me to her, locking her lips on mine. Her lips are soft and moist but, oh, so *urgent*. I feel her part them with fervour, summoning me in. I dart my tongue inside her mouth, feeling her breath hitch.

This is not the first time I've kissed a woman, but it's been a while... like a *decade*.

I forgot how good this feels.

My head screams that this *isn't* a good idea. But her mouth is *so* sweet, and what is this *current* drawing us together? I try and slow the kiss, savouring the little caresses of my tongue on hers. She moans softly and I can feel her hand on my knee. Gingerly, her hand moves higher, caressing my thigh and the sensation makes me want to combust.

My resolve to leave this at *just* kissing is waning fast.

My fingers long to squeeze and stroke the breasts that are being thrust against me.

Breathing hard I pull away. This is entering

very *dangerous* territory.

"Simone, I'm not sure this is a good idea."

Her pupils are dilated as she replies. "I know… but I want *this* so much." She gestures to the two of us and she takes my hand, placing it on her upper thigh. A loaded gaze passes between us, our breathing ragged. Simone's fingers reach into my hair, pulling me into another deep kiss. I cup her cheek and my fingertips brush the edge of her hair. Simone's spare hand explores me over my clothes and all my willpower slips away.

I'm *burning* for her.

My hands take on a will of their own as they snake under her shirt. A sigh of pleasure escapes me as I discover she is *not* wearing a bra today. I reach up to cup her in my hands and feel the fullness of her breasts. I groan into her mouth as I fondle and squeeze her, feeling her nipples harden even more under my touch.

I'm doomed.

Even if I wanted to, I can't stop.

Simone suddenly pulls back and hurriedly tugs her shirt up and over her head. Her nipples stand to attention under the sun's warm rays. I bend my head to her chest and pull one into my mouth. She moans loudly and reaches down fumbling with the hem of my shirt before pulling it up, over my head. She reaches around me and swiftly unclips my bra. I let it drop onto the grass and Simone tentatively starts rubbing my breasts.

"I've never done this before" she says

shyly. Simone gives my nipples a playful squeeze between her fingers, her eyes watching me intently. "Is this alright?"

"Mmmhmm" I sigh as the sensation stirs a deep ache within me.

Feeling intoxicated, I slip off the edge of the deck and stand facing her, the sun warming my back as I lean forward and flick my tongue over one nipple, then the other. Gently I nudge her thighs apart and nestle my hips against her. I pull her closer so I can bury my face in her body. My hips take on a mind of their own as I grind against her, the friction between us growing the exquisite ache below my navel. Her gasps spur me on as I work my kisses up to her neck.

I run my tongue from behind her ear down to her collarbone, then lightly, I blow on the wet trail. She pants in delight and pulls me into another deep kiss.

I feel her hands slither down and squeeze my behind, crushing me even harder against her. Reciprocating the gesture, I find her backside is round and firm and I can feel her hips rhythmically lifting against me.

Jesus, this is going to make me come.

Wrenching my hips back, I look into Simone's eyes breathing hard. Her deep brown eyes smoulder into mine and the thoughts of '*no, stop*' fade into internal sighs of '*yes, yes, yes*' as my primal instincts take over.

I place a long line of feathery kisses from the nape of her neck down to below her navel. I slip a finger under the waistband of her shorts, and Simone lifts her hips off the deck, offering permission to pull them down and drop them to the ground. My hands run up the outside of her thighs and I trace the elastic sides of her panties with my fingers. She subtly shifts her weight and her legs part for me, giving me access to pull the gusset aside. I drag my finger along her inner thigh, and she quivers beneath me. I lower my head and run my tongue along the line I've just traced, then pause.

I look up, finding her darkened eyes, I must ask, "are you sure?"

Am I sure?

"Yes, yes, a thousand times. YES!"

I hover a little longer taking in the sun-kissed sight of all she is, while also checking her expression matches her words.

"Please" she begs.

There's something in her voice that breaks me. A *wanting*. A deep *need.*

Unable to hold back any longer, I tug her gusset aside before plunging my tongue into her burning hot folds.

I kiss and flick my tongue into her velvet depths, feeling her node harden and grow with every stroke. My spare hand ravages her body as I feel her arousal building and growing beneath me.

"I need… *more* Evie. Please… use your hand… as well as your mouth."

A woman who knows what she wants.

Smiling up at the wanton siren before me, I withdraw my hand from her breast so I can wrench her panties from her hips. I drop them unceremoniously to the grass. Simone is now completely naked and spread before me, her chest heaving as she stares deep into my eyes. My fingers slowly circle her slick entrance as I hold her gaze. She moans with anticipation and I pause for a moment, enjoying the show. She squirms in frustration, inching closer to the edge of the deck. I sink my two slender fingers deep inside her and she lets out the most delicious sigh of contentment. Her molten core clamps around me as I slowly move inside her.

Her fingers run though my hair, pulling me closer. My eyes close as my lips and tongue find their target, dancing across her hard knot. I can feel she's getting close, her breathless moans spurring me on. Not wanting to miss a thing, I glance up from my task. I'm rewarded with a *gorgeous* sight as my tongue and hand incessantly pleasure her.

Simone's head lolls back, her breasts arch up to the sun as a delirious scream of ecstasy startles the nearby birds in the trees.

Her whole body shudders around me, then she flops backwards onto the deck, completely sated.

I wait for the waves to calm with a smile and the taste of her on my lips. Gently, I remove myself from between her legs then lean over her, placing little kisses from her pelvis up to her neck. As I join her on the deck, I prop myself up with my elbow, while the other hand strokes the soft skin of her hip.

Simone slowly opens her eyes and smiles up at me.

"Well, I wasn't expecting *that* when I said pop over for a cuppa".

I laugh. "Neither was I!"

She gazes at my breasts and runs a finger over a nipple.

"Mmmm my turn" she says as she jumps off the deck, grabbing my hips and pulling me to the edge.

She kisses me tenderly then murmurs "I never realised how perfect the height of this deck was, until *now*".

Eleven

Evie and the Confession

Reversing out of Simone's driveway my heart pounds in my chest.

Did that really just happen?

Licking my lips, her salty sweet taste dances on my tongue and the corners of my mouth twitch happily, until another thought strikes me.

Steve.

Fuck.

What have I done?

Collecting the kids is surreal. They gabber to me about their day and I nod, offering non-committal grunts at intervals. Hannah is talking about math, but she sounds so far away. Jackson is trying to contribute to the conversation, and they start arguing with each other. Their annoyed, raised voices become a hum in the background. I don't even bother to break it up, or understand what they're fighting about. My mind is whirring with what this means for our family, for my marriage.

Steve doesn't deserve this.

How could I have done this?

How have I just *cheated* on my husband?

Our beautiful home looms into view. It's an old villa that Steve and I have lovingly restored over several years. The old tin roof was replaced and painted a soothing cobalt blue which now shelters pale grey weatherboards. The veranda balcony and fretwork painted a crisp white.

How many hours did we spend painting before the kids arrived?

A memory of Steve flicking his paint brush at me swims to the forefront of my mind. His wolfish laugh at my indignation melting my resolve to remain grumpy at him. He made love to me then and there on the veranda. Lifting me onto the balustrade so I could wrap my legs around him. So carefree, out in the open.

We're lucky the neighbours didn't see… or maybe they've just never mentioned they did…

Our life, our home, our kids…

All of this is now in jeopardy.

Bile rises into my throat as our car pulls into the driveway. Hastily, I unbuckle the kids and race to unlock the door. Without checking to see if they are following me, I race up the stairs and just make it to the bathroom before I vomit into the toilet.

"Mummy? Are you alright?" Little Hannah's voice wafts in from a safe distance behind me.

Queasily I tear off a few squares of toilet paper and wipe my mouth before flushing the toilet. As I wash my hands I murmur 'yes darling, just feeling a little sick. Nothing to worry about."

She cocks her head quizzically for a moment.

"OK, can I have a biscuit?"

I smile weakly, the thought of food gives my stomach an unpleasant lurch and I fear I might be sick again.

"Sure thing, honey." I choke out. "Take one for Jackson too."

With the tasty snack cemented in her mind, Hannah skips over to the pantry and leaves me to dry my shaking hands.

Dinner needs to be started and Steve will be home soon.

Pulling ingredients out of the pantry and fridge is challenging. My hands are shaking so severely I keep dropping things on the floor. It's a good thing it's not breakfast time and eggs I'm cooking. As I return to the fridge for the tomato paste, a bottle of wine catches my eye.

Just one glass. It'll take the edge off.

Golden chilled perfection swishes into the glass. Raising it, my nose inhales its' crisp scent.

The first sip slides down *so* smoothly.

I close my eyes to savour the taste, but the taste of Simone and the sound of her climax play across my mind.

My second sip is more of a glug. The

memory of her enthusiastic face between my thighs as I reached my own orgasm sends an illicit throb deep in my core.

Tilting my head back, I skull the rest of it. Hoping the loud sloppy gulps will quiet her sighs teasing my every nerve.

The unmistakable sound of the door closing behind Steve stops me in my tracks. I hold my breath as I listen to his heavy footsteps coming up the stairs.

Fuck, I don't know what to do!

The kids hear him too and run to greet him on the landing.

"Daddy! Mummy threw up in the toilet!"

"Yeah! It was gross! Ewwwww!"

Steve looks up to find me looking sheepish in the kitchen with an empty glass of wine clutched in my hand.

"Oh. Was that before or after the wine, Evie?" His eyebrow raised comically.

Fearing my shaking hands will give me away, I place the glass on the bench then tuck my hands behind my back. The sight of him slightly concerned, yet on the verge of laughing because he knows I've attempted to treat vomiting with wine reminds me why I married him.

I have to tell him the truth…

"Just something I ate." I mumble.

Simone's open legs flood my mind and warmth floods my cheeks. I shake my head and turn back to my duty of preparing to cook dinner.

Unnerved, Steve pulls out his phone and

finds Netflix.

"Hey kids, who wants cartoons?"

"Me!"

"Me!"

Hannah and Jackson jump up and down with excitement then run into the media room.

Steve selects a cartoon at random and the theme song blares from the TV speakers.

He stands behind me at the kitchen bench and kisses my neck. Strong hands slide down my arms and hold my trembling hands still.

"What's up Evie?" Warm breath tickles my neck as he inhales me. "You smell... *different.*"

Oh no.

Of course I do.

My shoulders start to shake.

He barks in laughter for a moment until he realises, I'm not laughing.

I'm crying.

Steve spins me around in his arms so he can look at me.

"What's wrong Evie?" His voice is so gentle.

Looking up into his caring eyes, my throat constricts. I don't want to hurt this man.

My breath is suddenly ragged as large sobs escape me. Fat tears roll down my cheek as I prepare myself to murder our marriage.

"I'm so *sorry* Steve. I didn't mean for it to happen." It's a barely audible whisper.

"For what to happen Evie?" Bewilderment etched across his face.

I suck in air faster and start to hyperventilate. I must tell him.

Now.

I take a steadying breath in and count inside my mind. Counting again I slowly push the air out of my lungs.

Better.

"I… I had sex with Simone this afternoon."

Another large sob falls out of my lips and teardrops fall in earnest. They fall onto my bare feet, as I can't look anywhere else. I can't look him in the eye as I await his anger, his sadness.

The seconds drag out between us.

Waiting for him to tell me it's over, is torture.

"Wait…*What?"* Steve is stunned.

"Please don't make me repeat it." I stammer to his feet.

"I didn't even know you *liked* women." He runs his hand through his hair, taking a moment to process this new information.

I shrug non-committally at his comment. I don't know how much to give away about my life before we met. Prior relationships had never really been discussed because we wanted a fresh start… then the kids came along.

"Have you… have you had sex with a woman before?" Steve asks in wonder. Clearly amazed there was another side to his partner of ten years.

Memories from my early twenties flit across my mind. The parties, the late nights… and kissing girls in dark corners of bars. Often, it hadn't stopped there.

I realise I need to explain myself.

"I… have a past Steve. Before I met you, I… dated women. But that was ten years ago, I honestly thought that part of my life was finished. Of course, I never stopped *noticing* women… I just haven't been *intimate* with one since before I met you… until today."

Remorse is etched on my face.

"I cheated on you Steve, I didn't mean to… it just… sort of… happened… and once we'd started, we just couldn't stop… I'll…I'll understand if you want a divorce." I stare at the ground.

A long pregnant pause stretches out between us, and I look up to see Steve's mind-cogs cranking behind his eyes.

"Do you like sleeping with women?"

"Jesus Steve! Did you really just ask me that? Of course I liked it. But that's not the point!" I hiss.

Why is he being so flippant and not seeing the seriousness of my actions?

"Hey, I'm trying to look at this logically. So, you liked today, but you came home to me and our family right. We are important to you?" His voice is calm and reasonable.

"Of course you're important to me! Our family is my everything. You and the kids are my life."

"Right, and we make you happy?"

"Yes." I agree.

"But you also *like* women."

"Yes." The word comes out just above a whisper. It's always felt so taboo. A secret that

I've held so close, for so long.

"Did sleeping with Simone make you happy?"

I'm confused by his question, haven't I already answered him? I shoot him a puzzled look.

"What if I just want you to be happy?"

"I don't get what you mean, Steve. Yes, I was happy in the moment, but the fear of losing you had me vomiting down the toilet!"

Steve chuckles and shakes his head.

"We need to get rid of that anxiety, Evie." His eyes burn into mine once more, indicating the logical thinker has been parked. Steve wipes at the still wet tears on my cheek. The look in his eyes is not what I expected to see.

The confusion has evaporated. There's *humour... awe...* and *...a smoulder.*

"Was it good?" He asks, *sincerely*.

Visions of Simone flit behind my eyes and warmth spreads to my cheeks.

"It was *good* wasn't it?" His eyes are wide, his head nods as he takes in his blushing wife.

"Did you *come* today, Evie?" His voice low and intent.

Jesus, did he just ask me that?

Our eyes meet and it's like he can read my mind. A wolfish grin spreads across his face.

"Did *she* come?"

I make the slightest of nods.

A loud bark of laughter fills the kitchen and muscled arms pick me up and spin me around. My brow furrows and confusion floods me, replacing the sadness I felt mere seconds ago.

Where's the yelling?

Why is he so... *pleased?*

Steve sets me down, beaming from ear to ear. I shake my head, perplexed.

"Oh, come on Evie. This is brilliant!"

"Really?" I ask meekly.

"Yes!" He stands back to take me in, then he leans in closer. "I want *all* the details." His eyes burn into mine and a knot below my navel starts to unravel.

"So... you're... *happy* I slept with someone else?"

I'm incredulous.

He pulls me against his hips, his erection straining against his work slacks.

"I'm *delighted.*"

Oh.

"So, what does this mean Steve? Are you ok with me having a...*a girlfriend?*"

"Weeelll... no. I want to be your only constant. You married *me*, remember? But am I happy for you to have sex with other women in a casual capacity?" He pauses, then nods his head up and down. "Yes. Yes, I am."

"Wait... you want me to have sex with other women?"

He nods excitedly, then sobers. His hand strokes my cheek.

"You've gone ten years denying this side of yourself Evie. I can't believe you gave that up for *me.*"

"I don't know what to say."

"Say yes, that you'll do this for yourself...

and if I can ask just one thing in return?"

I knew there would be a catch.

"What Steve?" I hold my breath wondering what his condition could be.

"We're to *always* be honest with each other… and after each encounter, could you… tell me the *details*?"

I pause to reflect. This man should be ranting at me for cheating but instead he's giving me a part of my life back that I thought was long lost and over. I look up lovingly into his eyes.

"That seems a reasonable request."

I honestly don't think his smile could get any wider.

New possibilities swim across my mind as I take this new arrangement in.

He *wants* me to do this.

I have *permission* to sleep with Simone… and *other women* in a casual capacity.

I pull Steve into me and kiss his boyishly happy face.

"OK." I whisper into his mouth.

"If you *insist*."

Twelve

Evie and the Change in Perspective

I am still reeling from what happened last week with Simone. I just can't shake it from my mind. What surprises me was that it was so natural, and she was so willing to be swept away in the moment.

It makes me wonder if there are other women *like me,* out there. Mums who are in relationships with men, but secretly yearn for a female touch.

I hadn't kissed a woman since before I met my husband, I'd almost forgotten what it felt like. So sensual and soft. My issue now, is I can't seem to shake that exquisite memory from my mind. My mouth tingles at the mere thought.

My conversation with Steve replays in my mind. This *isn't* the end of our marriage, but a new *beginning*. A new chapter in my life where Steve is supportive of my *adventures,* provided I share my experiences afterwards. I didn't think it was possible, but since that conversation, our bedroom activity has ramped up as a result!

I want to see Simone again, but it's been *awkward.* There have been so many children and work commitments and Simone takes *so* long to respond to my messages. I'm no longer certain that another perfect moment will arise where we have an hour just to ourselves.

As the weeks roll by, I am starting to feel a little deflated. I have started questioning if that afternoon really unfolded so perfectly. Simone is leaving longer and longer pauses between messages which is pushing doubts into my mind.

It definitely happened…

I just need to carry on and not draw attention to it. This is our *secret.* We can't let the other mums know. They would have a *field day.* It would be the biggest scandal of the year! I hold our moment close but I'm starting to realise that maybe that is all it will be.

One moment.

There have been so many kids' birthday parties lately. So many opportunities to brush against other mums in innocent embraces. With Simone's distance, I'm starting to notice the *other* possibilities all around me. I've been to three birthday parties since I saw her last.

At each one I search for Simone, but she's

not there.

I can't say I'm not disappointed, but it does allow me the space to browse other women in my mind. There are a few mums who I know I find attractive.

Stacey with her sultry green eyes and gorgeous red hair.

She encompasses my Ariel from The Little Mermaid fantasy perfectly…It's a shame she's such a bitch.

Rachael with her beautiful buxom curves and friendly smile.

Too bad she's straight and I wouldn't want to ruin that friendship anyway.

…and then there's Lily.

I find myself chatting to her the most at each party. We have a couple of things in common, we are both juggling raising kids and working in customer services. She's gone back to work full time and coaches the school netball team on the weekends. I don't know how she keeps up with it all. With each subsequent party, we become more comfortable with each other, our laughter lighting up the room over the sounds of the kids playing musical chairs.

I love a woman who can laugh, I find it so *sexy.* Lily is very easy to like, but she frequently mentions her husband, so I lower my expectations and see this as a nice new *friendship.*

It's another Monday morning at the school

drop off. I sign Jackson into kindy and walk Hannah to the gate. She runs off without a backwards glance. I have so much on today that I don't linger to talk to the other Mums. The only Mum I *want* to talk to has stopped responding to my messages.

As I enter the carpark, I see Simone also climbing into her car. Our eyes meet and I make a beeline for her.

We need to talk.

Just the sight of her has a grin stretching across my face. But something is *off.*

Instead of happiness to see me, ice-cold fear is evident in her eyes. I watch as she rapidly buckles herself in and starts reversing.

She doesn't look back.

I feel sucker-punched, unable to move as I watch her zoom away from me.

What's going on?

Thirteen

Evie at Adventureland

Another two weeks have disappeared to the organised chaos of family life. Disappointedly, I realise it's been over two whole months since that blissful afternoon with Simone. A sigh escapes me as I rally myself for the activities of today.

It's mid-Saturday morning and the kids are excited for yet *another* birthday party. This one is at 'Adventureland'; one of those god-awful indoor playgrounds as the early winter rains have finally set in. I sit in the carpark and take a breath, trying to mentally prepare for what I'm in for. Jackson and Hannah are shrieking in the back seats.

"Let me out Mum!"

"The party has already started. We're Laaaaaate!"

I unbuckle myself and walk around to the back seats to help unclip Jackson while Steve opens the door for Hannah on the other side. Once on the footpath I straighten their outfits and hand Hannah the present to carry inside. Thank goodness Steve is here to help wrangle them. He's already off at a jog as the kids make a dash for the main doors.

I lock the car then make my way towards the main entrance. When I'm within a few metres I am assaulted by the noise of shrieking sugared up children. Like a warrior about to enter the midst of battle, I gather myself and walk headfirst into the throng.

It's even more of an assault to the senses once I'm through the doors. I have no idea how the staff can stay here for hours every day. They probably all have tinnitus.

I order two coffees then find the party table. Ours is in the middle, opposite the main entrance to the playground so the stream of happy kids going in and out is dizzying.

After saying hello to my fellow parents, I go back to collect our coffees and take one to my husband. He is dutifully on kid duty and stands watching them run amok. As I return to the party table, I scan the room. Simone's absence, yet again, noted on my radar.

I sit down at the table next to Lily, happy to see a friendly face. We embrace in a slightly awkward sideways hug. As we pull apart, she turns her chest and I find her breast has made its' way into my palm. It takes a second to realise I'm groping her. I'm so embarrassed and barely choke out an apology between my awkward high-pitched laughs. I can't understand how that just happened. It's then that I notice, she has her left leg in a moon boot, and it's slightly trapped under the table.

"What happened to you?"

"Netball. I tore my Achilles tendon last week. Looks like I'm in this for a few months." Lily gestures to the moonboot. "It's so frustrating, I have to get everywhere on crutches."

I'm waiting for her to say something, *anything* about the fact I just cupped her breast, but she's acting like it didn't happen. Trying to calm my pounding heart, I focus on what she has said. I make sympathetic noises and sip my coffee.

Despite her being clearly uncomfortable, she's made an effort for the party. Her hair is combed back into a butterfly clip and she's put on a little eye make-up. She's wearing a tight T-shirt that shows off her figure and slimming black leggings. The leggings clearly necessary so she can fit the moon boot over her clothing.

We chat about what our kids are doing at school, outside of school and their behaviour at home. I can't help but notice how animated she gets as she complains about the day-to-day grind of being a mum. Her cheeks have a subtle pink glow and her lips form this happy-tired smile in between sentences.

We are interrupted by platters being placed in front of us on very small tables pushed together. As we move closer to the table, I feel Lily's knee bump against mine. I expect her to apologise, but she carries on as if no bump happened. As we tuck into the cheese and crackers, we continue our conversation.

As we discuss extra-curricular activities, I feel her knee bump against mine, *again*. I try not to draw attention to it, then she starts brushing crumbs off her lap and her hand grazes my thigh. I think I glimpse a sparkle in her eye but I'm not sure. The cacophony of children having fun and a child crying somewhere from inside the fortress playground distracts me. I scan the room to check that Steve is watching our kids.

I hope that's not one of mine.

My thoughts are interrupted by a firm hand on my thigh. Startled, I look at Lily and she is leaning right into me. Her warm breath is on my ear, and I can tell she wants to say something, but she hesitates.

I'm listening intently, waiting... when we're interrupted by the loud voice of Zoe's mum, Susie.

"Cake time! Everyone round-up the kids, we're in party room two."

Lily and I exchange a *let's come back to this* glance and I help her stand up. She squeezes my arm in thanks, and I let her hobble ahead of me. I watch her toned behind skip hop with her crutches all the way to party room two.

Kids are darting everywhere as we all pour into a ridiculously tiny room. Zoe sits at the head of the table and the happy birthday song is sung. The cake is cut and handed out and within 20 minutes the kids are even more sugared up and running back to the playground.

The other parents run after their kids and Lily and I stay seated at the back, waiting for the stampede to filter out. Zoe's mum starts tidying up. Lily stands and steadies herself against me as she squeezes past to get to the other side of the table. She leaves her crutches leaning against the wall so she can hobble around with her hands free.

"Susie, you need a break. Why don't you go out and grab a coffee. Your hubby is watching the kids and Evie and I will clean up in here." Lily smiles at Susie and starts picking up cups.

"Are you sure?" Susie implores. "I really could do with 5 minutes and a shot of caffeine."

"Go, we got this" I smile and start stacking paper plates and napkins.

Susie leaves the room gratefully.

Lily and I work in silence, placing rubbish in the bin provided. I start musing about what Lily wanted to say earlier and my thoughts turn a little saucy as I remember her hand on my thigh and her breath on my ear. I'm depositing the final cup into the bin provided when I hear a subtle *click*.

I look up to see Lily push the bolt across the door, locking us in. I cock my head to one side and shoot a quizzical look across the room.

"I don't mean to scare you" she starts. "I just wanted to talk to you… alone…" Lily suddenly looks a little lost for words. Her cheeks flush and I notice she's a little breathless.

"Oh, umm well having the door closed definitely cuts out the noise. Is everything OK?"

She moves closer to me and we perch on the edge of the much tidier party table. My heart starts to race as I feel a frisson of electricity fill the small space between us. I have no idea what she wants to tell me, I'm wondering if she needs a girly heart to heart.

"I don't know how to say this…" she trails off and I rub her arm consolingly. I specifically aim for between her elbow and shoulder, a safe, non-sexual zone and try to calm my hammering heart.

"Whatever it is, I'm here. I'm a good listener."

Lily has leaned in so close I can smell Zoe's birthday cake on her breath.

"The thing is…" she whispers.

"Yes?" I say leaning in closer to hear her.

"The thing is… this.." Lily doesn't finish her sentence. Instead, she brushes her lips against mine then sits back, looking at me.

Waiting.

"Ohhh… that's a surprise."

Lily looks a mix between uncomfortable and eager.

"Was that… OK?" she asks quietly. "I've never kissed a girl before, but there's something about you Evie. I don't know what's come over me." She looks down at her hands.

I reach out, placing my hand on hers. Softly

I say, "yes, that was OK. I've noticed you too."

Lily lets out a sigh of relief.

Lily's lips are open, the briefest of quivers ripples across them and they look so *kissable*.

Steve's permission runs across my mind, followed by the image of Simone eagerly driving away from me on Monday. Here I am in a private room with someone who *wants* to kiss me. I push Simone from my mind.

I'm going to have some fun.

Chuffed, I say "So I'm your first girl kiss? That was just a peck. Shall I give you a proper kiss?" I lean in and hover my lips over hers, awaiting her consent.

"Yes please Evie" she whispers.

I close the space between us and gently touch her lips with mine. I taste sugar on her lips and I dart my tongue across them to get a better taste.

"Mmm, you taste good Lily"

A loud giggle escapes her, then she pulls me to her, her mouth hot and demanding. This time she parts her lips and I dart my tongue into her mouth. She pushes her tongue against mine and they swirl in a playful dance. Lily groans into my mouth. The sound travels straight to between my legs and I feel a delicious ache grow inside me.

I flick my tongue in and out of her mouth and I suck on her exquisite bottom lip.

She pulls my hand from the table and places it on her breast. It's warm and firm as I squeeze it. She sighs into my mouth as I fondle her. My other hand reaches behind her back and I deftly reach under her T-shirt and unhook her bra. I slink my hands around to her chest, sliding under her loosened bra and squeeze her nipples playfully until they harden in response.

Lily's hands shyly and hesitantly touch my chest. She rubs my breasts through the fabric and the friction feels amazing. I sigh, letting her know that it feels good. She gains confidence and before I know it, she is fumbling with the top of my trousers.

She makes quick work of finding entry and her fingers snake across the outer fabric of my panties. She starts rubbing me and I am amazed at her boldness considering this is her first time.

She pulls away from my lips. "Is this… OK?" she asks. "I have no idea what I'm doing".

"Yes" I breathe into her ear.

I start kissing her neck and as I move up towards her ear lobe, I can't resist giving it a playful nip. She sighs and I feel her fingers moving to the edge of the fabric of my panties. I turn and stand facing her, dislodging her fingers from their task.

She looks up at me with so much want and desire in her eyes.

It's *intoxicating.*

I lift her shirt and bra over her head to expose her beautiful breasts and place a nipple in my mouth while I fondle the other. She delicately takes my hand and leads it to the waistband of her leggings.

"Please" she whispers in my ear.

"Patience, Lily" I purr as I trail kisses along her smooth belly, slowly making my way south. I run my hands all over her body then squeeze her bottom, pulling her towards the edge of the table. She gasps excitedly.

I pull at her waistband with my teeth and use my hands to pull them down and off one leg, leaving them hanging against her moonboot.

She's wearing very sexy undies for a kid's birthday party. They're lacy and sheer and I can see they are already drenched with her anticipation.

I inhale her sweet heady scent as I move my face further down.

Memories of my first encounters with girls in my early twenties flit across my mind.

I've missed this.

She pulls the gusset aside and urges me forward. I kiss her gently, slowly, then I run my tongue in one long stroke along her very wet entrance. She tastes so good. I dive in ravenously, devouring every inch of her. She lets out a loud moan of delight. The sound charms and warms me to my core. I place a finger gently inside her, then two as I suck on her sweet, hardened node. I pulse my fingers in and out as I circle her clit with my tongue.

I can feel her mounting orgasm beneath me and suddenly she lets out a loud shriek of ecstasy.

Thank goodness the noise outside that locked door is enough to dampen the sound of her gloriously loud release.

I kiss her sweet spot and feel the spasms of her climax dissipate beneath my lips. As they finally cease I look up at her, a wolfish, satisfied grin plastered across my face.

She laughs heartily and it drives a delicious ache to my core. She pulls me up and wobbles to a standing position, I'm not sure what she wants to do next. She kisses me and pushes me against the wall, her hands are all over me, eagerly trying to get under my clothes.

Her hand finds the entrance to my trousers and this time she snakes her hand straight inside my panties. Her fingers find my molten moist centre and she sighs into my mouth. Her hands are soft and I am taken aback at how expertly she dances them between my folds.

She's a natural at this.

I close my eyes, allowing myself to relish in the mounting delectable pleasure rising between my legs.

She whispers in my ear "I've never tasted a woman before, can I go down on you?"

I smile at her and say, "You go right ahead".

Her eyes twinkle and she shimmies my trousers and panties down over my hips and they gather around my ankles.

I watch as she slowly stretches out her moon booted leg to one side and kneels on her good leg. Her face is so close, I can feel her breath on my thighs. She leans forward and kisses the very top of my opening gently. I feel her nervous tongue dart out and taste me. She hovers over me, savouring the new taste on her tongue.

I watch her curiously, looking to see from her expression if she liked it or not. She looks up at me with a devilish smile then dives in with a carnality I was not expecting. I am grateful for the wall behind me, holding me as I sag in bliss. I reach down, pulling her butterfly clip out and throwing it on the table. My fingers wrap into her silky hair which spurs Lily on. She is intent in her task and I am *burning* up.

I'm so, *so close.*

Suddenly I feel her fingers inside me as she sucks hard on my rigid knot. It's too much and I let out a delirious scream as I shudder and spasm in my blinding white-hot orgasm.

After the little waves inside me cease she gently removes her fingers and kisses my folds, then my thighs. She looks up at me with an elated smile.

I notice her lips are glistening with my nectar and it's so *hot*.

I help her up off the floor and I feel her eyes lingering on me as I pull up my panties and trousers. Silently I help her step back into the hanging fabric of her black leggings.

"You were as loud as I was" she murmurs.

"Thank goodness this place is loud enough to cancel us out!" I reply with a smirk.

She takes her fingers and places them in her mouth, a final taste of my salty sweetness. I pull her hand away and kiss her deeply one last time.

"Come on, I think the hour for this party room is up."

We quickly ensure the room is in fact tidy and after checking each other's clothing and hair, we unbolt the door. I poke my head out and look around at the chaos of running and screaming children. No one is looking our way. I give Lily's hand a gentle squeeze before I stand back and let her hobble through the door before me.

As she awkwardly moves back to our original tables by the playground, she glances over her shoulder at me. A soft smile plays on her lips and there's an evident a sparkle in her eye.

Who would have thought I'd have such a decadent *adventure* of my own at Adventureland.

Fourteen

Evie and the Distraction

Well, who would have known Lily liked women. I honestly thought she was just a friendly gal. As we drive home from the party, I think back to that tiny party room and feel an internal celebration inside me. It was so pleasantly unexpected. Lily had such a wonderfully infectious enthusiasm to please and… oh… that delighted glint in her eyes afterwards.

Steve is pleased too. As we were wrapping up the party, he kissed me, immediately noticing the slightly salty taste on my lips. The smoulder he gave me as he read me like an open book was sexy as hell.

As the rushing countryside whizzes past us, my thoughts stray yet again to Simone. I wonder if she would be upset about what I've just done with Lily? Then I remember all my messages that have gone unanswered… plus the look she gave me in the school carpark that day as she drove away.

She couldn't get away from me fast enough.

The reality is, Simone is clearly avoiding me, which hurts. I have tried a number of times to see her, but if she responds at all, it's after the suggested time has already passed. I can't help but feel a little… well… *rejected.*

Finally home, the afternoon is filled with the sugar-crash aftermath of the party. Our kids bicker and make continuous grumpy protests as we try and play a nice family board game.

When dinner is finally over, Steve and I rush the kids' bedtime routine so that we could have some alone time. As I relayed each exquisite detail of my party room encounter, the sex Steve and I had was *explosive.* Sated and relaxed, Steve turns to me. "I like Lily for you. Do you think she'd be up for more femme-sur-femme adventures?"

"Maybe. I guess I could ask and see what she says. Are you happy with me seeing the same woman more than once Steve? I thought girlfriends were not on the cards."

"You're right, I did say that… Hmm… what about if we make the boundaries really clear. You can have casual sex provided she knows you're happily married and not looking to break up any families."

I ponder this for a moment.

Would Lily be open to that?

"I guess I could ask… I'd also need to ensure she would be *discreet.* I know what the mums are like at school. If word got out it would spread like wildfire."

"That's something you'll need to discuss first then. Want me to watch the kids tomorrow so you can have a coffee date?"

He gives me a wink and I can't help but laugh. Spurred on by his eagerness I pull out my phone and hastily tap out a message to Lily.

'Hi Lily, how are you? Just wondering if you had time tomorrow for a coffee to chat?'

It's ten o'clock, so I'm not sure she'll get back to me tonight. I turn off my screen and place my phone on the bed next to me, snuggling back into Steve's chest. I breathe in his masculine scent, wondering if he would be up for round two. As I stroke my fingers across his torso the light from my phone interrupts my thoughts. Steve chuckles "looks like she got your message."

I sit up and reach for my phone. I'm actually surprised she's gotten back to me so fast.

Simone would have left me hanging.

I push Simone from my mind as I welcome the distraction of Lily's response, a small smile shapes my lips.

'I am still glowing from what happened earlier, Evie. What we shared… it blew my mind. I would love to have coffee with you. 10am? Camelia Café?'

I show the message to Steve and he nods. "I can watch the kids."

I quickly type out my reply.

'Yes, me too. I'll meet you there.'

Butterflies flit around in my stomach as I wait for Lily to arrive. I've ordered my coffee and a ginger slice. I drum my fingers on the table as I wait. Suddenly, Willow runs up to me and gives me a big hug.

"Hi Hannah's Mum. My mummy said I can have a hot chocolate and a treat if I play by myself afterwards."

I squeeze her back, affectionately.

Maybe I should have brought Hannah.

Lily looks a little harassed as she sits down opposite me with an apologetic look.

"You alright Lily?" I ask.

"Yeah. Sorry, Cam wouldn't look after Willow for me. I hope that doesn't bother you?"

I shake my head with a smile. "No, not at all. She's such a sweet girl, I wish I'd have known earlier. I would have brought Hannah so they could play."

Lily looks relieved. "Thanks. Have you ordered?"

"I have for myself, sorry I had no idea what you liked."

"No trouble I'll get myself something and I promised this one some sugary treats." She gives Willow a playful tickle and she giggles.

A few moments later we're all drinking our drinks and talking about how the girls are doing at school. Willow slurps loudly, finishing her hot chocolate. Lily leans over and nudges Willow towards the toys. A strange expression flashes across Willow's face, apprehension perhaps? It disappears in an instant, replaced with a big smile as she jumps down and heads to the children's toy area. My eyes follow her, not quite sure of what I just saw.

My thoughts are interrupted by Lily's foot rubbing my calf under the table, making me jump. Surprised I automatically pull my feet under my chair out of her reach. Even though they're under the table, *anyone* can see. A nervous laugh escapes me as I take in Lily's darkened gaze.

"Right... umm should we talk about what happened yesterday?" I try and sound confident, but my mouth has gone dry. I pick up my coffee, taking a calming sip, whetting my mouth with it's sharp flavour.

"Hmm I'd rather talk about when I can see you... *alone.*" Lily's words are heavy with suggestion and I'll admit it's turning me on. But I need to be an adult and discuss things before I jump into bed with her...*again.*

"I'd like that too Lily, but first, I need to check we're on the same page here."

"Of course." She purrs. "What's on your mind?"

"Well, we're both married. Steve knows what happened between us and he is supportive of us to...to..." I'm suddenly aware of the people at nearby tables and I can't quite get my words out for fear they will hear me.

"...to have sex? Is that what you wanted to

say?" A sleek eyebrow is raised playfully.

"Yes." I whisper. "But we need boundaries... and rules."

"Such as?"

"This is strictly casual... only us and our husbands are to know what we get up to. No one else can know Lily.... And we're not to mess up our families with this. I love my husband. I can't believe I have the freedom to even be having this conversation with you." I smile, thinking I've captured it all. Lily plays with the teaspoon sticking out from her plate as she considers what I've said.

"So you want this to be *a secret.*"

"Yes."

I suddenly wonder if she's not alright with my proposition.

Lily raises her eyes to meet mine and I'm taken aback by the fire within them.

"Yes, Evie. I think that's a wonderful plan. So, when can we have our next *secret session?*"

The messages have been firing back and forth between Lily and I like teenagers since that Sunday morning coffee. I've been to her house *twice* now, she is starting to become my favourite thing to do on a Friday. I don't know how she's worked her hours, but she's managed to organise late starts just so I can visit at 9am for an hour. I can tell you, sex with Lily is a *thrilling* way to start my day off. We *never* make it the bedroom. Today will be my *third* Friday visit in a row.

Steve dropped the kids for me this morning, so here I am, on Lily's doorstep, dressed in a raincoat that reaches my shins… with my sexiest underwear on underneath, playing out a high-class escort fantasy.

I feel the cold swirling around my ankles as I wait for her to open the door. Anticipation pooling in my lacy knickers. I wouldn't have thought to do this myself. I'm definitely out of my comfort zone here… but Lily wanted me to.

Lily begged me to.

Getting impatient I ring the doorbell again. It is the middle of fricken *winter.*

Why couldn't we try this one in summer?

Summer… Simone pops into my head and I feel a weight drop into my stomach.

Everything about that day was so beautiful.

Movement inside the house distracts me from my thoughts and Lily finally opens the door in a soft bathrobe, a wicked smile across her face. Her crutches are nowhere to be seen. She grabs the belt of my coat and pulls me inside the door, slamming it behind us. She pushes me against the wall and slowly undoes my belt. Thoughts of Simone fade quickly as she pulls at my buttons one by one. It's cold inside today and I shiver.

"Lily, why isn't your heat pump on?" I ask as she finally opens my coat, revealing my frigidly cold body. She runs her warm hands over my hard with cold nipples which are straining against my sheer bra. The sensation is *exquisite.*

"I want you cold, Evie."

"You have that. I'm freezing."

"Good. I'm going to warm you up... slowly."

I gasp as Lily spins me around and pulls the coat from my shoulders. She is slightly unbalanced as she pushes me against the wall, a little rougher than expected. I feel her tender kisses on the nape of my neck as she presses herself against my back and I relax. Lily's warm hands run up and down my body, burning me with her caresses. I want to kiss her so I push myself away from the wall and turn to face her. We're so ravenous for each other we forget about the role play. Lily drops her robe from her shoulders and thrusts her naked body against me. Her hand pulls at my underwear and within seconds I feel her fingers deep inside me, her spare hand pulls my fingers from her hair and pushes it between her legs. We grind against each other, the friction adding to our building orgasms. It's too much. I feel Lily's velvet folds pulse in pleasure at the same time as blinding hot waves envelope me, our cries dancing together in the cold hallway. Our bodies slump together, our lungs gasping for breath.

Lily disentangles from me and hobbles into the kitchen, flicking on the kettle. I pick up my coat and wrap it around myself again. Her house truly is freezing. I watch silently as Lily starts awkwardly pulling on her work uniform. Her moonboot still impeding her.

I offer my arm for her to hold while she

pulls up her skirt. Once dressed, she starts making us coffees and I lean against the kitchen counter, smiling as I watch her work.

"So" I venture, "how is Cam enjoying our little shenanigans?" I ask with a coy smile.

Lily fusses over the instant coffees, not meeting my gaze. She mumbles something non-committal as she stirs in the milk.

Her reaction is odd, but I push on anyway. "So, tell me, has your sex-life with Cam gone up a notch? Mine with Steve is incredible at the moment. He loves our *catch-ups.*" I smile saucily.

Again, Lily averts her gaze.

What's going on here?

"Lily, you have told Cam haven't you?" My heart starts to race as Lily turns to face me, coffees in hand. The look on her face says it all.

She hasn't told him.

"Lily, you *need* to tell him!"

Sheepishly she places one mug in front of me and slowly sips hers. "I will. I promise. As soon as he gets back from his business trip. He'll be home tomorrow."

"Make sure you do, Lily. I'm not sure I'm OK with us doing this if he doesn't know. It's not what we discussed."

Lily puts down her mug and takes my hands in hers. "I will tell him, I promise." She cradles my face in her hand and draws me in for a tender kiss.

"Tomorrow."

Fifteen

Evie and the Play Date

I never thought I'd be grateful for one of those ridiculous, teacher only days, but there's one coming up this Friday. My daughter Hannah is begging to have a playdate with Simone's daughter Katie, so in an attempt to at least, maintain the girls' friendship, I've invited them around for a playdate.

Simone has surprisingly agreed but told me that she can't stay. I'm disappointed. I was hoping we could chat while the girls play.

I'll be honest that despite my newfound enjoyment of Lily and our almost regular shenanigans, I still have a soft spot for Simone. I thought seeing Lily would push her out of my mind. I hoped time would dull my feelings for her... You'd think that after nearly four months of avoiding me the message would hit home, but I miss her. I'd like to have her in my life, even just as a friend... if that's all she can offer.

The days are dragging on as I internally will Friday to come faster. I am driving myself slightly crazy at the thought of seeing Simone in the flesh, wondering if we will get the chance to *talk.*

Thursday is filled with normal day to day mum and work stuff. But I can feel a subtle charge of electricity that propels me forward over the course of the day.

Before I know it, the day is over and I'm in bed with Steve with the lights out. I have a restless sleep. With every wakeful moment, I plan the conversations I want to have with Simone in my head. I think of all the scenarios of how I can rebuild our friendship as well as all the possible responses she might make to my points. I tie myself in knots and talk myself in circles until I finally drift back into an uneasy sleep.

My four-year-old son Jackson wakes us at ten to six in the morning and I feel hungover. Steve, my saviour gets up and makes us coffees and the kids' hot chocolates.

I lie in bed resting my eyes until the delicious smell of steaming coffee wafts over me, a soft kiss brushes against my lips.

"Good morning" my husband smiles a tired smile as I sit up.

Hannah is now awake, thanks to Jackson shouting his glee for hot chocolates throughout the house. I do love our morning ritual. The four of us piled into our bed, enjoying a quiet moment together as the winter sun rises outside our window. The quiet calm before the storm of the day.

After a blur of rushed morning activities, Steve leaves the house with Jackson.

Thank goodness for day care. I think to myself as the calm is slightly restored with the house half empty.

Hannah is so excited for Katie to come over. She fizzes about the house telling me all the games and arts and crafts she would like to do with her when she arrives. I encourage her to set a few things up while I finally make it into the bathroom for some time to myself.

As I step out of the shower, I catch sight of myself in the mirror, glistening wet with steam surrounding me. I see my own breasts standing to attention and can't help myself as I give them an appreciative squeeze. I find it fascinating that when I was younger, I was so self-conscious about my body. There were so many parts of myself that I wished were different.

Yet here I am, with my post-pregnancy body where I grew not one, but two little human beings inside me. My body has changed, along with my view of myself. I know I'm softer in places and rounder in the hips, but I look at myself now and I *love* my body.

I feel *sexy* when I move.

I feel *confident* in my skin.

My body is miraculous, it gave life and I appreciate it so much more.

I dry myself and complete my morning routine, glancing at my watch.

They'll be here soon.

I know it's just a playdate and Simone won't stay, but I put a flick of mascara on my eyelashes. Just to make me feel good. The sound of tyres crunching on gravel, along with a happy little toot-toot, tells me our visitors have arrived.

Hannah rushes down the stairs with me just a few steps behind her. Katie is barely out of her seat before the girls are jumping up and down with excitement. Hannah lists all the things they will do today as Katie looks over her shoulder to our large trampoline on the front lawn.

"Can we play on your trampoline first?" Katie asks.

The girls look at me pleadingly.

"Of course you can" I laugh. "Go right ahead."

They dash off up the garden path hysterically laughing and talking as they go. I share a contented mum smile with Simone as they rush off. Simone reaches into the back seat to retrieve Katie's bag. I can't help but notice the smooth curve of her behind as she bends over.

She brings it over and as she passes it to me our fingers touch. Our eyes meet and the heat between us is instant.

"Are you sure you can't stay for just one cuppa?" I pause wondering what she will say. "I can make it quick, the kettle's not long boiled."

My words hang in the air for a moment.

Simone looks at her watch.

"You know what, sure. I have time for a quick one. 20 minutes tops though, OK?"

"Great" I beam, a blush gathering on my cheeks.

Simone laughs. "Yeah, we probably need to talk anyway."

She follows me inside and up the stairs to the kitchen. I make sure I sway my hips, knowing that my behind will be at her eye level. I glance over my shoulder to see if she's looking and feel slightly giddy when I see that she is.

Our eyes meet and I see her desire change to fear and awkwardness.

It throws me.

Where did my free-spirited, confident Simone go?

Once in the kitchen I open the front window so that we can hear and see the girls playing outside. I push my feelings down, not knowing what to make of the murkiness between us.

"Coffee or tea?" I ask. I need to make myself busy so that my hands won't give me away with their nervous trembling.

"Coffee sounds good thanks. White, no sugar".

I make my way into the little nook where our kettle is and busy myself making our drinks. I like our nook, it's kind of a large walk-in pantry next to our fridge. Inside we have a shelf with a couple of electrical outlets for our toaster, kettle and microwave. I can feel Simone behind me, a mere meter from my body. I glance up and see her leaning against the door frame watching me work.

"I've tried so hard to stay away Evie." She starts, then stops.

Confused I ask, "Why are you trying to stay away?"

She looks exasperated, strained. Like I should already know the answer.

"You're a woman. I'm not supposed to like you, Evie. I'm not supposed to want you… or dream about your hands on me every night…"

Her words are anguished and I can see the turmoil all over her face. My mind flashes back to her deck, a place my mind flits to often, her words "I've never done this before" when she was pinching my nipples, rush across my mind. It suddenly dawns on me.

Simone had never been with a woman before.

Our moment together on her deck was so much *more* for her.

"Oh, Simone. I've just realised…" I breathe out "I was your *first.*" I reach out for her arm and heat sizzles between us. "That was a big deal for you. You were such a natural, I wasn't listening properly and got caught up in the moment. I'm sorry." Remorse floods me as I wonder if I took advantage.

She can see where my mind is going and she holds out a hand to stop my rampaging thoughts.

"*I* didn't know I could do what I did that day. I surprised myself with how bold I was with you." Her cheeks flush as her eyes meet mine, our lovemaking memory hanging heavy between us. A question nags inside me.

"Did you know you liked women before that moment?"

Her arms fold protectively across her chest and she can't quite meet my gaze.

"I loved Jonathan, but I always felt something was ...*missing.* After Katie was born, I took a long time to warm up to being intimate again. I tried to reason that I was tired, or had a headache, or Katie was sick and needed me. We tried, but I didn't enjoy it. I'm wondering now if I ever really did. When Katie was four the sex stopped and Jonathan stopped asking. I guess he'd finally had enough of my excuses. We were still amicable, all things considered, but something was broken and I didn't understand why. I was still shocked when he asked for a divorce... I should have seen it coming." She sniffs, holding back the tears welling in her eyes.

"Then I saw you, Evie. I saw you and something stirred inside me. It *scared* me… I'm not supposed to like women Evie! I shouldn't be feeling these *things*…But every time I saw you, this heat, this *spark* between us… it just kept growing…" Simone pauses, then whispers "it was burning me alive."

"Oh Simone, we should have talked about this before we were intimate. I had no idea you were struggling with your sexuality. It must have been terrifying for you."

"It was at the beginning, but then you kissed me and deep down, I just knew. It felt right for the first time in my life. That kiss brought my soul *alive*. Finally, my body was responding... but it was to *your* touch. I couldn't fight it anymore. There was no turning back."

Her arms fall to her sides as tension leaves her body along with her confession. But something about her admission niggles at me.

"So, if it felt so right, why have you been avoiding me all this time?"

Simone shoots me a frustrated glare. "Do I have to state the obvious? You're married Evie. I'm separating. It's a mess. We can't do this. We can't break up your marriage just because I find myself attracted to you. You're *lying* to your husband Evie." The statements rush out and she takes a big breath. She's clearly been practicing saying those words to me for a long time.

"Ohhhhh." I reply as the penny drops.

Had I not told her Steve was OK with this?

No... I realise I never had the opportunity.

"I'm so sorry Simone, I should have told you, but we never seemed to get a moment alone after that day. I have told my husband. Steve knows and he's OK with it."

"What?" Simone looks shocked. It wasn't the answer she was expecting.

"He's OK with you cheating on him?" She says it like an attack. A challenge.

"Well, he was surprised of course. But we had a big heart to heart. He thinks it's great, that women find women attractive. He was happy for me when I told him about you. But there are some rules of course...." I trail off as I watch her trying to take this new information in.

"Such as...?" She asks.

"Well, I'm allowed to explore this side of me, provided we continue to be honest with each other... and provided I tell him what I get up to.... In detail."

"In detail?!" Simone almost yells the words. I can see she's piecing the information together and she's not happy.

I reach out and take her hand. She snatches it away and I feel like I've been slapped in the face. She takes two steps away from me, breathing hard.

"Simone" I implore. "I loved my time with you that day. There was nothing sinister in that moment. It just happened and I honestly wasn't expecting it. Simone, it was beautiful what we shared. Don't you remember?" I feel my bottom lip quiver as tears sting at the corner of my eyes.

She stares at the floor and doesn't meet my gaze.

"I was so scared to tell him." I feel my voice thicken with the confession. "I even threw up before he came home. I thought it was going to be the end of my marriage. The fact that he's even open to me doing this is just mind-blowing. I'll understand if this is all too weird for you."

I watch her pace across my kitchen and can see her brain whizzing behind her eyes. The kettle pings and to give her a minute, I return to making our coffees.

I reach into the fridge to pull out the milk and suddenly I feel a soft hand on my shoulder. I turn around and Simone is inches from my face. I never realised that she was slightly taller than me, but I have to tilt my chin to look up at her. Her eyes are shining with the emotional rollercoaster of the last five minutes. I'm sure mine are the same. She gently pulls me back into our kitchen nook. Her hand brushes my cheek and her fingers interweave with my hair.

Simone's voice is low and throaty, barely above a whisper. "So what you're telling me… is if I wanted to kiss you right now, we wouldn't be cheating on anyone?"

"No" I'm barely audible. My heart is pounding so hard in my chest that I'm sure she can hear it. She grips my hair slightly harder. It pulls but doesn't hurt.

"You're sure?" Her lips have moved so close to mine I can taste her words.

"Yes" I whisper.

Her lips crush against mine. They're soft, yet urgent as they explore my mouth. The sensation stirs flashbacks to our first encounter, and I feel a delicious dull ache inside my knickers. We devour each other, our tongues twirling in ecstasy. I am completely lost in her. My hands find her hair and I twist my fingers into her soft tresses. Our bodies are pressed firmly against each other, and the friction is *delicious*.

"Come and see my room, Katie!"

I hear Hannah and Katie joyously slam the downstairs door shut before they start bounding up the stairs.

Fear rips through me and hastily, I pull away. Simone is dazed but swiftly gathers herself as she sees the look of trepidation on my face.

"Here's the biscuits Simone." Thrusting a packet of biscuits into her hands, I gesture to the table behind us in the kitchen. She takes the hint and makes her way over to the table.

I busy myself with finishing the coffees as the girls make it up the stairs to the landing. Simone is at least halfway across the kitchen, biscuits in hand, like everything is normal.

The girls dart about around us, taking biscuits as we sit quietly sipping our coffees. I try and keep things light and rouse a conversation about school and the events coming up. Simone listens, albeit absently, then glances at the clock on the wall.

"My goodness, is that the time?! I really must run. I have an appointment." She downs the dregs of her coffee and stands up.

She calls to Katie. "I'll see you this afternoon sweetie. You be good for Evie, OK?"

"OK Mum!" Katie responds from the depths of Hannah's room.

"I'll walk you out." I place my coffee back on the table and follow her down the stairs. At the door she puts on her shoes and glances around, ensuring the kids are still in Hannah's room and not lurking in the stairwell. She reaches out and takes my hand. I lean in for one last kiss before she rushes off. She chastely pecks me on the lips and gives my hand a squeeze. I can see the longing written all over her face.

"I'll message you later." A suggestive grin tugs at the corners of her mouth.

The strain that was etched on Simone's face on arrival has miraculously lifted and I'm relieved.

Standing in the doorframe, I observe her as she climbs into her car and reverses up my drive. My eyes following until I hear her chirpy toot-toot as she turns out of view.

The girls alert me to the merry ruckus inside and I sigh heavily, returning to my supervising duties.

If only I could have a playdate with Simone, *without* the children.

Sixteen

Evie and the Dilemma

My secrets just became complicated. I had no idea Simone had been having this internal struggle with her sexuality. She seemed such a willing participant, I just assumed she wasn't a complete novice. What a fool I've been. Looking back, it makes so much sense. I'm disappointed in myself for not realising earlier when Simone went so quiet. I was so wrapped up in feeling so confused and hurt myself that I never thought about what she might have been going through.

My new dilemma is *what do I do now?*

Lily is still very much part of my present… Simone clearly has a thing about cheating, which I do too. I'm really not happy that Lily hasn't told Cam yet.

I know I'm a hypocrite right now. I haven't told Simone about Lily. Another question strikes me.

Have I cheated on Lily with Simone?

Is kissing cheating?

I have *no idea* what I'm doing.

To be honest, I'm not quite sure I'm cut out for this polyamory thing. I keep jumping from being so excited, to feeling deathly anxious that someone is going to get hurt, quite possibly *all of us*.

I weigh up the events that have shaped my year so far… sleeping with Simone in Summer and then Lily in Winter. The settings and people involved are so *different*.

I'm not sure I like different.

The jury is currently out to lunch.

The truth of it all is that I have slept with two mums from my daughter's school.

Steve seems oblivious to my internal quandary. He is ecstatic that Simone and I made out in our kitchen and has loved every story about my Friday sessions with Lily.

My mind darts back to Simone grappling with her emotions as she shared her journey in my kitchen. The tears in her eyes evident for me to see. There are so many emotions swimming inside me, they flit through the full range, like someone shuffling a deck of cards. I don't seem to know which emotion will take hold next. It's quite overwhelming to *feel* so much for three different people.

Simone is messaging me again, which ignites so much hope. However, I think she's still coming to terms with things, as her messages are intermittent and sometimes cryptic.

Unlike Lily's.

Lily's messages are outright X-rated and I'm wondering what more I can do to communicate that we need to tone it down and keep our encounters *hushed*. I am *petrified* that Simone will find out about Lily… and that Lily will find out I've been kissing Simone.

It's sad, but every time I hear my phone ping, I get a little rush of hope that it's Simone. Then I feel deflated when it's not.

The last few days, it's just been Lily…

'Evie, can I come over?'

'Evie, my husband just left for work, I'm lonely. Could you be at mine in 15?'

'Evie, I can't stop thinking about your hands and mouth on me…'

'Evie, are you OK?'

'Evie, why aren't you answering?'

'Evie, did I do something wrong?'

'Evie?'

'Evie?'

'EVIE!'

After those last three, I finally respond.

'Alright. I'll see you Friday at 9am.'

I want to put an end to our arrangement as this is all just getting too hard. Her spirited face floats across my mind and I feel a pang of remorse. This might crush her, but I can't go on like this. Thank goodness she knows this is just casual. I'll go over and tell her I just want us to be friends. I have to do it in-person, she deserves that. I just hope she takes it OK.

Lily opens the door wearing her bathrobe.

Without a word she pulls me inside and slams me against the wall with a heated kiss. This is Lily's trademark move to initiate sex. She does it every time I visit. I kiss her back but Simone's kisses replay in my mind making me feel sick. I wrench my lips from hers and push her to arm's length.

"Don't I even get a hello?"

"Hello Evie" she says with a sultry low voice, then proceeds to kiss my neck, her hands reaching under my skirt.

Despite how heavenly her lips feel on me, I push her hands away and slip out from under her.

"Lily," I say pointedly, "we need to talk." I take her hand and lead her, hobbling with her ankle still in that moonboot, into the kitchen and flick on the kettle switch. I turn to face her, resolute in my task, holding her hand in both of mine.

"Lily, I've been thinking, I don't know if we..." I start, but my words are cut short as Lily grabs my face, locking her lips on mine. Her body presses up against me, pushing my hips against the kitchen counter. The body-to-body contact sparks the familiar pull below my navel. My body *knows* this, *wants* this, but I lean back, trying to put some space between us. I need to say what *I came here to say* before my desire takes over my brain.

"Lily, listen to me...I..." But Lily is not listening. She kisses me again. As I pull away for the third time, she holds on with her teeth, biting my lip hard.

"Ouch! What the fuck, Lily?" I wipe my mouth to check if I'm bleeding.

I'm not.

Lily shrugs, a glint of playfulness in her eyes as her fingertips trail up and down my sides. I shake my head as I try to find the right words.

"I don't think this is such a good idea anymore, Lily. My kids, Steve, it's all getting too complicated."

I'd barely gotten those words out when suddenly, Lily lifts my skirt and rips my panties down. She drops to her knees and plunges her face between my legs. I'm so surprised, it takes me a moment before I try to resist. Squirming my hips I try to move away from her, but my squirms spur Lily on. My body responds and for a moment I'm torn between enjoying what she's doing and following through on what I came here to do. Ignoring the warm sensation building beneath her tongue, I reach down to try and pull her up. I came here to *talk to her,* but Lily's hands pin me firmly against the kitchen counter. Her fingers dig into my hips, holding me still.

"Lily, *stop!* I'm trying to..." but before I can finish my sentence, my body betrays me, and I come hard against her mouth. Shock courses through me as Lily finally releases me, a satisfied smile swathes her face.

But *I* am not smiling.

"I was trying to talk to you." My voice cracks as I tug my twisted panties back into place and adjust my skirt.

Lily laughs. "You just came on my face Evie, I think that was *all* the talking we needed to do." Her voice and eyes are light, but there is something very *unsettling* about what just happened.

My eyes sting with tears and I feel *strange.*

I need to get out of here.

Frowning at Lily's impish face, I grab my bag and walk out of her kitchen.

Lily catches up with me as I open her front door.

"Evie, come on, I thought you liked that?"

"I was trying to *talk* to you." Flashing her a glare, I frustratedly ask "ughhh… have you even *told* Cam yet?"

Lily's face looks odd, like she's stifling a laugh, but trying to be serious.

"No… but I will. Come back inside Evie, it's my turn now." She pulls on my hand, pushing it under her robe where I find she is *very* naked.

This feels wrong.

I pull my hand back and step outside.

"Sorry, not today Lily. I… have to go."

I rush to my car, leaving a vexed-looking Lily in her doorway. I belt up quickly and screech onto the road, tears burning in my eyes.

I need some space to think.

I pull into the park near my home and sit in my car under a tall oak tree. My hips ache where Lily dug her hands into me and my lower back is sore from where it was pressed against the edge of the counter. I *can't* believe

I orgasmed. I can't believe I lost *control* of my body like that. I place my face in my hands as I allow my tears to fall.

I feel so *guilty*.

Guilty because Lily *hasn't* told her husband.

Guilty because I think I'm developing real feelings for Simone and Lily just fucked me in her kitchen when I was meant to be *ending it*.

I said stop…

Lily's reaction indicated that she thought I didn't mean it… and well… *I did come.*

Maybe I didn't want her to stop?

I'm so confused.

It dawns on me that I can't tell Steve what happened today, he's all about consent. He'd blow this way out of proportion and I'm still trying to figure all of this out.

All I know, is that this was meant to be fun… but I'm no longer enjoying this game.

Seventeen

Evie and the Proposition

The school drop offs are suddenly very problematic. I try not to get too close to either Lily or Simone as kids dart between our bodies in the rush to start school on time.

Once or twice, Lily has hobbled over and in a quick embrace she has pushed her body against mine creating an unexpected rush of friction. I'm still unsure how I feel after our last encounter, so I'm quick to extract myself. I know I need to talk to her, but school is not the right place.

Simone is much more discreet with her physical contact. This morning Simone hangs back with me as we wait for the throngs to dissipate, then she walks me back to my car. I open my door to create a shield for us to stand behind. It looks like we are finishing off a conversation about our kids, or school, but in reality, the car door conveniently blocks our hands from view.

We watch as numerous parents tear

through the school gates, wild eyed as they eject their kids from the back seats. With the briefest of hugs, they shove them towards their classrooms as the bell rings out across the schoolyard.

Simone and I observe each scene with our hidden hands entwined. The sensation of her fingers interlocked with mine, her thumb drawing circles on the skin between my thumb and index finger feels tantalisingly *thrilling*. The fear of getting caught tugs at me, attempts to suppress the desire that is building between us.

"Jesus Simone, I want to kiss you right now." I whisper, hoping that no other parent has super-sonic hearing, or can read lips from across the carpark.

She smiles beguilingly. "Oh trust me, I want that too… But, I have to go to work."

She traces a couple more circles on my hand then extracts her fingers from mine tormentingly slow. God, she makes me feel *alive*.

I watch her cross the carpark as I climb into my car, wishing we had the time and a private space to make out.

The interactions with Simone are so small but packed to the brim with explosive chemistry.

I just don't know what to do with myself.

Steve is loving it, *obviously*.

With each small interaction with Simone in the morning, Steve and I have the most mind-blowing sex as soon as the kids are asleep at night. All my senses are alive and pulsing with sexual energy.

I'm sure every pore of my existence is screaming for sex and I wonder if other people can smell my pheromones.

I have noticed a few extra appreciative scans of me from other mums recently. Part of me is intrigued when I notice them. I watch as they subtly shift their weight and gently arch their backs so their chest prominently shows off the curve of their bust.

I wonder if they even *realise* they're doing it?

I feel powerful and shit-scared by the attention at the same time.

Lily still doesn't know about Simone... and Simone still doesn't know about Lily.

I've had a lot of time to think over the past few days. Regardless of the fact my body might still *respond* to Lily, I've realised that I no longer *want* to be intimate with her after last Friday. Now I just need to find a way to make that *clear*.

I'm working from home today. It's always such a relief to have the house to myself. The early winter sun streams through our window and I can hear the birds chirping outside. I am so glad we bought out here. The only cars that come along our road are locals so there isn't the constant stream of traffic noises that I used to hear at our old home in the suburbs. I look back to my emails and start processing claims for our customers. I am so glad that I can do this from home.

Ping.

I glance over at my phone and I feel my heart flutter as I see it's Simone and *not* Lily.

'Hi Evie, Jonathan has Katie this weekend. Can I cook dinner for you on Saturday?'

...

I can see she's still typing so I wait. I'm also doing my best to play it cool and not appear that I am always waiting by my phone to respond to her.

'Would that be ok with Steve?... Could you spend the night?'

Spend the night?

Oh my! My heart is hammering in my chest, my fingers are itching to reply YES! YES! YES!

But I don't.

I can feel myself getting wet at the mere thought of spending a whole night with Simone. I can't believe it's been four months since I saw her naked. But there is this niggling feeling in the back of my mind.

Would Steve be ok with this?

This is not a secret squirrel romp with Lily on a Friday morning.

I don't respond.

I sit staring at the message for what feels

like an eternity. I hear my laptop ping at least five times with new claims from clients but I don't action them. Suddenly my phone is ringing. It's my boss, Abigail.

"Evie, what's going on? You haven't completed an order for over an hour."

She sounds pissed. *Jesus.* I think to myself. *What just happened?*

"Abigail, I'm so sorry."

Thinking on my feet, I tell her a lie.

"I think Jackson brought home a gastro bug. I've been in the toilet... But I'm feeling a bit better now. I should be able to complete those tasks before the end of day."

"Oh! That explains a lot." Her tone softens.

"Don't worry Evie, I'll assign those claims to one of the other team members. You take the rest of the day off, I'll put it through as sick leave. Enjoy the quiet before the kids get home."

I thank her profusely then we hang up.

Damn it, now I can't use work to distract me from Simone's text!

Ping.

'Evie, I can't stop thinking about you... and your lips... and your hands... on my body. God, this is killing me... I want you so bad.'

It's like Simone is speaking directly to my clitoris as images from our one time together replays yet again in my mind.

I glance around at the empty house. It is rare that I'm alone here, but today, I *am*.

I rush to my bedroom and fumble in the bottom drawer of my bedside table.

Please be charged. I beg silently.

I pull out my rabbit vibrator and turn it on.

It buzzes into life.

I aim a silent thank you to whichever Gods have granted me this sanction. I look over to the window and wonder if I should close the curtains. The winter sun is beaming through and my mind flits to a well replayed image of the late summer sun warming us on Simone's deck. Throwing caution to the wind, I leave them open. I want the sun on me like it was that afternoon. I pull my pants down, lying in the subtly warmed spot on my bed while I buzz myself into oblivion. I come so quick it even surprises me. I lie in the afterglow for a few minutes. Basking in the sun while knowing that it must be crazy cold outside. I can't lie here forever, so eventually, I get up and wash my toy before safely tucking it back into my bottom drawer.

Sated and now with nothing to do, I am forced to ponder Simone's question. Rationally, I know I must ask Steve if he is ok with me staying over with Simone. So, I send him a message as I just can't wait until he gets home.

'Steve, darling. Simone has invited me over for dinner on Saturday night. She is asking if I can stay over. Would you be ok with that?'

I wait impatiently for his reply. Within a

few minutes I get my response.

'Let's talk about this tonight.'

Dread surges through me and I feel a heavy weight drop into my stomach.

What if he actually says 'no'?

What would I do then? I suddenly feel the weight of our marriage and the vows we exchanged.

I hastily punch out a message to Simone. As much as she has left me hanging in the past, I think the two and a half hours I have sat on this are probably long enough.

'Simone, what a delightful invitation. I would love to, but I need to chat to Steve first.'

I watch the little dots cycling on my message tab, telling me she has been waiting and is now thinking of a response.

'Of course, I'll be waiting for your response… and I'll be thinking of you naked until then.'

My heart skips a beat. I know I came hard only 30 minutes ago, but I can already feel myself quickening with the anticipation of being naked with Simone again.

I can't believe I have the opportunity… and yet it might not happen.

My phone alarm interrupts my thoughts. It's time to collect the kids and I'm calmed by the necessary shift back to reality.

The afternoon is a standard affair of kids talking loudly, demanding snacks, me reinforcing manners and making them wait for dinner. I have so much time for them… ok I have more time for them when I'm not tired.

But now that they are both mostly sleeping through the night, I am enjoying them so much more.

Sleep truly is key.

Anybody that tells me their kids slept through since they were a newborn, I want to hurt them.

Physically punch them.

These parents *must* be lying. Parents talk about unicorn babies that magically sleep all night and never fuss and are just *easy*. Well, that is NOT the ride that Steve and I have had.

Steve and I have been in the trenches together when one or both of our kids are screaming inconsolably through the night. It could be a fever, or a bad dream. Or their teddy bear has been lost somewhere in the blankets and we must turn the lights on and find it *immediately*.

The urgency of small children is frightening. Nothing prepares you for the primal instinct to answer to your child's cries. It physically shakes you to your core and you will do everything in your power to calm the monster that has replaced your angelic child.

The sound of Steve's tyres on the gravel outside interrupts my parenthood musings. Once inside he kisses me tenderly before the evening routine ensues. We have a lovely family dinner, then we take turns reading to Jackson and Hannah in their own rooms. They get two books and a song each. As we finally close the bedroom doors, I feel relief that I can now sit with my husband and have a cuppa tea. We sit in the lounge, teas in hand and a small treat on the table. We only bring out the chocolate after the kids are asleep. I sip my tea appreciatively and I can feel the air grow heavy with the seriousness of the conversation we're about to have. I don't know where to start, thankfully Steve takes the reins.

"So, Simone wants you to stay over, does she?" Steve raises his eyebrow at me. His expression is playful which is a welcome reprieve from the discernment I was expecting.

"Yes." I feel we need to discuss this properly, so I tackle the obvious. "This is different Steve. You know I never stay over with Lily. Staying the night is *big*. This opens a door to questions from the kids about where I am and who I'm with. How do you honestly feel about that?"

Steve sips his tea and ponders all I've mentioned. This is one of the reasons I married this man. He takes the time to think about things, he doesn't make rash decisions. He considers all information and calculates accordingly. I await his answer and as he starts to talk, I realise I was holding my breath. I let it out in a soft whoosh as he lays down his reasoning before me.

"Yes, this is different. This is a big ask of us, our marriage, and our kids. But I don't think it's as hefty an ask as you imagine. You're allowed a girl's night out Evie. You go to parties and stay the night every now and then and I look after the kids. You do the same for me with my friends and when I'm away on business. One night is ok Evie."

He pauses and turns serious. "I might have a problem if staying over becomes a regular thing. Because then I would question where it is going. I love you Evie and I want you to explore your sexuality, but if this ever becomes more than just exploring; If feelings get involved, we need to have a serious talk. Because that could change things."

I take a deep breath. I agree with everything he has said. *One* night is no big deal.

"You're right, I think I have put more weight on this than I needed. I think the anticipation is getting to me because I've only slept with her once before, whereas Lily... well you know how many times I've been with Lily." The image of our last encounter replays in my mind. I push it down, I don't want to even think about it.

"It is just a bit of fun, thank you for understanding me better than I know myself. I love you, Steve."

I lean into him, and he puts his arm around me. A weight lifts off my shoulders as I snuggle into his warmth. I push Steve's line in the sand comment about feelings to the back of my mind.

I tell myself that this is still, just a bit of *fun*.

I feel a flurry of excitement as I anticipate

seeing Simone at the school drop-off tomorrow. I can't wait to tell her, that her proposition has been passed by the court and we are free to:

Spend.

The.

Night… Together.

Eighteen

Evie and the Revelation

My secrets are starting to get under my skin. I tossed and turned all night last night. I love the excitement of my encounters with Simone, but I'm not loving the guilt I feel for having slept with Lily. It's officially interfering with my sleep. Sleep comes in snippets and I'm no longer sure where my sex dream of Simone starts or my nightmares of Lily laughing at me as I ask her to stop, end. Dream or nightmare, I still woke up throbbing, adding to my restlessness. I really should have woken Steve so he could help a girl out, but he was so tired he fell asleep within seconds last night. I'm probably wearing him out.

I'm wearing *myself* out.

Thursday morning has arrived… *finally.*

I feel hungover yet supercharged as I rush through the morning routine. My heart beats faster and faster, the closer I get to the drop off time. I start to wonder if this is what anxiety feels like?

Finally with one last struggle to get jackets and shoes onto my protesting children, I bundle them into the car. Jackson has toothpaste on his chin and Hannah looks like she's been dragged through a bush because she wouldn't let me brush her hair. She's still glaring at me as I help her into her seat because I was a bit rough getting her jacket on.

"I'm sorry Hannah but we're going to be late. I didn't mean to hurt you."

Hannah sulks all the way to school. I try and placate her with her choice of music in the car. Once she's singing along loudly, and badly, I feel my thoughts drift back to Simone.

I'm so worked up, I can feel every pore *fizzing* to be near her. Within ten minutes I arrive at school. Hannah jumps out and with a kiss on the cheek she is already running off to her classroom. I hold Jackson's hand and walk him into the kindergarten and sign him in. He clings to my leg and looks up at me with sad blue eyes.

"Mummy I want a home day with you. I don't want to go to kindy."

My heart melts and I kneel down, enfolding him in a tight cuddle. I whisper "I know Jackson, I wish I could have a home day with you too. But look, I see your friend Elijah over there and your teachers have so many fun things planned for you. I'm sorry I have to go to work. But I'll be back to get you at 3pm,

I promise."

I give him one last squeeze then signal for one of the teachers to help. A lovely lady named Cassie comes over and takes his hand. I smile appreciatively at her as they walk away.

Back outside, I scan the front entrance for Simone.

Where is she?

I walk towards the gate, feeling like I'm on the prowl.

I'll do one quick loop, and if she's not there I'll just message her from the car.

I see a group of mums I know, so I say hello and join the conversation. They're discussing the Agriculture day which will be here soon. I know all the details from the last committee meeting and we need a few helpers for the day. I'm just getting into my recruitment plug when I feel a warm hand snake around me and pull me into a hug.

Chilled by her touch, I find myself in a very tight embrace with Lily… in front of lots of *mums*… in front of the *school.*

I give her a quick squeeze back and act like we're just good friends. A strange fear bubbles inside me but I push it down as I attempt to continue with my spiel. I manage to get at least two mums fully committed to running stalls. As I'm talking, I glimpse Simone getting out of her car in the carpark with Katie. I fight a massive urge to start waving maniacally to get her attention. It takes every fibre of will power

I have to pretend that I didn't see her.

I say my goodbyes and as I make my way back to my car, Lily is by my side, keeping stride with me.

I stop.

Something is different.

Normally I'd be able to get away…

"Lily! You're out of your moonboot!" I'm genuinely happy for her.

"Yes, came off on Monday. I can't believe how good it feels to walk at a normal pace again." She smiles a happy-relieved smile. "My physio is really happy with my progress, now I just need to make sure I don't over-do it. No netball for me for at least another month or two."

We start walking again towards the carpark and I can see Simone pausing. Waiting for *me*.

How can I get rid of Lily?

I immediately feel guilty for thinking it. We've been intimate for two months; she deserves better from me.

Lily reaches for me but before she can touch me I shoot her a *'don't even think about it'* glare with my head cocked to one side and my eyebrow raised. She knows how I feel about public places, plus my recent memory of how she ignored my request to stop is still raw.

I start to walk faster to my car, but Lily keeps pace.

Damn she's quick.

"Evie, what are you doing tomorrow? I

know you don't work Fridays… Want to come over? I'll call in sick" She winks and gives me a mischievous grin.

Normally an offer delivered like that would have me melting on the spot, but not now.

"Sorry Lily, I can't."

She senses something is off as I look over her shoulder to Simone. She is opening her car door.

She's leaving and I haven't had the chance to tell her!

In a desperate move, I push Lily aside and wave at Simone eagerly. I mouth the words "I'll call you" while making the universal symbol with my hand against my ear for a telephone. I see Simone nod and continue getting into her car.

I catch sight of Lily's face and it *scares* me.

"What was that about?" she demands. Jealousy and uncertainty flash in her eyes. She looks formidable.

Thinking on my feet I reply "Oh, I was going to organise another playdate for Hannah and Katie."

"Ohhh." Lily's face softens, evidently relieved by my response. I feel a jolt of empathy. I realise for the first time that she might be becoming emotionally invested in whatever this *is* between us.

"Hey Lily, I think we need to talk. But *not here.* Message me later and we can set up a time. Ok?"

I reach out and touch her upper arm just below her shoulder. A *safe* place to touch another mum in public. Lily nods and leans in for another hug. I hear her sigh sweetly into my hair, her hand brushes against my hip.

"Lily, *boundaries.*" I admonish through clenched teeth. "I'll talk to you later ok." I force a reassuring smile as I climb into my car. I'm relieved when she smiles back and heads to her car too.

Anxiously, I wait until she has driven off. I make it look like I'm setting up my mirrors and listening to the 9am news on the radio. But really, I just want to make sure Lily can't see me pick up my phone and dial Simone. Simone picks up on the first ring.

"Simone." I feel so much loaded anticipation fall out of my mouth as I breathe out her name.

"Evie." Simone murmurs back. My name sounds so *sexy* on her lips.

I don't beat around the bush.

"Steve said yes."

Simone lets out a long, sighing lungful of air. My heart thrashes in my chest and I wonder if it's audible through the phone.

"Where are you, Evie?" She asks.

"Just leaving the school gates. Where are you?" I wonder why she's asking my exact location.

"I'm at the park just down the road. Parked under a tree. Will you join me a moment? I know you start at 10am today and

I have a late start on Thursdays…" She trails off.

I glance at my watch. It's such a small window but I think I can squeeze twenty minutes.

"I'll be right there." I turn left and hang up the phone.

A few minutes later I pull up next to Simone's car. The park is almost completely deserted apart from a Mum and her child far in the distance on the playground. Simone gets out of her car and climbs into my passenger seat.

"I'm so sorry Simone, I was looking for you. But I got stuck talking about Ag day."

I feel a chill run through me. I've stretched the truth. I shove it down and focus on the here and now.

Simone reaches over my center console and takes my hands in hers. She grips me tight and we just stare into each other's eyes. A whole conversation passes between us without uttering a single word. Our gaze feels so *loaded.*

Loaded with all the things that have passed between us already, and all the things yet to *come.*

I feel Simone's hand slither down to my thigh. My breath catches in my throat. I nervously glance around the empty carpark. The only living things within our immediate vicinity are the birds swooping between the trees. The road behind us is deserted. I note the Mum and her child are walking away from the playground to the exit on the other side of the park. Their backs are to us and they look so far away.

Simone starts rubbing my thigh up and down.

It feels *so* good.

I make one last furtive scan for anyone that might see us, then I reach for her face and plant my lips on hers. We're so hungry for each other, we could be swallowed whole by this moment.

God, she's an amazing kisser.

I can feel my tongue zinging against hers and I lose sense of all time as we kiss. With my eyes closed, my ears fill with the sound of our urgent whimpers, which emit each time we come up for air. I notice a tug as Simone's fingers pull on the waistband of my work trousers and my top button pops open. Her fingers slip inside over the top of my lace panties and I hear her sharp intake of breath as she discovers how wet I am. I moan into her mouth with my need for her. With one hand in her hair, I reach the other down to her waistband.

"Yes." She breathes between us, shifting in her seat to help me get closer. The song playing on the radio comes to an end and the babble of the radio announcer reading the 9:45am traffic report breaks through the lust filled haze in my brain.

9:45am! Shit!

I rip myself away from her, extracting her hand just as I felt her finger slip beneath my gusset. Breathing hard, I sit back in my seat, pressing myself against my door as I try to put physical distance between us.

This is crazy *intense.*

I stare at her from the driver's seat, panting. Her eyes are sparkling with delight, her hair tousled from where my hand was just entwined.

I need her to get out of my car. I'm going to *lose* my job if I'm not there on time.

"I'm sorry Simone, I have to go to work. I'll see you Saturday, ok."

Breathing hard, Simone nods. "6pm. I can't wait."

Her words drip with lust and for a moment I wonder if I have the strength to drive away.

Could I be late to work?

No!

I shake the thought from my head. I reach over and grab Simone's hands and bring them to my lips. I give her fingers a chaste kiss.

"Simone, you have to get out of my car, or I will lose my job." One side of my mouth twitches into a grin. It's the truth, but a delicious truth at that.

I let go of her hands and do up the button on my trousers. She gets out of my car, not breaking eye contact until she has to turn and open her own door. Once seated she looks at me and waves. I buckle my seatbelt and reverse out of the carpark.

Damn.

I really need to start packing a spare pair of knickers in my handbag.

I hope I can get through the next two days without imploding from sexual combustion.

It's Friday and I am so relieved to have a day off. I need to clear my head and really, I need to reset this horny monster inside me. I do some gentle yoga at home, meditate, then head to the local park for some fresh air. I breathe in the smell of damp grass thawing with the winter sun. The birds are singing and swooping between the trees above me and I feel a wonderful sense of calm. The air is crisp and I pull my coat tighter around me. I see the odd runner as they bolt pass me.

I admire them.

I'm *not* a runner. But I can hike and walk long distances *if* I wanted to.

My hand in my pocket feels my phone vibrate. It's not a message, it's ringing.

Please don't be school asking me to collect one of my children. I silently pray.

I pull out my phone and see it's Lily.

I swipe it off, sending her to voicemail. I just need some time alone with my thoughts.

My phone buzzes again, ringing. I pause wondering if I should answer.

I'm allowed a moment to myself.

I swipe Lily off a second time. Then the

messages start coming.

Ping.

'Evie, why are you sending me to voicemail? I know you're not working today.'

I don't answer. We haven't spoken about that moment in her kitchen and suddenly I feel so unsure of myself.

'Evie, are you alright?'

Her concern breaks me.

I know I need to end this.

Right *now*.

I call her.

"Hi Lily, I'm sorry I'm just trying to enjoy a quiet walk. We really need to talk. Are you on a break?" I ask.

"Yes, I have my coffee in my car. I wanted some privacy to talk to you. Evie, when can I see you again? I'm going insane over here without your hands on me." She giggles and I hear the warmth in her voice.

This is the Lily I like. Carefree, *sexy* Lily.

I can't help myself. "Well, your skin does feel so good on mine Lily..."

What am I doing? I need to end this. Not set up another secret date.

"But Lily, I don't feel comfortable with what we're doing. Have you even told Cameron about us yet? You know you're cheating on him."

Lily sighs. "I know... but he's such a *bastard* Evie."

Woah, she's never said that before.

Alarm bells ring in my mind.

"What do you mean Lily? What's going on?"

Venomously she spits out "He's cheating on me Evie. He's been doing it since Willow was born. That's six years Evie. He thinks I don't know, the cocky bastard!"

Stunned I say nothing.

Lily's voice is hoarse, "Evie, I need you. I need your hands on me. You're the only hands I want… and the only hands I know, that want to touch *me*."

I can hear it in her voice, she's about to cry.

"Lily…" I placate. "What an asshole!" I feel so angry for her. All the moments she acted so cagey now make pristine sense in my mind. Maybe that moment in her kitchen was just her *need* for me. Maybe it wasn't as awful as I imagined it… I did come after all.

"Yes! He is an asshole!" Lily half cries, half laughs into the phone.

I'm awed by her strength. I don't think I'd be laughing after six years of a cheating husband who wouldn't touch me.

Her voice returns to sultry sunshine. "Evie, Cam's away again tonight. Please come over… You're the happiest part of my week."

I can't see her before I see Simone. It would be too *close* and after our encounter two weeks ago I don't think I could stop her from taking charge and that honestly *scares* me.

"Lily, I'm so sorry but I can't this weekend. Steve and I have plans." I pause. I need to even out the lie with the truth. "I am still married Lily and Steve is happy for me to see you sometimes, but I have a life and a family with him. I'm sorry I can't offer more, but that wasn't the deal."

Lily sniffs. "I know Evie, you told me. But *damn girl*. I'm burning up waiting to see you."

"Lily, I don't know what to say. I'm so gutted for you that Cam is cheating… and has been for a long time, the *prick*. But do two wrongs make a right? We're cheating here too Lily."

"I know I'm cheating Evie." She sounds exasperated. Her voice turns unexpectedly cold. "I *want* to cheat on him. He's not the only one allowed some *fun*. I *saw* the way you looked at women Evie. Other mums might not notice, but *I* did. *I* knew you liked women and I wanted to show you how much *fun* it could be... with *me*."

Her words unnerve me. My mind spins back to our first time in the party room.

She *was* so confident.

"Wait," I stammer. "You told me you'd never been with a woman before."

Lily lets out a tinkling laugh. "It wasn't my first time. Come on Evie. It clearly wasn't yours either."

She's right, but I still feel played.

Lily's voice turns back to sugar and spice. "Hey Evie, I've got to go back to work. But I look forward to seeing you again soon… *real soon*."

The call disconnects.

The wind whips up the leaves in the trees and a chill wind caresses my cheek. I stand in the middle of the park, reeling with the revelation.

I do not know who Lily truly is.

I have been the hunted and *not* the hunter.

Touché Lily.

Touché.

Nineteen

Evie and the Sleepover

My secrets are making me uncomfortable.

The revelation that Lily lied to me during our first time together makes me feel very *uneasy*.

Why did she feel she needed to lie? So what if it wasn't her first time? It wasn't mine either.

But... *she lied.*

My mind is racing on a hamster wheel, around and around. I feel sorry for Lily, her husband is clearly undeserving of her.

Why is *he* cheating?

Lily is clearly a sexual creature. I get the impression that she wouldn't withhold from him.

Why did she take so long to tell me that he's cheating?

She seemed to revel in the fact that I'm helping her to cheat. I wonder if she's relishing having a *secret* of her own.

Something feels *off*.

Malaise sits heavily on my chest since our last encounter. I need her to understand I want to stop being intimate with her.

How do I tell her that?

Plus, how would Simone feel if she knew there was another woman?

The weight of my complicated situation sits like a bag of bricks in my stomach.

My mind whirrs all Friday night and Saturday morning.

I've been honest.

Lily knows this isn't a relationship, I am not beholden to her… but I can't let her think we will be intimate *ever* again. I know this isn't the right way to do this, but I don't want to give her an opportunity to change my mind… nor do I want to find myself in a scenario where she forces herself on me again. Officially I *had* ended it that day in her kitchen, but Lily didn't listen.

I need to make it clear this is over.

I pull out my phone, callously ending our arrangement with a text.

'Lily, I don't know how else to say this. I can't sleep with you anymore. This is too complicated. I'm sorry. I hope we can still be friends.'

I send the message before I lose my nerve. Then I put my phone on silent. Guilt washes over me as I know Lily will be upset, but I need to have a clear conscience before I see Simone tonight.

At least it's been three weeks since Lily and I have been *alone*. I tried to do the right thing, but sometimes things just don't work out the way you'd hoped.

I know I've been lost in my thoughts and behaving absent at home, so I take my kids to the park to enjoy some late winter afternoon sunshine. I cultivate my mindfulness practice and focus on my present moment. I can hear the tinkle of Hannah and Jackson's laughs as they swing on the swings and race up and down the slide. The wind whips at my hair and I watch my breath escape me in a cloud of warm steam. I shove my hands in my pockets to anchor my mind into the tangible feeling of the warm fabric lining. The sound of little gumboots stomping on the ground and climbing the metal playground bars becomes a beautiful melody.

"Look at me Mummy!" Jackson cries as he shoots down the slide.

"Push me higher Mummy!" Hannah calls from the swing.

I engage with my children. I watch them enthusiastically and enjoy their joy.

I do love being a mum.

I'm pushing Hannah on the swing when I hear a squeal that twists into a cry of pain. Jackson has shot out of the slide on his stomach and landed on the ground with a thump. His little bottom lip quakes and he starts to howl. I pick him up and inspect the damage. He's completely fine apart from a small graze on his hand. But if you went off the performance he was giving, you'd think he'd broken his arm. I soothe him with tight cuddles, gentle hushes and feathery kisses on his face and sore hand. After a few minutes he calms and snuggles into me. He clearly just gave himself a fright.

"I want to go home" Jackson says, looking up at me with watery blue eyes.

"OK Jackson" I signal for Hannah to join us. "Let's all go home."

The afternoon disappears amidst the whirr of our normal routine. I get the fire going, then put the kids pjs in front of it to warm while they have showers. I help Steve make the kids dinner. At 5:20pm I realise I haven't done a thing to get myself ready.

I hastily shower, my heart rate increasing with every passing minute. Standing before my wardrobe with a jar full of butterflies in my stomach, a thought suddenly strikes me.

What will I wear?

No particular outfit is speaking to me and I feel conflicted about whether I should dress up or be comfy casual. I settle for somewhere in between. Jeans that make my ass look great, a going out top, nice jacket and I style my hair so it falls softly around my face. I duck into the bathroom and apply moisturiser to my face and hands. Then, I put on the subtlest of eye make up to make them sparkle and pop without smearing under my eyes if it gets hot and heavy later on...

Which I hope it will...

With a final spritz of perfume, I'm ready. I emerge from the bathroom transformed from the mum I am, to the sexy woman who I know still lives inside me. Steve gives me an appreciative scan up and down with his eyes. He whistles and embraces me with a tight hug and a squeeze of my bum.

"Have a good time tonight" he growls into my ear and nips my neck.

My hands snake down and give his behid a tight squeeze too, his member twitches against my pelvis. I feel a bit bad, knowing he will have to wait until tomorrow night for the juicy details and a romp with me. I flash him a knowing and slightly apologetic smile and pull away. I head into the lounge and kiss my children on their foreheads, their eyes glued to the television set.

I murmur 'be good for your Dad' as I head towards the door. I give Steve a kiss in the doorway and whisper "Thank you" as I pull away. Then I step out into the cold, ready to drive the five minutes to Simone's house.

I pull into her driveway and see the porch light is on for me. Her chimney smokes happily in the early evening twilight. I take a deep, steadying breath. I haven't even gotten out of the car and my heart is thudding in my chest. I close my eyes and count to five as I let my breath out slowly. My heart calms and I unbuckle my seatbelt. I pick up the bottle of wine and chocolates I'd purchased earlier, wondering if it's too much.

I laugh softly to myself.

I'm like a schoolboy on a first date!

I grab my bag and walk as confidently as I

can to her front door. I raise my hand to knock and the door swings open to reveal a beaming Simone.

"I heard your car pull in."

Her cheeks are slightly flushed and she's wearing an apron that shows she's been busy in the kitchen. A nice dress peaks out from underneath. Simone's hair is twisted into a mop of curls, pinned to her head with a large clip. Her face is fresh and clean, her skin glowing. She radiates such a natural beauty that I stand in the doorway, so mesmerised I forget to speak.

"Wine and chocolates! For me! You shouldn't have!"

Simone opens the door wider, and I offer a lopsided grin as I pass Simone the gifts and remove my shoes. I follow Simone into the kitchen, and I am enveloped in the delightful aroma of dinner being cooked for me. Simone reaches into a cupboard and pulls out two wine glasses.

"Let's crack this open shall we?"

"Hear, hear!" I laugh, then look down at my hands. "I don't know why, but now I'm here, I actually feel kinda nervous." I shyly steal a glance into Simone's warm mahogany eyes and I am relieved to see my own nervousness echoed in their depths.

"Me too." Simone confesses quietly as she pours the wine then hands me a glass. "This will help. To a fun night!" She toasts with a wink and a smile.

"To a fun night!" I concur.

I take a seat at the breakfast bar on a tall stool and I watch her move gracefully around her small kitchen. She proffers a spoon so I can sample a taste of our dinner.

"Mmm that's delicious."

As Simone returns the spoon to the pot, I spy mini chocolate lava cakes ready to go in the oven for later. Silence stretches between us as Simone focuses on adding the final touches to our meal. I sip my wine while I watch her work, not knowing what to say to fill the space. Bringing up Jonathan feels wrong and I feel like we've already cleared up our misunderstanding. I'm halfway through my glass of wine when Simone exits the kitchen and sidles up next to me. She spins my stool towards her, parting my legs as she stands between them. She takes my wine from my hand and places it on the bench. The sudden proximity of her makes me light-headed.

I breathe her in.

The aromas of cooking spices along with the soft smell of floral soap on her skin make me wilt before her.

"Can I… kiss you, Evie?" she asks as her eyes flick down to my lips.

I nod my assent.

She leans in and places the most delicate of kisses on my bottom lip. Her hands press down on my thighs as her lips suck gently at my mouth. Every fibre of my being ignites and my heart hums in my chest. I return her kiss while my hands reach behind her and pull her against me, enjoying the soft curves of her behind. After a short, blissful moment, she pulls away and returns to the kitchen.

Glancing over her shoulder she asks. "Better? More relaxed now Evie?"

I shift in my seat and nod. "That certainly helped. But you realise if you do that again you might end up burning the dinner". I smirk with a mischievous challenge in my eyes.

"Well, lucky we stopped then, because dinner *is* ready."

Simone smiles sweetly and starts dishing up a curry onto ornately decorated plates. It smells delicious and I notice the subtle fragrance of cinnamon, coriander and cumin.

"Follow me if you're hungry." She sashays past me to the dining table.

"I'd follow you anywhere Simone." The words escape my lips completely unchecked.

They surprise me as I feel the multitude of layers within those words. I brush off the emotions bubbling under my skin and follow her to a small table, set for two. There are candles lit and place mats. I bring the wine and our glasses and place them down on the table before taking my seat. Simone removes her apron and hangs it on a nook by the kitchen entrance. I can't help but notice the curve of her bottom as she reaches up to hang it there. She returns to the table but before she sits down opposite me, she leans down and cups my face in her hands. Without her apron, I notice her dress has a plunging neckline which shows off the curve of her... *oh my goodness*... unsupported breasts.

She's *not* wearing a bra.

My breath snags in my throat as I raise my eyes to hers. Simone's eyes twinkle at my unveiled desire, then she kisses me again. Her velvet tongue darts into my mouth and I can taste her sweet, wine tinged, breath. My hands reach up and rest on her hips as the kiss deepens.

I want *more.*

So much more.

I can't help myself. I reach up and squeeze her right breast. Under the thin fabric, I feel her nipple harden into my palm as twin lust-filled moans are swallowed by our kiss. My fingers twist towards the hem of her dress as the urge to rip her clothes off and have her on the table *right now* consumes me.

As if she is telepathic, Simone agonisingly puts on the brakes. She takes my hands in hers, squeezing my fingers as she pulls away from my still puckered lips. Hazily, my eyes flutter open to find her gazing at me with such a lascivious stare that it feels like a match has been struck between my legs.

"Let's eat". A roguish smile tugs at her lips as she makes her way to her seat.

Wait... what?

Every molecule of my being is screaming to get up from my seat and touch her, *right now*. I know my mouth is hanging open so I close it quickly. Simone picks up her fork and nonchalantly nods towards my own cutlery. I cross my legs under the table in an attempt to suppress the heat that's spreading like a wildfire within me.

I look down at the beautiful meal in front of me as I will my brain to focus on the present. Not wishing to appear impolite, I pick up my cutlery and try a mouthful. It's delectable and I can't help but let out a sumptuous moan of pleasure.

"Damn Simone, you can cook!"

I pick up my glass to toast her meal. Our glasses clink and we sip our wines with an amorous, interlocked gaze.

We eat our meals peacefully. Apart from the scrape of cutlery on our plates, the only sounds are the soft crackle of the fire and the dulcet tones of classical music playing in the background. I have a few more mouthfuls then push my plate aside. Despite the soothing atmosphere and how heavenly the meal is, the butterflies in my stomach don't want me too full.

I enjoy watching Simone place a few more bites between her lips, slightly jealous of the fork. She pats the corners of her mouth with a napkin while I refill our wine glasses.

"Shall we take our wine to the couch?" I suggest.

She nods and the sound of our scraping chairs sound harsh against the recent quiet. We sit down opposite each other, our knees facing but not quite touching. Our arms rest on the back of the couch as our bodies twist towards each other. I can't help but notice her dress riding up her thigh, one dainty ankle crossed underneath her.

To distract myself, I let my gaze take in the room. Her home is quaint, a perfect country cottage with the kitchen, dining and lounge all connected with a central fireplace as the main feature. I know the other half of the house consists of three bedrooms and a bathroom. If it wasn't so dark, I'd be able to see the deck that overlooks her beautiful back garden. The very same deck where we were intimate in the full afternoon sun on that beautiful summer's day. I shift in my seat and Simone notices my nostalgic look at her darkened window.

"Reminiscing back to summer Evie?" she asks quietly.

I chuckle. "As a matter of fact, yes. That was quite the afternoon Simone." I feel my eyes twinkle as I sip my wine.

"Yes, it was an afternoon I'll never forget. In fact, I think about you every time I walk out that way. You sure leave a lasting impression." She says as she demurely studies the wine glass in her hand.

I reach out and take her spare hand in mine, tracing circles with my fingers while we sit quietly. I don't want to rush anything, but I can't help but notice I feel slightly uncomfortable within these little silences. My mind starts to wonder if I'll be able to live up to the standard I set on that summer's afternoon… plus the guilt of not telling her about Lily tugs at me, but I don't want to ruin our evening. Pushing it down, I take another gulp of wine to try and still the nerves growing restless inside me. It's barely 7:30pm and we have a whole night to get through.

"Do you have any games?" I blurt out. "Like card games or… board games… or video games?"

I feel an internal cringe as I say it, but I need to fill the space with *something*.

"Sure… umm I recently bought the latest 'Just Sing' for the kids on their playstation. Could be a bit of a laugh."

"Sounds great! Who needs nightclubs when we can sing and dance at home?" I'm genuinely delighted by this suggestion. I'm not the greatest singer but I love dancing and it will get us into a lighter mood. I help shift the coffee table to give us a bit more of a stage and while I'm bending over I feel Simone give my ass a playful smack.

Now this is more like it.

I laugh and can feel the tension I was feeling just moments ago melt away. The classical music is switched off and the game starts up. We select a song to sing, one that's currently thrashed on the radio, so at least I know the chorus. We stand next to each other, microphones in hand and follow the words and notes on the screen. I sing along trying to hit the notes as I go, but I'm shocked to hear Simone belt out the words pitch perfect.

She's kicking my ass!

We complete the song and her points are a good two thousand more than mine. I watch her as she starts selecting the next song. Her eyes are bright and her lips slightly parted. The nape of her neck is exposed due to her soft curls being piled on top of her head. It looks so exposed, so *vulnerable*.

I can feel my lips tingle with the ache to kiss her there. I slink closer and place my lips on her neck. I trail soft kisses up to her ear and give her lobe a playful nip.

I breathe into her ear; "Your neck has been demanding that I kiss it all evening."

"Well, I'm glad it finally received what it was asking for." Simone purrs in response.

We face each other, our hands entwined once more. I feel the familiar spark of electricity in the space between us as we look into each other's eyes. I can't wait any longer. I plunge one finger deep inside my mouth then trail it along the shoulder of her dress.

"Let's get you out of these wet clothes." I lustily whisper.

The delight at my roguish gesture is evident on Simone's face. She leans in and kisses me hungrily. I can feel her gently pushing me towards the couch and I stumble backwards, ungracefully separating our mouths in the process. Simone playfully pushes me onto the couch and stands in front of me. She reaches down and grabs the hem of her dress, crossing her arms and lifting it up and over her head. She stands before me, naked, with the exception of a very small and lacy pair of panties. My breath snags in my throat, she's so stunning. She leans towards me and tugs at the hem of my shirt.

"Your turn. May I get you out of these?"

"Please" is all I can utter as I feel her lift my

top over my head.

I sit there, exposed in my best lacy burgundy bra and feel Simone's hands slither down to my jeans. She undoes the button and slowly unzips me. I lift my bottom off the seat to help her shimmy them down off my hips. She can now see my matching underwear.

"Look at you, you've wrapped yourself up beautifully for me." Her eyes sparkle, drinking me in. My cheeks grow hot as I blush in response.

"I aim to please."

Reaching up, I pull her onto the couch beside me, devouring her with my eyes. A goddess like her needs to be worshipped, slowly. My mind flashes back to her dainty ankles and I know where to start. I position her feet on my lap then lift one foot and bend my head to kiss the top of it. I cup her heel in one hand and trace small circles around her ankle with the other. Simone lets out a small gasp, then a giggle. The corners of my lips twitch smugly, I know how sensitive a woman's ankles truly are. I start planting feathery kisses on the ankle I'm holding, so that I can caress the other at the same time.

A soft moan escapes her, and it urges me higher up her legs. I rub my hands along her smooth skin with my lips following in pursuit. I reach the apex of her thighs and look longingly at the black lacy barrier. I place a gentle kiss at the base of her panties and look up into her eyes. She squirms beneath me and reaches down to hook her fingers in her waistband. I see she wants them off but I'm in no rush.

"All in good time Simone." I chide while pushing her hands away.

I lay kisses on the soft curve of her belly and let my hair tickle her sides as it drapes wispily across her. Simone's fingers twist into my tresses as she arches her belly towards me. My hands wander further, cupping a breast in each. I feel her nipples harden beneath my fingers as I give them a spirited pinch. My hair drags over her as I move my face north, shifting into a kneeling position on the couch so I can reach her nipples better. I give one a teasing flick then suck it into my mouth. I let my teeth graze over the sensitive skin and Simone gasps deliciously.

I smile into her chest as I make my way to the other side. Simone's hands glide around to my back. It feels exquisite as her hands tickle me up and down before finding the clasp of my lacy bra. In one swift motion she slips it off my shoulders and tugs it from my chest. Simone pulls herself up to kneel opposite me and our breasts brush against each other. The sensation is so tantalising, a low sigh emits from deep within me. Simone traces her fingers across my clavicle. She pulls me tightly against her as she dips her head into the crook of my neck. Her sophisticated lips suck gently against me as she moves towards my ear. My pulse throbs rampantly against her lips and my knickers pool with my desire.

Simone pulls my face towards her and

seizes my mouth once more. Her tongue pirouettes against mine as her hand snakes between my legs. Suddenly her fingers pull aside my gusset and plunge inside me, making me lose track of where I am.

As I gather my decorum from my lust-induced daze, I locate the elastic waistband of her knickers. I pull it open and delve my hand under the dainty fabric. Her folds are slick as I trace her entrance. My middle finger easily finds its growing target as I move inside her. Simone's mouth pauses on mine, losing herself in my touch.

I think this is going to be quick for both of us. Simone's fingers deftly work magic circles between my thighs spurring me closer to release. Our tongues entangled, I urgently stroke her, *in and out*. The pleasure of being so close to her is overwhelming.

She's close, so I apply a smidge more pressure as I loop around her hard knot. The spasms of her orgasm clench around my finger and pulse under the palm of my hand. Simone's release pushes me over the edge as my own climax ripples through me. Our cries of ecstasy entwine and dance through the air of her quiet cottage.

Our bodies wilt against each other, our heads rest on each other's shoulders, our breathing hoarse. Lazily, I kiss her and tickle her back with my free hand. My other hand stays deep in her panties so I can enjoy Simone's small aftershocks as we cling to each other. I'm sure she's enjoying mine too.

As the storm of our racing hearts ebb, we slowly remove our hands from each other's folds. Our smitten giggles ring out across the room as we notice the wet stickiness on our hands.

"Follow me." Simone stands up and pulls me off the couch.

My muscles are slightly stiff and I stretch before following her. She leads me to the kitchen and pulls my hands into the kitchen sink. She turns on the tap and pumps hand soap into my palm. She stands behind me, her breasts pressing against my back as she washes her hands with mine. Her fingers slip and slide as the bubbles lather between us. She breathes on my neck and I wonder if it's too soon to have her again. She rinses our hands under the warm water.

"Ready for dessert?" She breathes in my ear as she hands me a tea towel to dry my hands.

"Round two already!" My eyes light up at the invitation.

"No silly... well not *yet*. I meant the pudding." She chuckles.

"Oh! That would be nice too." I give her a *thwarted* grin then my mouth waters at the thought of the gooey chocolate dessert.

Simone turns the heat up on the oven and places the lava cakes on the shelf. She sets a timer and we move back into the lounge to wait. We snuggle in front of the crackling fire and pull a blanket over our still mostly naked bodies.

This feels so nice, so *comfortable.* All awkwardness from earlier has dissipated as we talk about our kids and what we got up to during the day. I tell her about my wardrobe plight, then giggle affectionately as I tell Simone that Steve bit my neck before I headed out tonight.

"Poor Steve, he will have blue balls until I get home tomorrow." I laugh heartily but trail off as I notice that Simone is not laughing with me.

She looks away and I feel her shift uncomfortably under the blanket.

"Are you OK? Did my mention of Steve kill the mood?"

"Yeah, it has a bit." She pouts. "You've just reminded me that tomorrow morning you'll go home to him and he's going to get off on the *details* of our night." Her words a mixture of moroseness and scathing.

I lift her chin, so her eyes meet my gaze.

"Simone, are you upset with me?"

"Not you, not really. I'm upset with myself." She looks away again.

"Why would you be upset with yourself?" I ask bewildered.

A moment ago, we were so cosy and content. I want that feeling back.

"Because… because I feel a connection with you Evie… and I'm fucking jealous of Steve who gets you every night." She wipes at a tear that is forming in her eye.

Woah…

I hold her hand in mine.

"Simone…" I falter.

I try again.

"If I'm completely honest with myself… well… I feel a connection too."

Her eyes light up with hope as she turns back to look at me.

I could get lost in those eyes.

"So, what does this mean?" She implores.

"I don't know." I shake my head because I can feel us crossing a forbidden line just talking about this. I should have known that this could never be *just sex* with Simone.

Beep-beep, beep-beep, beep-beep.

The timer on the oven goes off. I can't help but feel that our time is up as well.

Simone pulls on her dress as she heads into the kitchen to get the desserts. She dishes them up into little bowls and spoons a little vanilla ice-cream onto each one. I follow her lead and pull my top over my head, but I don't bother with my bra. I slip back into my jeans and join Simone who has just arrived at the table with our dessert. It looks delicious but I can't bring myself to taste it.

"Simone, all of this…" I gesture at the dessert, her cosy home, at us. "I've had a wonderful time, here, with you…"

"Stop." Simone demands putting her hand up. "Don't say it. Don't say this is all we get."

"But it is Simone. This is all we get… I love my husband. Our kids, our family…"

"Enough" she whispers. She looks so heartbroken.

I feel *heartbroken.*

How can we possibly carry on from here?

"Simone, we can have more nights… like this… if you want to that is… But, Steve will need to know…"

"And you must go home afterwards." She finishes for me. She takes a steadying breath, mulling over our future.

"Yes… I don't want to hurt you, Simone. If you have feelings… if I have… feelings. Then it complicates things." I'm trying to be as honest and adult about this as I can. But even though I want to keep seeing her, I don't think it's wise for either of us. I don't want to, but I take a breath and deliver my blow.

"I don't know if it is wise for us to continue after tonight."

"What?" She looks at me, her eyes narrowing. "Right, so was this just a *booty call* Evie? I cook you dinner, we're intimate on *my* couch, in *my* house. I'm honest about how *I feel* and now that's it?" Her voice rises as she slams her hand on the table, making the cutlery jump.

I recoil in my seat. "Woah, just wait a minute there Simone. You invited *me* here. I didn't ask… for all this."

"Agghhhh. Don't give me that crap, Evie. You did ask. You asked *that* day. On *my* deck." She gestures dramatically towards her window. "You asked *me* when you kissed me and made love to me in the sun." She spits the words out with such venom but her bottom lip quivers.

"You started this Evie" she whispers.

I put my head in my hands as I gather myself. She's not wrong and I feel terrible. I look up with remorseful eyes.

"You're right. I'm so sorry Simone. I couldn't stop myself that day and I didn't put any boundaries in place to protect you..." under my breath I whisper "...or me."

Simone's eyes glisten.

We sit in silence as the enormity of our conversation hangs in the air.

"I should go". I stand and start gathering my things. I look at the wine glasses and count how many I've had in my mind. I feel sober enough to drive home but if I'm breath tested, I'm probably at the threshold for a DUI. It's risky, but I don't want to inflict anymore emotional turmoil on either of us.

It's best I leave.

Simone stands and crosses the room to me. Her hand grabs my arm as I'm trying to stuff my bra into my bag.

"Evie, stop."

"Me staying here is not what's best for either of us Simone. I don't want to hurt you any more than I already have." Tears form in my eyes and I hang my head in shame.

She places a finger under my chin, raising my glistening eyes to hers as she searches my face.

"This is hurting you too." She breathes her revelation.

I nod and look away.

"OK Evie." She strokes my hair and puts her hand on my waist. "Just tonight. Then that's it."

"You want me to stay? Are you sure?" My mind spins as I question if this is a good idea.

"If this is all we get, I want you as close to me as possible until you have to leave tomorrow."

She embraces me in a crushing hug. My mind is still reeling but I can't stop myself from nuzzling her neck. Her scent is so intoxicating. My eyes close as I inhale her.

The weight of our talk sits heavy in my chest. My emotions are singed and suddenly I'm exhausted.

"Where's your bedroom Simone?"

"This way." She takes my hand and leads me down the hallway to her room. I see her bed is made with crisp fresh linen. The pattern on the duvet is feminine and colourful. Before I move further into her room, I excuse myself to grab my bag of toiletries and head to the bathroom to freshen up. Once I'm done Simone brushes past me to do the same.

"Make yourself comfortable." She purrs before she places a chaste peck on my cheek.

So many things whirl inside me as I pull back the blankets. I discard my jeans, deciding to sleep in the spare cotton shirt I'd brought with me and my underwear. I haven't slept in a bed with anyone but Steve since before we met. It's a strange feeling… her sheets are soft and smell freshly washed. Her pillows are just the right height for my neck. They smell new and I suddenly find myself questioning how much effort went into tonight. I feel guilty about the desserts. Melting and growing cold, untouched on the table. Simone returns and my meandering thoughts are halted. She stands in the doorway, *naked.*

Without a word between us, we make love again.

We touch every inch of each other's bodies, with our hands, with our mouths.

We ensure there is constant contact between us, as if our very skin cells are committing this moment into their memory.

We climax again… and again.

I lose track of how many times we are intimate. I no longer know where my body ends, and Simone's begins.

We are *one*.

I secretly wish that the dawn will never arrive. I'm not ready for this sleepover to end.

I'm not ready for this to be *over*.

Twenty

Evie and the Morning After

This secret hurts. Lying awake I gaze upon Simone's serene face as she peacefully sleeps on the pillow beside me. A glorious slither of golden sunlight pours through the gap in the curtain, announcing that dawn has arrived. I haven't slept a wink. I know this is the last time I will lie next to her. As the realisation cements in my mind, I feel a proverbial knife twist in my heart.

Ouch.

I knew I liked her, but I wasn't prepared for how quickly my heart would swell to... dare I say it? ... *Love?*

I shake my head. *Is* it even love? Or am I just allowing my jagged and raw emotions to take over in my lust-intoxicated and sleep deprived state?

My eyes sting with the threat of tears.

What a sorry mess I have made here.

Simone's naked chest gently rises and falls with even breaths. My hand is itching to move the curls that have draped over her eye, but I'm fearful I'll wake her.

I don't want her to wake.

Not *yet.*

When she wakes it will be time to get up and I feel like my entire body is filled with lead, pinning me down to this exact spot. I couldn't move if I wanted to.

Ping.

Fuck. Who is that?

I realise that my 'do not disturb' function has turned off now that it is 7am.

Ping. Ping. Ping.

I carefully turn away from Simone and reach down to where my phone was stowed in my bag for the night. I had unmuted it just in case Steve needed me before I left home, but my automatic 'do not disturb' is always on from 9pm to 7am. Thoughts of something going wrong with the kids flood my mind as my phone continues to ping. As I lean over the bed, I pull the phone towards me. I see the home screen flash with several messages and missed calls… from Lily.

Ohhh. She got my message.

I quickly turn my phone off to stop the incessant flood of messages.

I'll deal with that later.

As I throw my phone back into my bag, I feel Simone's gentle hand rub my back. Turning to face her I snuggle back into my pillow. Our hands find each other, our fingers interlock as I gaze into her sleepy eyes.

"Good morning, Evie" Simone murmurs,

the corners of her mouth twitching upwards.

"Good morning" I smile back.

Simone yawns, pulling her hand from mine so she can perform a big stretch.

"Did you sleep?" she asks, a flash of mischief in her eyes.

"Not a wink." I return her playful gaze.

"I can't believe how fast the morning has come." Simone admits with a sadness in her voice.

I sigh. "I know. As beautiful as the dawn is, I wish it hadn't arrived."

"Yeah, me too. But it's here. I wish things were different Evie." Simone averts her gaze and I feel her eyes scan my body.

A warmth aches between my legs and I wonder if one more time together would be appropriate. With nothing left to say, I pull her towards me and envelope her in a full body embrace. I breathe in her scent as we lie in silence, watching the sunbeam move slowly across the room.

The minutes tick by.

I'm committing to memory how her body feels pressed against mine.

The air hangs with unspoken words.

Unasked questions.

Suddenly my stomach emits the loudest gurgle you can imagine. The silent spell is broken, and we both erupt with laughter.

"Are you hungry there Evie?" Simone laughs as she props herself up onto an elbow and gazes down at me.

"Just a little." I admit, sheepishly.

"Come on. I need coffee and you clearly need food". Simone slips out of bed and pulls on a bathrobe. I note there was a second floral silk robe hiding under her cotton waffle one and my eyes linger on it. Simone follows my gaze and pulls it off the hook, throwing it at me as she laughs.

"What, did you think I'd expect you to walk around my house naked?"

I flash her a wolfish grin. "Thanks." I slip out of bed and slink the robe up and onto my shoulders. It feels silky and cool against my skin as I tie it in a bow around my waist.

Simone leads the way to the kitchen and turns the kettle on. I survey the aftermath of our night as I glance around the room. The playstation is still out, but the TV is off. The couch throw is crumpled in a heap on the floor. Our empty wine glasses sit next to each other, just touching on the small side table. The fire has gone out and the room has a brisk chill to the air.

I wish I'd brought my slippers.

Under the curtains, I glimpse the deck where it all started. Sunlight streams onto it, creating a glow on the lounge floor. The memory of our first time floods my mind and I wonder if it's too cold to have a re-enactment.

Yes, it's too cold!

I chide myself as I carry out my stocktake of the room. Two desserts stand untouched and sticky with melted vanilla ice-cream swirled around the sides. They still look delicious and I'm so disappointed that we didn't eat them. I start to wonder if they would still be safe to eat…

It's cold enough…

I stand next to the table eyeing up the dainty ramekins. While Simone's back is turned, I quickly dip my finger in one and have a taste. Before I can stop myself, a happy moan escapes my lips. My eyes close as I relish the layers of velvety rich dark chocolate paired with the sticky-sweet vanilla and … what *is* that extra taste?

My eyes flutter open as I realise the slightly salty taste is Simone. I pull my finger from my lips and giggle as Simone catches me in the act.

"You couldn't wait for toast?" She laughs.

"Mmm Simone you have to try this! It's still good!"

Pulling back the chair, I sit down and pick up the petite dessert spoon taking a bite, then another. In less than a minute the dessert is gone and I am licking the sides of the tiny bowl. Simone watches from the kitchen with a grin.

Finished, but still hungry I rise and make my way to Simone. I pull her against me and place my sticky, chocolatey lips on hers. She pushes me back.

"Ughh! You're so sticky!"

Laughing, I give her a playful nip on her neck.

She throws her head back in laughter and the sound is so *sexy*. I just can't get enough of her.

I want her… now.

I pull at the strings on her robe and it falls open in front of me. Her naked body is exposed and illuminated by the morning glow coming through the kitchen window. My hands slink behind her back and I trail kisses down her chest. A dulcet sigh greets me from above, which spurs me on. Continuing my journey, I head south, kneeling to get more comfortable. I am now face to face with the small strip of her downy hair. It smells heady from last night and I dart my tongue inside her folds for one last taste. Simone leans against the kitchen bench, shifting her weight, allowing me better access. I hungrily devour her, her bud hardening beneath my dexterous flicks. I'm amazed at how ready and quickly she responds to me. Just hearing her sharp intake of breath ignites a glorious pulse deep inside me.

My tongue ravages her clit and she comes violently, much quicker than I was expecting. I pull my mouth away so I can witness her post-orgasm afterglow.

Cheeks flushed, her eyes closed, lips parted.

Simone braces against the kitchen bench, her chest and chin are arched towards the ceiling. The bathrobe softly frames the sides of her body. Golden morning sunlight streams through the window, the glow backlighting her hair and body like a halo.

Yes, I will remember this.

I slowly rise off the floor, winking cheekily as I make my way to the kettle to pour our coffees. Simone gathers herself and re-ties her bathrobe closed. I hand her a cup and we both sip in silence. After a moment, Simone moves about the kitchen, making toast for us.

There's nothing awkward between us. The morning ritual feels relaxed and natural. After breakfast, I excuse myself to the bathroom.

Once I'm in the shower Simone joins me. She washes my back. I wash hers. She rubs her wet breasts against mine and her hand finds my centre. Her dexterous fingers give me one last climax to remember her by.

We dry ourselves, dress and complete our bathroom rituals. Before I know it, I find myself standing at her door with my bag in hand.

"Simone…" I start.

"Don't say anything Evie. Just kiss me and go." Her eyes glisten.

"It's not goodbye." I feel my voice falter and tears sting my eyes. As brightly as I can, I say, "I'll see you for playdates and at the school drop-off."

Simone smiles. "Yes, you will."

I kiss her one last time. It's soft and chaste with a hint of tongue. A lovely kiss to end it with.

"Last night will forever be etched in my mind." Simone's voice cracks with emotion.

I squeeze her hand. "Mine too, and the morning after." I smile sadly and let her go.

Taking a deep breath, I turn and walk out the door. I can feel her eyes on me as I climb into my car. It takes every ounce of courage I have, to not look back. I start the ignition and slowly pull out of her driveway.

It *is* the morning after and it's time to go *home*.

Twenty-One

Evie and the Rough Landing

Secrets suck. I don't understand what just happened. What is this ache in my chest?

I pull over at the start of our street to gather myself. Gripping the steering wheel, I try and take a few steadying breaths. Closing my eyes, I feebly attempt to push Simone from my mind. I try and think of my husband, who has been so supportive.

Our kids, our home, our animals swim to the surface of my mind. I think about how awful it would be if I didn't have my life with *all* of those things in it.

Maybe awful isn't the right word.

Different?

I can't imagine my life without my husband and kids and I don't even know what a life with Simone in the mix would look like... I shouldn't even indulge that possibility.

We've called it.

It's *over.*

Gathering myself, I pull away from the curb. I focus my mind on my kids and my husband.

They're waiting for me.

As I approach my driveway, I see a silver car parked opposite. It looks familiar. I draw near and see that it's Lily sitting behind the wheel… and she looks *pissed.*

My mouth drops open in shock.

What is she doing here?

Suddenly the silver car screeches away from the curb. Lily drives past, flipping me the bird.

She screams 'FUCK YOU EVIEEEE!' through her open window.

I catch a glimpse of her daughter Willow in the back seat. She looks pale and scared.

Waving frantically with my hands, I signal for her to stop so we can talk, but it's too late. She's already fleeing my street like a bat out of hell.

From my rear-view mirror, I watch her car gain momentum and speed wobble as she turns the corner out of sight.

Unnerved, I pull into my driveway and see my husband working in the garden. The kids are bouncing on the trampoline. As I exit my car I hear Hannah and Jackson squeal "Mummy's home!" in delight as they rush to open the zip on the trampoline safety net. Beaming, I meet my kids halfway up the stone path where they embrace me tightly.

Hannah looks up at me with her arms tightly around my waist. "We missed you

Mummy."

Looking into her beautiful eyes I murmur, "I missed you both too."

Steve puts down his spade and makes his way over to me. "Out of my way kids. It's my turn to give Mum a cuddle."

The kids reluctantly let me go and Steve pulls me to him and places a kiss on my lips. His chin is stubbly, and he smells like petrol, sweat and fresh cut grass. It's such a contrast to the floral softness of Simone that for a moment, I feel conflicted as to whether I like it. I place my head on his shoulder and breathe him in again. My brain flicks a switch and suddenly I feel *home*.

Steve looks down and pulls me to arm's length. "Are you OK?" His eyes searching mine. He can tell something is up.

"I…"

I start then look down at the kids who are still awaiting another turn for more mummy cuddles.

"I have a lot to tell you, but not right now…. I… I just saw a certain someone parked outside our house. But they sped off before I could talk to them."

"Oh?" Steve's eyebrows furrow. "OK… yes we will talk about this later."

Steve lets me go so the kids can get another cuddle in. As I feel two pairs of little arms wrap around me, I glance around the garden and see there is a bit of work to be done.

"OK kids, it's so good to see you." I give them both a squeeze. "But it looks like we have a bit of work to do today. Let me go and get changed into some more comfortable clothes so I can help Daddy in the garden."

The kids let me go and race back to the trampoline. I can tell they aren't going to be much help in the garden today.

Returning to the car, I grab my bag. Once in my room I pull my phone from the side pocket and switch it back on. As I wait for it to start up, I find my gardening tracksuit bottoms and an old T-shirt to get changed into. Then I sit on the bed as the home screen bursts into life. It's filled with dozens of messages and missed calls from Lily.

'Evie. Where did this come from? Let's talk about this.'

'Evie. Come on, we need to discuss this. Please.'

'Evie, why aren't you answering me?

'I do not accept that we're over. Call me!'

'Evie what the actual fuck? Call me. NOW!'

I can see the messages started coming in around 9:15pm. At 10pm the phone calls started. I can see she tried to ring me fourteen times between 10pm and 1am. From 1am there is nothing until 6:30am when the texts start up again.

'Evie, please. I haven't slept all night. What's going on? Why aren't you answering me?'

'Evie, I think I have feelings for you. Please. Why are you being so cold?'

'Evie…'

'Evie!'

The next message sends an ice-cold shiver down my spine. It's sent at 7:02am.

'Evie, your car is not at home. Where the fuck are you?'

'There had better be an explanation for this…'

'You're with someone else aren't you? Admit it!'

'Who is she? Who is the damn whore?'

'You slut Evie. I HATE YOU! FUCK YOU!'

The messages end there at 8:30am. I feel nauseous and my heart races in my chest. I don't even know where to begin. My emotions have gone from shame and guilt to chilling fear and worry for myself *and* Simone.

What if Lily finds out that it's Simone?

What would she do?

My thoughts are interrupted by another incoming text.

'So Evie. This is how you want to play it? Well, you just fucked with the wrong girl. I will get you back for this Evie. Just you wait.'

My blood runs cold. I have no idea what this woman is capable of. The fact that she had been outside my house with poor Willow in the back seat from 7am makes me wonder if she's having some kind of mental break down. Who would put their six-year-old daughter through an early Sunday morning stake-out? I didn't get home until 11am.

My hands start shaking.

I have to show these to Steve. He'll know what to do.

Leaving my phone in the bedroom, I head outside. I don't want to have Lily's messages anywhere near me.

The pale sun warms my face and the early

signs of spring greet me as I pull out the late winter weeds. New growth and buds are starting to appear on our trees and I can't wait for the show of blossoms which will arrive in a few weeks. I listen to my kids' happy chattering and playing. Steve starts up the weed-eater at the bottom of the garden and I take a deep steadying breath. Parking the emotional rollercoaster of Lily and Simone I focus on what I have right in front of me.

The kids are asleep, and Steve has poured me a Baileys on ice. I sit opposite him on the couch, carefully watching his every facial expression as he reads the messages from Lily. He finally gets to the last one and lets out a low whistle.

"I'm actually at a loss Evie." He looks bewildered and disgusted as he throws my phone on the coffee table.

"What happened? Why is she freaking out like that?"

Jesus, had I not told him?

"Didn't I tell you yesterday that I sent Lily a message? I… I called it off. I told her I was sorry, but I couldn't sleep with her anymore."

"OK… Why did you call it off?" His brow furrows.

I take a deep breath. We're entering dangerous territory here. I don't know how he will take this.

"I couldn't sleep with Simone while Lily was still in the picture." I look away. "I didn't think it would be fair."

Steve says nothing. He just watches me squirm in my seat. I take another sip of baileys and opt for honesty as the best policy.

To front foot my confession, I start with, "Simone and I have also called it Steve. I won't be seeing her in *that way* again. We talked last night... I didn't realise it before, but we discovered that we have some... *feelings*... for each other... which complicates things. Also, there's something else I should have told you... about Lily."

Steve sits mute, sipping his Baileys while he waits for me to carry on. After all those dreadful messages, I know it's time to tell him.

"The last time I visited Lily's house, I tried to tell her in person that I wanted to stop sleeping with her...it no longer felt right as she still hadn't told Cam and with Simone back on the scene... it was just too much trying to handle *two women*. But as I tried to tell her, she... she... wouldn't listen. She kind of... forced herself on me... even though I asked her to stop."

"What?!" Steve bellows. He is no longer pensive. He looks enraged. "Why didn't you tell me this when it happened?"

Ashamed I talk quietly into my glass. "Because I still *came* Steve. I was so confused. I didn't understand what was happening. She pinned me in place... I was so shocked by her strength... I didn't struggle hard enough...she... she said I liked it... because I came."

Steve's nostrils flare and he puts his baileys down as he gathers me in his arms. I can actually feel him trembling with wrath as he holds me.

"You said stop. I don't care if she thought you liked it. Something is very wrong here."

His words make all the emotions I've been experiencing feel valid. My relief opens the floodgates and big sobs fill the space as I cry against his chest. Through my tears I murmur "Steve, I never meant for any of this to happen… Lily… Simone… I choose you, Steve. I choose our family. I just want this *crazy mess* to go away."

I listen to his heartbeat through his shirt. It's beating faster than his normal steady pace. I hear him take a deep shaky breath.

"Evie, I had no idea any of this was going on. I can't believe Lily…I can't say it…" He pauses for a moment, his furious eyes drift to the messages still alight on my phone. "I thought you all knew about each other…"

Sitting back slightly, I know I need to explain.

"Well, Simone went so quiet after our first time. I thought she wasn't interested. Then Lily kind of preoccupied all my spare time…. Then when Simone told me how she had been struggling with her sexuality and how the thought of us cheating on you had kept her away… I realised she didn't like cheating. So… I didn't know how to tell her about Lily… But I *tried* to do the right thing. I had to end it with Lily… before I could be intimate with

Simone… so I could have a slightly clearer conscience… I am an awful slut, aren't I?" I cover my face with my hands.

Steve's face softens. "No, you're not an awful slut, Evie and you're not a mind reader. You thought Simone wasn't interested… but yes, her coming back into the picture changed the dynamic. I see that now." Steve ponders a moment as his eyes glance again to my phone. "What do you think Lily will do if she finds out it's Simone?"

"I have no idea, Steve. Those messages… and our last encounter…I don't know what to do."

"Well, there's nothing we can do until she actually follows through on her threat. I suggest you keep the messages and missed phone calls. If things get a bit heated, we can always put a restraining order on her."

The thought of filing a police report scares the hell out of me. Plus, *would* Lily really do something that would warrant that consequence?

"I don't think she believes she did anything wrong that day… I'm sure she's just super pissed that I broke up with her via text… even though she knew this wasn't a relationship. I kept that clear right from the start…. But yes, I should have called her. I know it's a cop-out, but the last conversation we had kind of *frightened* me… and I didn't think I could trust myself to be alone with her again. It was just easier to get my words out in a text."

Steve rubs his chin in thought.

I can see he's still deeply unsettled, his brain evidently churning the information behind his eyes. Suddenly, Steve sighs. "I don't have the answers tonight. Tell you what. Let me do the school runs this week. Put some space between you and the ladies while the dust settles. Plus, I don't feel comfortable about Lily being *anywhere* near you."

Nodding, I realise it is a good idea for me to lay low. I pick up my phone to look at my calendar. It's full of meetings and working bees for the upcoming Agriculture Day. Hannah has been raising a lamb in the rear paddock and is so excited. As a member of the school committee, I have a lot of responsibility in the lead up and on the event day. I groan. Why couldn't it be further away?

"Steve, it's Ag day in three weeks."

We share a look of understanding. We both know I will see Lily and Simone there.

"We will tackle it together on the day. I can hang close if you need me."

"Thanks." I feel a surge of security wash over me. Knowing that my husband will be there and is being so supportive allows me to see a glimmer of hope for everything to blow over and just go back to *normal*.

"So, this is it for you and your femme-sur-femme adventures?" He asks with a wary raised eyebrow.

I feel a pang of sadness pull at my heartstrings as I think of Simone, but I know this is best for everyone involved.

"Yes, that's it. I don't want to do this anymore." I can hear the tired defeat in my voice.

"Then that's it." He kisses me on the lips. "Come on, you look shattered. Let's go to bed."

I climb into bed, exhausted. I feel like I have crashed back down to earth and bounced along the tarmac. This has to be the roughest I've felt emotionally in years.

What a rough landing.

I snuggle up next to my husband letting his strong arms embrace me.

Protect me.

Emotionally battered and bruised, I am officially grounded and do not wish to depart on any crazy adventures *anytime soon*.

Twenty-Two

Evie and the Deafening Silence

My mornings feel *different.* They are still full of the morning rush of helping the kids get ready, packing lunch boxes and brushing their teeth. But it's Steve who is bundling them into the car and taking them to school. Our house feels empty and oh, so quiet.

I click on my phone to light up the home screen. There are no new messages. No missed phone calls.

It's been five painful days since that Sunday morning when I kissed Simone for the last time. I feel strange. I would even say I feel slightly *numb.* I'm going through my daily motions, but something feels missing.

Something feels...*Lost.*

It's Friday, my day off and I find myself slightly on edge. Lily's threat still looming over my head like a black cloud. I search all the online group chats that are connected to the school to see if there is any gossip brewing.

The anticipation that Lily may be spreading vile rumours in my absence makes my heart pound so hard it feels like it will burst out of my chest.

I close the chat windows, disappointed and relieved that there are no cryptic messages for me to be afraid of. I check my emails and find a dozen Ag Day committee planning emails. I sigh and open them one by one. There truly is so much to do. I will be the treasurer for the day but also need to purchase a few items for raffles and prizes. I open the Committee chat group and advise the members that I will complete the purchases over the weekend.

'So nice of you to join us Evie…'

Stacey's sarcasm drips from every word.

'Where have you been this week?'

Her question is so direct, making me bristle.

'Just having a quiet week, Stacey. I haven't shirked my responsibilities. I know what jobs I need to do.'

Hopefully that will appease the power-hungry bitch.

'Oh, lucky for some, Evie. We've all been here flat tack making props since 8am.'

Her words remind me of the working bee today.

Fuck.

'Oh yes, the working bee. I hadn't forgotten.' I lied. *'I'm just running late. Will be there in 20 minutes.'*

'Great, bring five flat whites with you. Two with coconut milk. Get them from Charlie's Café,

not the petrol station.'

Ughhhh she makes my blood boil!

'No problem, Stacey. I'll get a receipt.'

'Good-o. See you soon.'

It truly is a miracle I haven't snapped her head off yet. I have the patience of a saint!

I gather my things and head out the door. I feel my heart flutter in my chest as I hope that Lily is not at school during the day… and part of me secretly hopes that Simone *is.*

She won't be though.

Simone's face swims clearly into my mind. I can see her serenely resting on her pillow with her curls strewn around her. She's smiling her coy, happy to see me smile. I feel a pang of regret, knowing that I'll never see her like that, again. I sweep the image from my mind as I lock the house door and climb into my car.

Let's get this working bee over and done with.

I show up with six coffees as I decided to include myself, seeing as Stacey hadn't mentioned my need for caffeine. I pass them out to the ladies and hand Stacey the receipt.

Stacey tuts and glances at the clock, then back at me.

I can't suppress an eye roll before I look around the hall to see which project looks the easiest for me to help with.

Rachael is working on some bunting and beckons me to work with her. Grateful, I take my coffee and sit next to her. It is so good to see a friendly face.

As I take my seat next to her, I roll my eyes

in Stacey's direction. "She's such a dictator."

I smirk, expecting Rachael to join me in a bit of Stacey slander, but she sits back, folding her arms unimpressed. My smile falters as Rachael lays into me in hushed tones.

"I know she's bossy, Evie, but she's been running ragged trying to get this event organised. If you actually spent some time getting to know her, you'd see her a bit differently." I'm taken aback by her sudden defence of Stacey and I sit there bewildered.

"I know she does a lot, but she doesn't have to be so mean about everything." I counter.

Exasperated, Rachael adds "you know she's a legal secretary right? She does all the legwork for some uppity male lawyer in town and he takes all the credit for her work. She's treated like a servant and it's made her grow a thick skin. At least with the committee, she's in charge, but she never takes all the credit. Haven't you noticed that?"

I think back to previous events and the praise and thanks she's gushed in newsletters to all the helpers and I realise that no one has ever thanked her. Understanding crosses my face and I nod.

"She's curt and efficient. I know she rubs most of us the wrong way, but she gets the job done."

"OK, you're right. I'm sorry, I'll keep my grumbling to myself." Chastened I sip my coffee as I look at the task on our table.

Stacey aside, I can see there's something

else on Rachael's mind. In a low voice she asks me "is everything alright Evie?"

I feign surprise. "Yes, why?"

"You haven't been making the drop offs and pick-ups. You're an hour late today. It's not like you. I wondered if you've been unwell?"

Ohhhh. Of course Rachael would notice.

Thinking fast on my feet. "Yes, actually, I've had a bit of a stomach bug. Jackson must have brought it home from daycare on the weekend."

"Oh no, that's awful!" Her face is etched with empathy and understanding.

I feel bad for lying but there is no way I could tell her the truth. I change the subject and get Rachael to show me where to join my flags with the bunting string.

Rachael starts talking animatedly about what has been achieved so far and how Archie is getting on with raising a chick for Ag day. We laugh as we share stories of raising farm animals with our kids.

I scan the room and I notice Jennifer and Sandra have their heads together deep in conspirational whispers. When they look up I smile, raising my coffee in toast but they share an uncomfortable glance and avert their eyes. They don't toast back.

What was that?

My heart starts to hammer inside my chest as I frown into my bunting. Hopefully no one saw our interaction.

Rachael moves closer and I can smell her

perfume. Her closeness makes me feel uncomfortable and I shift in my seat. Her hand brushes against mine and she smiles an awkward smile at me.

What's going on here?

Rachael is my friend. I tell myself. *It was an accident.*

I put my coffee down and excuse myself to the ladies.

Once in the bathroom I sit alone in a stall and put my head between my hands. I take a deep breath to calm the thrumming in my chest. I feel so *anxious*.

I hear the bathroom door open, and someone enters the room and starts washing their hands. I feel myself holding my breath and my bladder.

I wait until the door opens and closes again and I let out a sigh of relief. I finish up and exit my stall and start washing my hands. Suddenly I sense movement behind me. I whip my head around to see Rachael standing behind the door. I jump and water splashes all over the sink.

"Jesus Rachael! What are you doing? Creeping behind the door like that?" I shudder, but wear a smile as she really got me this time.

I return to rinsing my hands and she takes a step closer to me. Turning off the faucet and grabbing some paper towels I'm expecting her to start laughing and tell me that she got me good, but she doesn't.

"Evie?" Rachael takes a breath.

"Yes, Rachael?" I ask bewildered by what she is doing in here.

"Evie… is it true that you *like* women?"

I am stunned. My mouth drops open, yet no sound comes out. I close my mouth. Then it drops open again. I realise I probably look like a fish out of water.

I *feel* like a fish out of water.

Rachael moves closer to me.

"Is it true Evie?" She enters my personal space and is so close, I can taste her breath. I back up, my behind hitting the sink.

"I think I'll take your reaction as a… yes?" She says the last word like she's still not sure, but I can hear in her voice that she wants it to be true.

I still can't speak.

"I don't know what it is about you Evie…" Rachael has placed her hands either side of me on the bathroom sink and I feel myself leaning back between her arms. Suddenly her lips are on mine and as I pull away, I hit my head on the wall behind me.

The pain gives me the shock I need to find my voice.

I push Rachael to arms-length. I look into her eyes, which are searching mine for approval.

"Rachael, I'm so… flattered…" I start.

"Shit! Shit! Shit!" Rachael starts to freak out and I can feel her struggling to pull away from me.

"Rachael, it's OK, it's OK!"

She's my friend. She needs to hear this. In

lowered tones I hiss. "It's true. I do like women. But I'm sorry Rachael, I'm happily married."

Rachael looks down at her feet. I can see her lower lip tremble and her cheeks turn scarlet.

"I'm so sorry Evie. I don't know what I was thinking."

"Hey… Rachael. Please don't be upset. I find you very attractive… I'm just dealing with some stuff and… you've caught me by surprise. Please don't tell anyone. I don't want to make any mums uncomfortable… *or* feed the rumour train."

"What stuff Evie? You don't talk to me anymore." Her eyes are glistening with unshed tears. I realise that since Lily and Simone came onto the scene I hadn't spent as much time with Rachael as I have in the past.

"There *is* a rumour, Evie. I think you should know." She wipes at her eyes, composing herself.

I can feel the blood drain from my face.

"What is it, Rachael? Tell *me*."

She takes a breath. "I don't know where it started. But some mums are saying that you came onto them, *aggressively*."

"What?"

That wasn't quite what I expected. I thought maybe there would be something specific to do with Lily.

Aggressive?

Me?

"Who? Which Mums?" I demand.

"I'm not sure which mums, they all seem quite hush hush about it. They said they're protecting the mums' identity as they're so shocked that it happened...They're wondering if they should report you." Rachael looks away.

"Report *me?!*" I'm incredulous. I start pacing the small space in front of the stalls.

"Ughhh. She threatened she'd do something like this." I place my hands on the sink as I groan into the mirror.

"Who?" She asks. "What *happened* Evie? I'm starting to think you haven't had a stomach bug this week." She shoots me a hurt and accusatory stare.

I throw up my hands. "No, I haven't had a stomach bug, Rachael...I'm sorry... I.. I just don't know how I got into this mess." I feel contrite but I truly wasn't planning on having this conversation... *ever*... with Rachael. The fact that she just kissed me in the bathroom is making my mind buzz in confusion.

She folds her arms across her chest, waiting.

She looks so cute when she's cross that a chuckle escapes my lips. Despite this crazy moment between us I realise I could do with a friend.

"Please don't be upset with me Rachael. If I can still call you a friend, I would love to tell you everything. But it's a *big* secret. Can I trust it will remain just between us?"

She uncrosses her arms. "Of course, Evie, you don't even have to ask."

Relief floods through me knowing I can unload safely with a friend.

"Thanks Rachael. But we can't talk here OK. Let's meet for coffee tomorrow, but let's drive out a bit hey. Put some distance between us... and this town."

"Sure. I know just the place. I'll send you the details." She smiles and comes over for a hug. It feels familiar again and I'm relieved that the awkwardness from a moment ago has dissipated.

I pull away. "I'll head back first. Let's not start any more rumours hey." I give her a wink as I open the door.

Feeling slightly guilty that I've dashed Rachael's hopes of getting to know me in *that* way, I make my way back to the hall. As I enter the room, I suddenly notice the volume drop. All the mums glance up then start busying themselves awkwardly, doing everything they can to not look at me.

Great. It's spreading faster than I thought.

Pretending that nothing is wrong I return to my task. Rachael joins me a few minutes later and we chat about our kids more loudly than required, in an effort to return some level of normalcy amongst the group. I am hoping amongst all hope that this rumour will fizzle into nothing.

I work fast to complete my props, then make the effort to help the other mum's finish theirs. They allow the help, but the conversations are subdued. By the end of two hours, we are all finished.

I say my goodbyes and head to the carpark. As I approach, I see an ugly deep scratch running down the side of my car.

Someone has keyed my car!

My brain automatically flashes to Lily. Who else could it be? I stand there fuming as the other mums arrive behind me. I can hear the shock in their hushed whispers. I spin around.

"Did any of you see who did this?" My words come out loud, accusatory.

Sandra, Jennifer and Stacey band together. They share bewildered glances.

"No." They respond together.

Stacey, surprisingly throws in "That's *awful* Evie." She genuinely sounds concerned, which throws me even more.

I throw my hands defeatedly in the air. "You were all with me, of course you didn't see." I sigh. "I'll call my insurance company."

With nothing left to say, the mums awkwardly shuffle to their own cars, furtively glancing at me before driving off.

I look at the angry gash with my hands on my hips. I'm beyond upset. I love my car.

I climb in and with a set jaw I start thinking about how I am going to prove that Lily is the aggressive one.

Not *me*.

As I drive away, I mull over the brewing rumour, and I feel a tug in my chest.

What if Simone hears the rumour?

I think back to the lack of messages this week. Even though we called it, I thought we would still be friends. Which would mean that it's OK to text… surely?

I pull into the park near our home. The same park where Simone and I made out in my car. The same spot where I said I could spend the night with her which spurred us to almost have sex in a public place. I open my phone and type out a message.

'Simone, I miss you and I am feeling so lost…'

I feel stupid for saying how I feel so I delete it and start again.

'Hey Simone, how are you? You all good?'

Well, that's stupidly cavalier. I delete that one too.

I take a breath. I just want to know that she's thinking of me… like I'm thinking of her. I know it's wrong to stir things up, but I just want to know if she's still hurting?

Like I'm still hurting.

Plus, I am praying that she hasn't heard that god-awful rumour.

Would she know it's a lie?

I try again.

'Simone, I'm sitting in our park and I'm thinking of you. I know we're putting some space between us, but, I need to see you. Would it be alright if I come over?' I hit send before I lose my nerve.

I see that it's delivered, and the three dots start cycling.

Then stop.

I sit there staring at my phone. The seconds tick by. Then the minutes.

I hear the rhythmic thud of a runner's

shoes on the track that circles the park.

Is that the second time he has passed?

I stare hard at my phone, willing the dots to start cycling again. Willing there to be a 'yes come over'.

But there's *nothing.*

She doesn't respond.

And her silence is *deafening.*

Twenty-Three

Evie and the Confidante

I'm still fuming about my car. How could she? Steve is angry too. In fact, I don't think I've ever seen him this livid before. He called the school yesterday and demanded the CCTV footage but of course there's a blind spot on the row where I parked. How did she know that she wouldn't be caught?

I've called the insurance company and sent through the pictures. Thank goodness it's obvious that this was an act of vandalism. Otherwise, I'd lose my excess.

In bed this morning, I tell Steve about the rumour. He scoffs "How are they going to report you without proof? And to whom? Without evidence the police would take a statement then throw it in the bin."

I love his rational thinking. He knows just what to say to make me feel better.

I remind him that I'm meeting up with Rachael this morning, but he doesn't think it's a good idea.

"Spreading a rumour is one thing, her pride is obviously hurt, but vandalising your car... That's unstable behaviour. We don't know what Lily's capable of, Evie. Why don't we all go to the garden centre café instead and I can keep the kids distracted while you and Rachael catch up." I can tell he's rattled. He puts his arms around me and holds me tight.

Protectively.

"I had no idea... I shouldn't have encouraged...." He trails off.

"Hey, Steve. *I* had no idea. How were you supposed to know? It's not your fault." I look up into his blue eyes and mull over his suggestion of the Garden Centre Café.

"I don't really want to go to the garden centre Steve. I wanted to get out of town, even if it is only thirty minutes away. I doubt she'll be there, and I'll be with Rachael."

He looks down at me with pursed lips. I can see he's not convinced.

"I'll wait in my car until I know Rachael is there and we will do the Ag day shopping together. I won't be alone. We will stay in public places. I honestly don't think Lily would try anything if I did come across her. She'd have to be full-blown psycho for that and I don't think she is." I smile bravely at him and he sighs, hugging me tight again.

I hear thumping footsteps coming down the hall and our bedroom door swings open with the extreme force of a four year old on a mission. Jackson jumps up onto the bed and pushes Steve out of the way while bellowing

"Mummy cuddles!"

Steve gives me an eyeroll as Jackson hugs me tight. I hug him back fiercely. He will only be four for a short time. Steve climbs out of bed and opens the curtains for the sunrise to stream into the room.

"I'll get the hot drinks." He smiles at me and ruffles Jackson's hair.

A moment later Steve returns with coffees for us and hot chocolates for the kids. Hannah has arrived at the foot of our bed bleary eyed. She glares at Jackson until he finally moves into the middle of the bed so Hannah can take his place for a morning snuggle on my lap.

This is bliss. It's a beautiful morning with my family.

The only thing that would make it better would be seeing Simone.

The thought pops into my head before I can stop it. She still hasn't responded to yesterday's message and a bubble of dread settles over me. I would be so upset with myself if she got hurt.

It's dawning on me that it's going to be harder than I thought to stop thinking about her.

It's still early days. I remind myself.

Hell. It was only last weekend that we made love *all night*. A myriad of erotic images rush through my mind. I shake my head and sip my coffee. It is *so* inappropriate to be picturing Simone in the throes of passion while I'm having my morning family time.

The morning moves along. Breakfast.

Showers. A relentless stream of questions and demands from our children. Before I know it, I'm at the door kissing Steve goodbye.

He squeezes my hand. "I'm still worried about you."

"I have a plan, I'll be fine. I'll call if I need you." I kiss him again and climb into my car.

'I'm on my way.' I message Rachael.

I pop the coordinates of the café into my GPS and pull out of the driveway. My hands-free pings and reads Rachael's reply in robotic monotone.

'OK. Me too. See you soon.'

I put my music on to help calm the nerves. I start singing and I feel better going through the autopilot motions of driving my car. I'm almost onto the main road when I hear a new message ping.

I push play, expecting another message from Rachael.

'Evie. Evie. Where are you going today? Off to see your whore?'

The robot mispronounces the last word, so it sounds even more sinister.

I almost swerve off the road as I look around for Lily's silver car. She's nowhere in sight. My heart races inside my chest and I wonder if I should turn around and return to the safety of Steve.

I hear another ping. This time it's a voice message via messenger. I realise it's really unsafe to be listening to these while I drive. I turn off my notifications and focus on getting to the café.

I'll be in a public place. I reason.

I nervously glance around me at every stop sign.

Every corner.

There is no one following me.

I continue out of town once I am convinced Lily isn't within my vicinity. I still check my rear view mirror every other second.

She has me *so* on *edge*.

I am relieved when I see Rachael in her car in the café carpark. I pull in next to her and beckon for her to jump into the passenger seat. I turn off the ignition and as she climbs in, I lean around her, searching for a sign that Lily could be hidden behind her somewhere.

"Evie, woah. You look rattled. What's going on?"

I say nothing while I fumble with my phone. I haven't told Rachael anything yet, but I need to know what is in this message.

With trembling hands, I push play. Lily's voice rings out from my phone speaker.

"Why good morning, *my Evie*. I've missed you this week. I think I'm having withdrawals from our *secret sessions*. I think we should start those up again. In fact, I *insist* we do. Why don't you call me and we can sort out this whole misunderstanding. You know that I'm the only girl for you Evie. I know every secret button to push and oh how I love making you *come*. So come on Evie. Be a good girl and call me."

Lily's voice tinkles melodically, but her words chill me to my core.

Rachael stares at my phone in disbelief.

"Lily? … You've been sleeping with *Lily?"*

There's something slightly off in Rachael's tone of voice. I can't quite put my finger on it.

"Yeah, I guess I have a bit to fill you in on."

"You think!" Rachael looks at me in wonder and concern. "OK. Let's order coffee to go. We can sit in your car, and you can tell me all about it."

"Sounds like a plan… But can we sit in your car?"

"Of course." Rachael looks bewildered at my request, but I'm grateful she doesn't push me for a why. She might think I'm crazy if I tell her the truth, that I think Lily might somehow hear us from inside my car.

We enter the café together and the wonderful coffee aroma wafts over me, calming me. Coffee is my vice of choice. It takes me to my happy place with every sip. I take a deep breath in and browse the cake display window.

Damn, they all look so good!

When it's our turn to order I select the chocolate brownie and a tall latte. Rachael gets a flat white and a blueberry muffin.

We take our treats to her car, and I climb into the passenger seat. Her front seats are tidy but the rear seats resemble a post-apocalyptic mess of crumbs, wrappers and sticky smears. Rachael shrugs.

"I used to clean it. But now I've given up. It turns into that within minutes of the kids jumping in the back."

"Oh I feel you. My car is in a similar state." We laugh and it feels good to share a lighter topic of conversation.

I sip my coffee and its heaven. It's just the right temperature. The staff in this café clearly know their stuff. Some baristas have no idea regarding the correct temperature of a latte. You shouldn't have to wait for it to cool down. It should be warm and not burn your tongue on the first sip. If it's bitter, they've clearly burned the milk or *worse,* burned the beans. A latte should be creamy, rich in flavour and should *not* need sugar.

I smile at Rachael from my seat. "Good choice on the café. This is delicious."

I close my eyes as I savour the flavour rolling around inside my mouth. I taste the brownie and as the sweet chocolate melts on my tongue and merges with my coffee, I feel myself transcend into a world of tastebud bliss. An involuntary, soft "mmmmmm" escapes from behind my closed lips.

Rachael snorts next to me.

"You see Evie. This is why women like you. Everything you do is so *sensual*.... I think you just turned me on by eating a brownie!"

I'm so taken aback by her comment that I almost choke. I can feel a big belly laugh coming from within me and as it erupts a small spray of brownie crumbs come with it. I try and catch it with a napkin and nearly drop my coffee.

Rachael bursts into laughter. She bends over as she holds her sides and her forehead connects to the horn on the steering wheel letting out a loud 'beep' across the carpark.

A couple walking past jump and cast us sideways glares, making us laugh harder.

Our mirth eventually settles, and Rachael turns serious again.

"So, start at the beginning, Evie. Tell me everything."

I look down at the coffee in my hands and take small sips as I pour my heart out, telling her the whole story. I start with when Lily and I became involved. How our intimacies became almost a weekly saga at Lily's house. As I told her about our last intimate encounter and Lily's confession of how she lied to me, Rachael gasped. I do my best to show that it wasn't all sinister and that there was a friendly relationship there… until I ended it. I show Rachael Lily's messages on my phone and her eyes widen as she takes in the sheer number along with the disturbing content. Quiet and pale, she hands the phone back to me.

I sigh apologetically.

"I just don't know what changed Rachael. One minute we were having fun and Steve was supportive. Then the next it just didn't *feel* right. Especially after she didn't stop when I asked her to."

"That sounds horrific, especially that last time with her. I'm so sorry that happened to you, you know it's not your fault right?" I nod and stare at my coffee cup. After a moment Rachael continues. "I think I'd be just as confused as you… She clearly took offence to you calling it off… but you'd made it clear this wasn't a relationship."

"I know!"

"So... Evie… Is there another woman? Or is Lily just jumping to conclusions?"

I exhale heavily. I was hoping to leave Simone out of this confession.

"No, she's not." I pause to gather myself. "Before the first time with Lily… Like, two months before, I had a moment with Simone. Then she went quiet on me. I now know she freaked out about what had happened between us. It was quite unexpected…"

"Evie! You were sleeping with two women at the same time! You *hussy!*" She says it playfully, as she throws a napkin at me.

I flash her a wolfish grin but set her straight.

"As I said, two months b*efore* Lily. *And* I called it off with Lily before I was intimate with Simone again. I couldn't sleep with Simone, knowing that Lily was still in the picture… I may have…kissed Simone while Lily was still in the picture. I feel bad about that… but this is all such a grey area as I'm married! Steve is happy for me to sleep with women but I'm realising I'm just not cut out for this polyamory thing. There's too many repercussions."

I pause, not sure if I should confess my feelings for Simone.

"Not cut out? You mean you didn't expect the repercussions with Lily?" Rachael tries to make sense of it all, this is clearly new territory for her too.

"Well, yes that... and I care about Simone. To be honest, before Lily went a bit crazy, I cared for her too. My concern is, what if Lily figures out it's her? What would she do to her?" I put my head in my hands.

"Evie, I honestly have no idea... I've never been in a situation like this. I've never slept with a woman... but I've thought about it... Lily actually... I..." Rachael gets flustered and her cheeks flame red.

"Lily what Rachael?" Alarm bells start ringing in my head.

Rachael looks embarrassed. "It was nothing really. She just keeps getting *close*. Brushing against me when she sees me... and sometimes she kisses me on the cheek... but it's more the corner of my mouth. We've kind of laughed it off but she has started messaging me too. I think she likes me."

Hearing her words make several puzzle pieces slot into place in my mind.

"Rachael, she's positioning you! She's lining you up to seduce you. Ughh she did the same to me... I just didn't realise it!"

All the early interactions with Lily flash through my mind. The lingering hugs, the 'accidental' brushes of her hands down my body when saying hello and goodbye. I realise she had been doing it for at least two months before we were intimate.

"Can I see the messages, Rachael?"

She nods and flicks through her phone and hands it to me. My eyes scan rapidly over several messages from Lily.

'Rachael, how are you? You look so nice today. What are you doing later?'

'Rachael, Cam and I are fighting. I sooo need a girl's night. Fancy a wine?'

'Rachael, loved your outfit today. Navy is definitely your colour.'

'Hey, I've got the place to myself tonight, do you fancy coming over?'

'Come on Rachael, you need a night off. Let's let our hair down.'

Rachael had shorter responses in between. Polite, friendly responses that never agreed to go to her house or meet her anywhere, usually because she had the boys. I breathe out a sigh of relief.

I reread the messages again, then notice the dates and times…

"Rachael, when did she start being extra friendly?"

Rachael thinks hard. "Umm I don't know. Maybe a month or two ago?"

"Right… so while she was sleeping with me, she was flirting with you in the hope she'd get you too…" My mind whirrs.

Who is this woman?

"OK. Rachael. Stay friendly with her but never let her get you alone. *Ever*. I think she's got a problem… like mentally…" I pause then add, "don't delete her messages. If things turn bad you have evidence that she has been trying to get you alone."

The colour drains from Rachael's face.

"Do you really think it's that bad? She

seems so harmless…"

I scoff. "Yeah, tell that to my car!" Quietly I add, "she left bruises on me after our last... encounter." I physically shudder.

That last piece of information sends the message home for Rachael and we sit in stony silence as we mull over the heavy situation. I wonder if Lily is grooming anyone else.

A question niggles at me. "Rachael, how long have you been curious about women?"

"I don't know… a while… The thought of acting on how I feel terrifies me." Her eyes meet mine then flicker to a tree outside.

"You shouldn't be scared or ashamed Rachael. You're single and have complete free reign over who you choose to date."

"I know… oh Evie. Why can't it have been you sending me messages and brushing against me?"

Rachael's eyes burn into mine. I feel so vulnerable right now. We've just shared some very intimate information.

Rachael's hand comes to rest on my knee. I put my hand over it, squeezing gently before placing it back on her lap.

"Rachael, I'm sorry. If I wasn't in this situation with Lily and Simone, then yes, I might have liked to explore this. But this is *really* not a good idea."

"I know." Rachael looks crestfallen. Her eyes linger on my lips then flick up to search mine. "Would one kiss be out of the question?"

I know I shouldn't.

"One?"

"Just one. I promise to leave it there. I just want to know what it's like."

I let her words hang in the air for amoment. I *think* she's rational enough to leave it there...and who knows? Maybe she won't like it and return to dating men?

"Are you sure Rachael? There can't be anything more between us. I really don't want to blur the lines here. I need a friend Rachael. I'm not looking for another lover."

"Oh of course! I know that. I just really want to know what it feels like... I might even hate it. I trust you, Evie." After a moment she adds "...and you can trust me. I won't go crazy on you." She smiles and it's reassuring.

I draw a deep breath. I still don't know if this is wise but I know what it's like to be curious. If I can help her get this out of her system, she can move forward. I scan the carpark for anybody that might see us, the last thing I need is an audience. Thank goodness our cars are facing a tall hedge and not the cafe. I'll make this short and sweet.

I reach out and touch her cheek. She leans in and I can smell the coffee and muffin on her breath. Tilting myself closer I brush my lips against hers, my mouth slightly open. Rachael's tongue gently licks my top lip, then she retracts it sharply. Possibly startled by how soft it feels. She breathes heavily, her forehead resting on mine as our lips hover apart. After a moment she leans in again. This time, she timidly parts her lips, inviting me in.

Our kiss is gentle, tender, and in no time her tongue is dancing with mine. Rachael starts to shift in her seat, trying to get her body closer to mine. I can sense things are moving away from a friendly exploration, so I delicately end the kiss and pull away.

"Are you OK?"

Rachael looks dazed, her eyes linger on my lips for a few seconds before dragging them to meet mine.

"Woah Evie" She breathes. "… I can see why you were worried. Fuck, I want more!" She laughs and shakes her head.

I laugh too. "I did warn you. Kissing girls is addictive!"

"Wow! Yeah, I wasn't expecting it to be that good. I hoped… but yeah." She blows air out of her cheeks as she tries to shake it off.

She looks over at me again with a flirtatiously raised eyebrow. "Just one?" She asks.

"Just one. I told you. I can't get into anything with you. I need to dig myself out, not further in. You need to go online, see if there's anyone you might like to go on a date with. I can probably help you with your profile if you like?"

"Yeah, that's not a bad idea. Thanks." Her face is pensive and I can see she has taken on board what I've said.

"So.." she says brightly. Clearly trying to move things along. "Now that I've got that out of my system, what do we need to buy today?"

I glance at my watch. We've been here for

two hours, and we still need to get things for Ag day.

"Oh shit. Yes. Umm... I have a list." I fumble in my bag and retrieve the shopping list and hand it to her. Her eyes scan over the items.

"Right, we can get all of this in the mall just down the road. Shall we take my car and I can return you to yours afterwards?"

"Sounds like a plan."

Rachael turns on the car and we head out of the carpark.

The afternoon is filled with purchasing items (and begging for a few freebies) from the vendors in the mall. An hour and a half later, our trolley is full and we are thankfully, finished.

Rachael drives me back to my car and we transfer the goods into my boot.

She gives me a hug. "Thanks for confiding in me today Evie..." Shyly she adds "...and thanks for letting me down gently."

"Of course." I pull her into a hug. "And thank you Rachael, for listening... and please, be careful with Lily."

"I will." She gives me one last squeeze and climbs into her car.

I climb into mine and start the engine. Relief floods through me as Rachael follows me all the way to our town before heading her separate way.

Going over our conversation in my head, I'm positive that Rachael is being groomed... and it's starting to dawn on me that I'd been caught...

Hook, line, and sinker.

I have a lot to tell Steve tonight. I wonder how many other mums are trying to keep the flirtatious Lily at bay.

I also wonder who else she's sleeping with…

Rachael's lovely, friendly face swims in front of my eyes.

Thank goodness I could warn her.

I see my driveway and I'm relieved that there is no silver car lurking on my curb. It took a lot out of me, telling Rachael everything today. I am relieved that she took it all so well.

I no longer feel alone in this crazy scenario.

I'm so grateful to have her as my *confidante.*

Twenty-Four

Evie and the Breakdown

I'm starting to suffer from anxiety. My hands keep shaking and my heart is almost constantly fluttering in my chest. I've started drinking a glass of wine after the kids have gone to bed, just to settle the nerves. Steve is picking up on it and is worried. He can't do all of the pick-ups and drop offs this week so I'm trying to do what I can... and it's Ag day next Friday.

Every time I leave my house I am scanning for Lily. Scanning for her silver car.

I don't know how she does it, but I get a message *every* morning as I pull out of my drive.

'Where are you going today, Evie?'

I starting to wonder if someone can have a heart attack from *fear*?

My kids are picking up on my irritability. I'm snapping at them when I don't mean to. I cry at the smallest of things. I'm not sleeping well. They must think I'm going crazy.

I wonder if I am going crazy.

I'm doing all the drop-offs this week and every day I've noticed the scared glances from mums at the school gate. I see them in my periphery having hushed conversations after I've walked past with my children. Whenever I make eye contact, they look away to avoid engaging in conversation with me.

I want to scream at them: "It's not true! None of it!"

But I don't as I don't want to upset my kids… or cause a scene.

I carry out my committee tasks as required, but I'm much more subdued. There's no more friendly banter as I drop off supplies and make my rounds to check what needs to be done.

Oddly, apart from Rachael, the only person still talking to me is my nemesis, Stacey. It feels so strange to have her speak to me politely. I feel like the whole world has tipped upside down and I'm in some strange alternate universe.

I'm still trying to talk to Simone. I scan for her in the school carpark, but never see her. I've messaged her each day in hope she'll respond.

'Simone, we really need to talk. Can I come over? Or call you?'

'Simone, please. I don't know if you've heard that stupid rumour, you know it's not true, right?'

'Simone, please let me see you so I can explain. You can decide where and when we meet. I don't want to put you in a position where you feel

uncomfortable. You know me. You have to know whatever is going around isn't true.'

'Simone…'

'Please…'

'Talk to me…'

'Your silence is killing me.'

It's taken all my strength to not just show up at her house. I can see my messages are starting to sound *desperate.* I also *know* it looks like I am becoming a stalker. With every non-reply from Simone, I feel like I'm *becoming* the rumour.

I just don't know what to do.

Lily has been messaging me every day. I can't help but start to notice a similarity between her messages to me, and my messages to Simone.

'Evie, I miss you.'

'Evie, please call me. We have some things to discuss.'

'Evie, please. I'm sorry. Let's meet at a café. A public place if that makes you feel better?'

Then I get the following and I don't think I'm quite as stalkerish as Lily.

'Be a good girl and call me Evie. You know I can help you if you do. I can clear up this whole misunderstanding.'

I feel so vulnerable and ostracised right now. A flurry of questions sweep through my mind.

Would she stop the rumours if I call?

Will Simone talk to me again if things are cleared up?

…Maybe I should call Lily and 'sort out this

misunderstanding' as she put it.

Everything has been via messages. Could it possibly get any worse if I spoke to her?

Another week has passed and I just don't know how much more I can take. My nerves are shot, and I might actually need to see my doctor to get prescribed a sleeping pill.

It's Monday today and Ag day is *this* Friday. I'm barely going through the motions at work. Thank goodness the phones are quiet today so I can just plod along answering emails and lodging claims. The office is quiet and the only sound I hear is the quiet tap, tap, tap of fingers on keyboards and the quiet hum of the office air conditioner. The tranquillity is broken as I hear laughter coming from the direction of the break room as two colleagues emerge with mugs of coffee, their break-time over.

I glance at my watch. It's my turn for a break now and I know Lily will be at lunch too. Her latest message is still fresh on my phone screen.

'Call me Evie.'

I've had enough of these games and it's time I tried a different tact. Keeping my head down and hoping it will all blow over clearly isn't working. I grab my bag and head outside, then slip into my car for some much-needed privacy. I pick up my phone with trembling hands and hit call.

On the second ring Lily picks up.

"Evie! You finally called!" Her sweet voice drips with honey.

"Lily." I respond as coldly as I can. I want her to know this is *not* a social call.

"Oh Evie, it sounds so good to hear you say my name."

I don't want to get caught up in another ruse. I want this over and done with. I decide to appease her first. Maybe if she sees I'm contrite it will be enough for her to retract her rumour.

"Lily, listen. Firstly, I want to apologise. I should never have ended things with you by a text message. That was wrong. I should have called you. I am *so* sorry. Could you ever forgive me?"

"Evie, shhh. Thank you for your apology, I really appreciate it.... But I think what you meant to say was that you never should have *ended* it with me."

"No.. that's not what I me..."

Lily cuts me off with a tinkling laugh. "Yes it *is* what you meant to say Evie. Now, I know what you want. I know what you *like*. You are a sexual creature Evie and I know you like to *fuck.*"

I don't want to play these games.

"I told you from the beginning Lily. What went on between us could never be more than temporary. I'm married, Lily."

"That didn't stop you before. Now listen to my proposition Evie. Listen well. I know that you want to be able to show your face at your children's school. You want the other mums to *like* you. *I* can make that happen Evie. I can make all those rumours vanish. Poof! Just like that." Lily snaps her fingers into the phone.

The jarring sound sends a message straight to my brain that this is not right.

"Please Lily, stop this. Why are you doing this to me?"

"Why? Why? Why?" She sings manically. "Oh Evie. You still don't get it. You're *mine.* I *own* you. If you don't do as I say I will turn every single person in this town against you."

Her words are so *menacing.*

"Lily, that's crazy. You don't own me. No one owns me."

Calmly and matter of fact, Lily says "I *will* have you back in my bed Evie. If you don't come *willingly,* then I might just have to start *another* rumour… But first, tell me Evie. Who is the other woman? I see you're spending more time with Rachael. Is she the other woman? Is she the one you cheated on me with?" Her questions are soft, like she's coaxing a small child to share their toys.

The question in my mind is *how does she know I've been hanging out with Rachael?*

"Rachael is a friend Lily. There is no other woman."

"Liar!" Lily spits the word out with such venom I physically recoil in my seat. The whiplash from Lily's personalities finally breaks me.

"Lily, you're scaring me. I don't know who you are anymore. Please. Stop the rumours. I said I was sorry. No one is talking to me, I know it was you who keyed my car. I want this all to stop." My voice cracks on the last word and I feel my eyes prickle with tears.

"Ohh Evie, my poor little Evie. I'll stop."

"You will?" I feel a glimmer of hope.

"Of course I will. Just reinstate our regular sessions and I'll make all of this disappear."

"But I don't want that anymore." I sound so meek, so *pathetic*.

"If you want your happy little life back, you will."

"No… I" I start.

"Let me know when you're ready to make a playdate darling. Now get out of your car and toddle back into the office. Your break is over." She clicks off.

I try not to completely fall apart. My heart is pounding so hard, it's in my mouth… or is that a lump forming in my throat? I try to compose myself as I need to go back into the office... How did Lily know I was in my car *outside* my office?

A loud sob escapes my lips. Before I can stop myself, tears are flowing freely and my shoulders heave with distress. I'm crying so hard I can't catch my breath. I gasp and splutter all over my front seat. There's no way I can go back inside.

Suddenly there's a knock on my window. It startles me and I jump in my seat, hitting my head on the visor.

Is it Lily? Is she here?

I look out the window to see my team leader, Josie. She opens my door.

"Jesus, Evie. Are you alright?"

She asks so sincerely, with so much concern that I leap out of my car and hug her. She stumbles slightly but returns the hug as I sob uncontrollably on her shoulder.

"Evie, what's going on? Has something happened to the kids? Steve?" I can hear the worry on her every word.

My throat is so constricted I can barely get my words out. Between heaves I manage "No, they're... fine. Just... having... a... rough... time."

Josie tries to make eye contact with me and holds my shoulders at arms' length.

"Evie, you need to go home." I look at her with consternation. As if reading my mind, she adds "Don't worry about Abigail. I'll talk to her. You need to take the afternoon off. I'll arrange for you to work from home this week. OK?" My eyes well up again knowing I can take things slow at home. She's such a good Team Leader. With a caring smile Josie gently adds "we have counselling services... if that's something you'd like me to arrange? It's free."

She is being so compassionate. A counsellor actually sounds like a good idea. I nod my assent.

"Please." I manage.

She helps me back into my car. "I need to get back to the team now. Will you be alright? Take a moment hey. Don't drive until you've stopped crying. I'll make some calls and organise a counsellor to call you." I nod. "Do you want me to call Steve?" she asks.

"I'll call Steve. Thank you, Josie, I really appreciate it."

She casts me one last worried glance then heads back into the office building. I take another stilted breath in and my shoulders shake. I wipe at the tears on my face and catch a glimpse of myself in the mirror. My cheeks are glistening red and my nose is dripping.

Oh, you're a sight Evie.

I put my head in my hands and let out a frustrated "ugghhhhhhh". I can't believe I'm reduced to this... this… feeble person.

I used to be so strong.

I pick up my phone and call my doctor's office. I need to get this under control. Thankfully they've had a cancellation at 1:30pm so I take it.

I don't call Steve. I don't want to worry him, he's already apprehensive about the whole situation. However, I do need him to pick up the kids. I quickly punch out a text and hit send.

"Steve, I've booked a doctor's appointment this afternoon, getting off work a little early but I won't make it to get the kids. Can you pick them up today?"

The dots cycle and a moment later I receive his response.

"Sure thing. Love you."

It's the best feeling in the world to have a response come back that quick. I sigh in relief.

"I love you too." I flick back.

Once I'm in my doctor's office she takes one look at me and knows something is wrong.

"You're not sleeping are you, Evie?" Dr Goldfinch asks gently as she puts a blood pressure cuff around my arm.

I shake my head.

"Big day? It looks like you've had a good cry recently." Her voice is so calm and soothing. Before I can stop myself, I'm crying again.

"Hey, it's alright Evie. You're in a safe place. Do you want to talk about it?"

I don't know if I should... maybe I'll tell her the G rated short version...

I puff out my cheeks and blow the air out slowly before I start. "There's an awful... rumour about me amongst the mum's at my daughter's school. No one... is talking to me and one mum in particular is being just so... *awful.*" I'm still finding it hard to get the words out amongst my tears. As I say it, it doesn't sound as bad as it feels. It almost sounds petty without all the sordid details that led up to this point.

She hands me a tissue so I can wipe my eyes. She removes the blood pressure cuff and listens to my heart and breathing with her stethoscope. She then checks my ears and inside my mouth just to be thorough. She pulls down a small cup from her top shelf and offers me a lollipop.

I laugh at the absurdity of offering a grown woman a sweet, but I pick a red one and twirl it between my fingers.

Dr Goldfinch smiles kindly. "OK Evie, I can see you're clearly under a lot of stress. Your blood pressure is higher than your normal and your heartbeat is behaving slightly erratic. How much are you sleeping each night, Evie? And how long have you been feeling this way?"

"Oh, umm… I think I haven't been sleeping well for maybe a month… but the last two weeks I just toss and turn all night. I'm so short with my kids, I feel so guilty for it… I feel jittery and jumpy *all* the time. I think I need to go to a sleep spa… do they exist?" I chuckle meekly.

"Sign me up for one of those!" She laughs, then resets her face professionally. "Now seriously Evie, I think you're suffering from a bit of anxiety. Now, I've known you a long time, so I know this is a temporary thing for you. Let's get you a short course of diazepam for when you feel extra anxious and I'll prescribe a sleeping tablet for a month to see if that helps reset you. I think once you're sleeping again, you'll feel much better. I want you to book an appointment to come and see me in two weeks to check in and see how you're doing. OK?"

"OK, thanks." I hate taking medication, but I know I need it this time. I stand up as she hands me the scripts.

As I'm opening the door she says "and Evie, gossip and rumours are always short lived. Laugh it off and show them whatever it is, is not true. Be the bigger person. I know you've got this."

I offer a half-hearted smile as I walk out the door. It's nice she has faith in me… I just don't have much faith in myself right now.

As soon as I get home, I take a diazepam. I know I'm not going anywhere else today, so I pull on my comfy pyjamas and within fifteen minutes I feel a wave of calm wash over me. I feel so relaxed that I turn off my phone and climb into bed.

I close my eyes with relief and swiftly drift off to sleep.

Twenty-Five

Evie and the Discovery

Tuesday morning rolls around and I feel like I've been hit by a bus. My eyes feel puffy and every word uttered by my husband and my children feels like nails scratching down a blackboard. Why do they have to be so loud? I thought the sleeping tablets were meant to make me feel better? Not *worse*.

Steve brings in my coffee and as he opens the curtains I wince and screw my eyes tight.

It's so bright this morning.

I turn my face to the window with my eyes shut, trying to slowly acclimatise them to the light before I open them at a snail's pace. Steve's mouth is hanging slightly open as he stares at me.

"Jesus, do I look that bad Steve?"

He clears his throat. "Umm... no."

"So convincing." I tut, sitting up to view myself in the dresser mirror at the foot of our bed.

Yikes.

My eyes are puffy and the skin on my cheeks is blotchy. Dark purple crevices form shadows under my lower lashes.

I grimace at my reflection and reach out for the proffered coffee. Caffeine will be my saviour today. Our morning cuddles and drinks are short. Steve opens the window to let some fresh air in then bustles the kids out of the room.

"Come on kids, let's give mum some space this morning." To me, he says, "I'll get them ready. Take a moment then jump in the shower. I'm sorry Evie but I have a meeting in the city today, so I don't have time to do the drop off."

I've just realised that Steve is already freshly showered and dressed in his good suit. I look at my reflection again and groan. I nod to Steve, so he knows I've heard. As he closes the door behind him, I flop back against the pillows and cast my eyes out the window. The sun is casting a beautiful glow on the trees and grass outside. Small silver-eyes jump amongst the dew-covered branches and twitter happily as they drink the nectar from the spring blossoms on our trees.

The stunning scenery makes the bleak feeling inside me twitch. I feel a flicker of serenity and calm until the conversation with Lily rushes to the forefront of my mind, filling me with dread.

I drink my coffee down to the dregs and attempt to focus on my breathing.

"Deep breaths. Find my inner calm. I am

the bigger person. I will not succumb. I am better than this." I say the affirmations under my breath, not quite believing them, but really wanting to.

With one last deep breath, I climb out of bed and stagger to the bathroom for a shower. I know I'll feel better once I wash away the grime and tears of yesterday.

Afterwards, I stand in front of the steamed-up mirror and wipe it clean. The shower has helped. I don't look nearly as puffy, but the dark circles remain.

Once dressed I enter the kitchen and my star of a husband hands me a second cup of coffee and a plate of toast. The kids are dressed and have had breakfast. Steve helps them brush their teeth while I half-heartedly force a few bites down. My appetite has been suppressed the past two weeks. I noticed after my shower that my jeans are a little loose and I needed to add a belt.

The kids emerge ready to go. I brush my teeth while Steve helps them with their shoes and straps them in the car. He's made everything so easy for me this morning. If there was an award for being the most supportive husband ever, he'd win first prize.

Steve jumps into his car and exits the drive before me. He turns right, heading towards the city and I turn left, taking the country roads to school.

I make the short drive and find a carpark in a row where I now know the school cameras can reach. The angry scratch mark is still there looking raw and ragged. I wince every time I see it. I'm still waiting to hear back from the insurance company on when I can take it in to be repaired. I walk Jackson and Hannah to the front entrance and Hannah skips off when she sees a friend. I take Jackson to the kindy and sign him in, giving him a tight squeeze before letting him run off to play.

A number of mum's eyes are on me, their expressions a mixture of discernment and confusion by my appearance.

None of them speak to me. They just watch as I walk past.

As I make my way back towards the carpark, I see something that stops me in my tracks. Lily is talking to Rachael *alone.*

They haven't seen me yet, so I observe for a moment to see how the interaction will unfold.

Lily is stroking Rachael's upper arm and Rachael appears tense through her shoulders. I can see Lily clearly. She looks so friendly, so natural, that no one would ever suspect the *shit* she is putting me through right now. I edge closer so I can overhear their conversation.

If I just get behind this car…

"Rachael, I've noticed you've been seeing a lot of Evie lately. She's bad news, you know that right?"

I can tell Lily's testing the waters. Trying to see how much I've confided in her.

"No Lily, you're the bad news. You need to stop this. Leave her alone."

I do an internal whoop. *Thanks Rachael!*

"You think she wants *you*, do you?" Lily chuckles. "Ohh Rachael, she'd never go for *you* in a million years."

"It's you she doesn't want Lily."

She says it through clenched teeth so other mums won't hear her, but I'm just close enough. From my vantage point, looking through the passenger window, I see a flash of anger cross Lily's face.

"Oh and I suppose you know who Evie does want then? At least I've had a taste. You'll never have anything with her."

Don't take the bait Rachael, I plead.

"Actually, Evie has kissed me and it's only because of the drama with you and Simone that she won't go any further!"

Lily looks triumphant.

"*Simone!*" She hisses with glee.

Rachael gasps and covers her mouth.

"Shit! Shit! Shit!"

My phone starts to ring loudly from my pocket. With cold trepidation I watch as Lily and Rachael both spin around to look my way. I stay ducked down then make a crouched run for my car, the happy melody giving away my every move. As I flee, I fumble in my pocket and flick the caller to voicemail. I know they know it's me by my stupid ringtone. When I'm far enough away, I stand up and walk as calmly as possible to my car. I feel their eyes on me from across the parking lot, but I pretend not to see them. I open the door and climb inside.

I am the bigger person. I will remain calm.

My car tyres crunch slowly along the gravel until I am at the gate, then I let out the breath I am holding as I pull out onto the road.

In a trance, I make my way to the park down the road and come to a stop under a tall oak tree.

Our park.

The ghost of Simone sits in the seat next to me, haunting me. I take a steadying breath and close my eyes. I can hear the distant laughter of children on the playground, the thud of shoes on the track from two runners, and birds twittering overhead in the ancient oak.

My phone's cheery ringtone disrupts the tranquillity and with a heavy sigh, I pick up.

"Hello, is that Evie Monroe? Owner of a car that was keyed two weeks ago?"

"Yes, that's me." I dejectedly sigh into the phone.

"Oh good, it's Michelle here from Joe's Auto shop. I called about five minutes ago, but you must have been busy. Your insurance company has been in touch, and we can actually fit you in today if you come down. If you need a courtesy car, we have one lined up for you. It might take a few days for the repair to be completed."

"Oh, right. Sure, I'll be there in fifteen minutes."

Michelle rattles off the address, but I know where it is. I say "Thanks, see you soon" before clicking off.

I rest my forehead on the steering wheel

for a moment to gather myself. My heart is still hammering from the conversation I overheard between Rachael and Lily. I fumble in my purse for the diazepam but as I check the label it says quite clearly 'do not drive or operate machinery while taking this medicine.' I throw it back in my purse in frustration.

Well, that's inconvenient.

I line up the facts in my mind, wondering what I should do next.

1. Lily knows it's Simone.
2. I don't know what Lily will do with this information.
3. Simone is not returning my calls or messages.

I *need* to protect her. I just don't know if she will let me…

I put my car into reverse and head to the mechanics. Beautiful scenery rushes past my window. Green fields with corn half a metre high. Orchards in full bloom. Paddocks with calves on one side of the road, paddocks with sheep and lambs on the other. I turn onto the main road that will take me into town. The houses grow closer together until I hit suburbia with their 500 square metre sections.

The houses are so close to each other here. It makes me wonder if the neighbours can hear every conversation despite closed doors. It baffles me that people want to live so close to each other. Give me my five-acre property *any* day. I'd hate to feel like my neighbours were breathing down my neck… *or* could see into my bedroom.

The houses disperse again as I enter the industrial part of town. I turn into a narrow road that leads to the mechanics, then pull into the shop. A woman comes out to greet me, Michelle I presume. She holds a clip board and beckons me to drive forward over the hoist. Once in place I grab all the things that I might need for the next few days.

Michelle introduces herself, then helps me remove the car seats from the back. She's very bubbly as she natters away about the weather and how child seats are so important.

"To think that forty odd years ago these didn't exist!" She exclaims.

I smile and nod as she helps me install them in the courtesy car parked outside. Once secured, we head back inside to fill in the paperwork. The smell of petrol and grease are all encompassing as we cross the shop floor. Glancing over my shoulder I watch the mechanics hoist my car up off the ground so they can look at the damage without bending down. They run lights over the angry long scratch, assessing the best way to repair the damage. I leave them to it and enter the side office. Michelle hands me the clipboard so I can enter my details. I fill everything in quickly and hand over my licence for identification.

I notice the office smells a bit musty. Like it needs the windows opened.

"Help yourself to a coffee if you like." She nods to the table against the far wall. "It's a proper machine. Milk's in the fridge. I just need to photocopy your driver's licence and process this paperwork on the computer. I won't be long."

"Thanks."

Gratefully I head to the machine. It's a Nespresso and I select a pod from the bowl and pop it in. The machine buzzes into life and the merry sound and smell of coffee brewing briefly drowns out the tinkering from the auto shop.

Coffee in hand, I select one of the grey couches that faces the workshop. From here I can watch the lads work through a large viewing window. One of the mechanics calls another one over and they peer at something under my car. The first mechanic scratches his head, then glances over at me sitting in the office. Raising an eyebrow, I encourage him to come and speak to me. The lad comes over and leans a muscled arm against the door frame. He must be in his early twenties. A black mark is smeared across his left cheek and his hands are stained with engine oil. His branded shirt has the name 'Ben' written on it and when he smiles, he's devilishly handsome.

"Umm, sorry to bother you miss." He flashes me a cheeky smile with a mouth full of perfect white teeth. "But the boys and I are wondering why you've put your GPS tracker under your car instead of installing it properly on your dash inside?"

The question takes me completely by surprise.

"GPS tracker?" I ask puzzled. "My car has an automated one, linked to my phone. It's built-in."

"No, this one is one of those after-market ones. It looks like it's been glued in place..."

The colour drains from my face and the coffee cup in my hand starts to shake so I put it down. I can't help it, but my eyes fill with tears as I realise *this* is how she knows where I am.

This has gone far enough.

My resolve is absolute in my mind.

Through tears I ask "Ben, don't touch it. We need to take photos for the police and get it fingerprinted."

"What?" He asks surprised. "Shit, I asked Dean to remove it so we could install it properly for you." Over his shoulder he yells "Hey Dean! Stop what you're doing!"

"Stop what?" He yells back. I can see he's holding the tracker in his hand.

Thinking fast I call to Michelle. "Hey, do you have a plastic bag?"

"Ah, yes, yes I do." The seriousness of the situation dawning across her face as she hastily rifles in a desk drawer before retrieving a small zip lock bag. I hastily take it from her, rushing it out to Dean as I angrily swipe at my tears.

"Put that in here please." He obliges but looks flabbergasted. I pull out my phone and take a picture of where it was located. The glue residue still evident. I put the tracker and phone back inside my handbag then head back into the office.

"Are you finished with my licence yet Michelle? If it's all ready, I need to go to the police station."

"Right, yes, sure." She fumbles around on her desk and hands me my licence and the keys to the courtesy car.

I call "Thanks everyone!" as I stride out of the shop. I climb into the car and adjust the seat and mirrors to my size. Rage courses through me and for the first time since this whole drama started, I feel *compelled* to do something about Lily.

Feeling secure with the evidence safely tucked away in my handbag, I make my way to the local police station.

No more games Lily.

No more.

Twenty-Six

Evie and the Slip

I stand outside the local police station and gaze up at the building. It's a bit run down.

Funding must be tight.

The exterior is brown brick and the entrance is uninviting. Dark shadows overhang the electronic doors and the interior looks bleak from my position. Gripping my evidence, I purposefully walk inside.

It's now or never.

I enter the foyer and glance around. To my left are two rows of chairs for… what?... customers?... criminals? It smells odd in here. Damp is my first thought, yet hospital grade disinfectant accosts my nostrils. A woman behind the reception desk beckons me forward.

I approach the desk and she motions for me to use the hand sanitiser. I put my things down on the desk so I can rub the acrid germ-killer into my hands.

"How can I direct you?" She asks in a

bored, 'ready for the end of the day', voice.

"I… umm… I'd like to… provide evidence for…"

"Would you like to report a crime?" She interrupts, clearly wanting me to get to the point.

"No… Yes… I think so… I found this GPS tracker under my car and I have messages…I just want her to leave me alone." My voice grows thick with my vulnerability.

The woman looks up at me and her face softens. "Harassment hey?` OK. Fill these forms in and I'll organise an officer to talk to you."

Grateful I no longer have to explain myself, I take the forms and sit down. It doesn't take long to fill them in and within a few minutes I hand them back to her. I return to my seat and stare at the ceiling. It's clearly dated as it's covered with perforated tiles. It takes me back to my teenage years when I used to count the holes after I'd finished an exam.

"Evie Monroe?" A commanding voice breaks the silence.

I stand to attention then feel foolish. I flash a lopsided, embarrassed smile and the officer beckons me to follow him. He leads me into a small stark room and offers me a seat. He takes the opposite and I realise he's too big for the room. He looks like an adult playing tea parties in a playhouse. A smirk tugs at my lips as I watch him try and get comfortable. His hair is cropped closely to his head, his jaw clean shaven. Large biceps bulge through his police uniform and I'm tempted to reach out and touch them.

"I'm officer Dan Jones." He interrupts my bicep squeezing thoughts. He busies himself with setting up his laptop. I wait until he's ready.

"Right, Evie. How can I help?"

I start by placing my phone and the tracker on the table. He picks up the plastic bag and eyes it warily.

"Tracker?" He asks, matter of fact.

I nod.

"Let me guess, not yours?"

Again, I nod.

I open my phone to the thread of messages from Lily and allow Dan to scroll through.

He sighs. "When did this start?"

I start at the beginning. I don't want to tell him I've been intimate with her, but I feel like I'm on a stand in court. I tell him when it started, when I tried to end it, and the aftermath that has ensued. I relay all the issues calmly and I'm surprised that I'm not breaking down.

Why is that?

It dawns on me that perhaps I'm finally over her *shit*.

Dan listens intently and takes notes.

"Do you mind if I copy these onto the police server?" He motions to my phone.

"Go ahead. I can't wait until I can delete them once and for all."

"I bet." Dan plugs my phone into his laptop and starts running software to lift the sordid missives.

As the laptop hums between us, Dan explains the law.

"OK Evie. I can open a case file, run some forensics on the GPS tracker, but these messages indicate that she planted it. This will need to go to court. If Lily is found guilty, she faces up to two years in prison."

"What would happen to her daughter?" Worry for Willow wreaks havoc in my heart. A child shouldn't be without a mother.

"She would go into her husband's care."

"Oh right, of course... I've never met him."

"There are laws in place to protect the innocent Evie. Her daughter won't be overlooked. In the interim, I'm going to issue a restraining order on her. She won't be allowed within 50 metres of you."

A whoosh of air escapes my lips.

"Thank you, Dan. For taking this seriously. How long until this goes to court?"

"The judicial system isn't as fast as we'd like. Maybe a few months. If she had physically harmed you, we would be able to expedite the case and put her in jail until the trial. But as it stands right now, we have to wait for a judge to view the evidence and make a ruling."

My face falls. "Ah, OK. I understand."

"Tell you what Evie, I'll deliver this restraining order today, personally. What's the bet, her messages stop cold turkey." He gives me an encouraging smile.

His laptop beeps. He glances back at the

screen and unplugs my phone. He slides it across the table to me.

"Thanks." I murmur as I tuck it back into my bag.

"If you have no further questions, I'll start the paperwork this afternoon."

I shake my head and we make the short journey back to reception.

Back in the foyer he turns and shakes my hand. "Call us if anything else happens, especially if you're in danger."

"I will, thanks."

I head towards the exit and I suddenly feel freer. Less anxious. Like a weight has lifted off my shoulders.

The sun blinds me as I step outside. The spring air is still cool and I pull my jacket tighter around me, wondering what I should do now. I climb into the courtesy car and sit in the carpark for a few moments as I try and gather my thoughts.

My first thought is *Simone*.

How can I protect her?

Flashes of her beautiful, honest face rush into my mind. I wonder if now is the time, to just show up at her house. I check my watch. It's 2:15pm.

I was in the station for nearly 3 hours.

I realise there's not enough time to pop in before pick up… at least not enough time to have the conversation we need to have.

I pull out my phone and text Steve.

'Hi Steve, the mechanic found a GPS tracker under my car door. That's how Lily has known

where I am. I've just handed it in to the police and made a statement. They're issuing a restraining order as we speak. I'll tell you more when you get home.'

I hit send and my stomach rumbles loudly. I realise I haven't had anything to eat or drink since that sip of coffee at the mechanics. As I'm in town I have time for a dirty drive through.

I eat on the way to school, hoping the kids won't smell the evidence in the car. I crack all the windows, just in case. There's nothing worse than children feeling like they've missed out on a treat.

I'd never hear the end of it.

I park up, then make my way up the school ramp. I spy a bin and hastily dispose of the incriminating packaging. It seems so silly that I need to be so stealthy with fast food, but I don't want to be caught being a contradictory parent.

Apprehensively, I observe the other parents in the pick-up zone. Lily isn't there, nor Simone. I see a few sideways glances from a couple of mums and this time, instead of looking away, I hold their gaze. Daring them to say something to my face. I have evidence now. I don't have to take this crap anymore. I'm about to say something to the group, but I see Hannah skipping happily down to the meeting point. She embraces me in a tight hug and I laugh as she makes me stumble backwards. I signal to her teacher that I'll take her from here. She holds my hand and chatters away while we walk to the kindergarten to sign out Jackson.

Once home, I start the usual afternoon routine but today it doesn't feel quite so monotonous. I feel lighter than I have felt in weeks. I find myself laughing and chatting to my children like I used to. They can sense something has changed and they are all over me. Long lingering cuddles and requests of reading books and eating snacks. I feel like everything is right with the world again.

Steve comes home and helps with dinner, then the bath, teeth and bed routine. The relief is evident on his face too. As he passes me in the kitchen, his hand rubs along the small of my back as he takes Jackson to bed. A loving gesture that makes me feel warm inside.

With the kids in bed, Steve and I head to our bedroom and close the door. In hushed tones I relay the day's turn of events. Steve fixates on the conversation I overheard between Lily and Rachael.

"I can't believe Rachael fell right into Lily's trap," he muses in disappointment. "The question is what will Lily do now? Will she attack Simone? Or tell her another lie?"

Steve pensively gathers his thoughts for a moment before I interject with my own supposition. "Surely Lily knows she's in trouble now. I'm guessing the police have issued the restraining order... if not, she will believe my car is at the police station."

"Good point. We still need to do *something*. We need to warn Simone, just in case."

"I agree." I check my watch. It's 8:30pm.

It's not too late to call. "Let me try and ring her. Maybe she'll pick up?"

Steve nods and sits patiently beside me as I dial her number. I listen intently for her voice but she doesn't answer. As her voicemail message issues instructions, I take a deep breath and as calmly as I can, leave a message.

"Simone, it's Evie. Please don't delete this without listening. I need you to know the truth. Lily came onto me about two months after our first time. It turned into a…a… casual fling. I had no idea you were struggling with what we did… I thought you didn't like me. But as soon as you told me what was going on, I called it off with her. But Lily got angry. She spread nasty things about me and has been harassing me, *daily*. Not to mention keying my car and tracking me by GPS. The police have issued a restraining order on her. Simone, Lily is *dangerous*. She discovered today that you're the reason I called it. I have no idea what she will do with that information and I would never forgive myself if you were hurt. Simone… I … I think I love you."

I hastily hang up as soon as those three words fall out of my mouth.

I want to take them back, but it's too late.

Steve has been beside me this whole time and now he sits in frigid silence, staring at the floor.

"I'm sorry Steve, it just came out…"

I watch my darling husband's eyes flick from left to right as he stares at the floor. He is thinking hard, and fast.

My hands start shaking as I realise the enormity of the situation unfolding before me. I slip off the bed and kneel in front of him. I desperately grab his hands.

"Steve, you know I didn't mean it. I was just so worried for her. I love *you* Steve. I just got swept away in the moment."

His eyes glisten with unshed tears as he gazes at me.

"Steve, please say something." My voice cracks and I feel like my heart is shattering into a million pieces.

Is this it?

Is this the proverbial straw that will sever our marriage?

Tears stream down my face. There should be grooves in my cheeks after all the crying I've done the past few weeks.

Steve grips my hands tight. "You're under a lot of stress. We've warned Simone… that's all we can do for now." His voice is thick and shaky from held back emotion. He is clearly trying to be rational.

"It's late Evie. You've got to get through the next two days, then it's Ag Day. You should take a sleeping tablet and head to bed, you need some rest." His words are caring, but he struggles to connect his eyes with mine. He stands up and pauses at the door.

"Tea?" he asks, like nothing has happened.

"Please." Is all I can murmur in response.

The void he leaves behind as he departs the room feels like it will swallow me whole.

I can't believe I let that *slip*.

What have I done?

Twenty-Seven

Evie and Ag Day Part One

"Mummy, can I have some TV?"

I feel a little nose pressing against my cheek and his soft breath on my ear. I can sense it's morning as the room feels bright, but my eyelids do not wish to open. They feel heavy and gritty.

These sleeping tablets make me feel hungover.

"Mummy?" Jackson says my name again and I feel his little fingers probing my cheek.

My brain slowly cranks into gear, but I feel like there's no lubrication on the cogs.

Then the voice message I left for Simone two nights ago replays perfectly in my mind and Steve's heartbroken face swims into focus behind my closed eyes.

Steve!

I reach out for him on his side of the bed, but my hand sweeps across empty sheets. I bolt upright in bed and Jackson stumbles back. I force my eyes open and I am blinded by the light in the room.

"I opened the curtains for you Mummy."

Jackson climbs onto the bed and snuggles against me. He pulls my top down so he can rest his face on my naked chest and listen to my racing heartbeat. I thought he would have grown out of this behaviour by now, but I'm secretly glad he hasn't. Having him near calms me. I breathe in his little boy scent. He is my last child and he will never be this age again. I hold him tight, gleaning as much emotional support from him as he needs from me.

Hannah bounces into the room and she's already dressed in pink and blue flannel. "Mum, can you do two plaits in my hair like you did last year?"

*Two plaits… flannel…*AG DAY!

The realisation of what day has finally arrived sends a jolt of electricity through my entire body. The haze of the last two days flits dreamlike across my mind. It was spent mostly working from home, with a couple of diazepam to calm my nerves outside of office hours. Steve and I had a couple of small chats, but my anxiety is not quite acquiesced.

The silver lining is that Lily *has* stopped messaging. Officer Dan must have delivered the restraining order as promised.

I gently move Jackson to the middle of the bed and fling back the covers. I stand but need to grab the wall for support.

I'm a bit wobbly this morning.

I stumble to the bathroom and turn on the shower.

I need to wash off this sleep.

Fifteen minutes later I feel refreshed and revived. I dress in my best country attire, little denim shorts to accentuate my ass and legs, a black tank top and an unbuttoned flannel shirt tied in a knot at my waist. I quickly put two plaits into my own hair then I stand back to admire my reflection.

I could pass for 25!

Then I look at the dark circles and see the strain of my almost broken marriage etched in my eyes, reminding me I'm 34.

Makeup will be required today.

I sigh and pull out my concealer. With a few quick brush strokes, a little lightener on my eyelids and flick of mascara I look a little better.

I take a steadying breath before I leave the sanctity of the bathroom and search for Steve. I find him in the kitchen preparing lunch boxes. He glances sideways as I enter the room and murmurs "good morning."

I tentatively get closer and wrap my arms around him and hug his back. I feel him stiffen slightly, then I hear him take a deep cleansing breath. My heart starts to race as questions about the safety of our marriage race through my head. After what feels like a mini eternity, he swivels in my arms and pulls me against his chest.

"Are you OK?" I ask, not raising my eyes to his face for fear I'll see the pain I've caused.

"I will be Evie." He reaches under my chin and lifts my eyes to his. "Let's get through today. I made you coffee." I see a flicker of warmth in his face, and I feel a slight reduction to the weight on my shoulders. I flash him a watery smile and beam as much love as I can muster towards him. He pulls me tight against him and I feel his hands reach down and squeeze my bum.

This is the Steve I know. Some of the stiffness around my neck magically disappears. I reach both my hands up to his face and kiss him. I pour my love into his mouth to show him that what we have is real. To prove that my love for him has never faltered. I feel the twitch of his growing member against my navel and a delicious pull, tugs between my legs.

"Ewwwww Mum and Dad! Stop it!" Hannah cries repulsively, interrupting my thoughts of taking this to the bedroom. Steve and I reluctantly pull apart and share a *'thwarted by our children'* smirk. The silent promise of *'finishing this later'* echoes in our eyes.

I take Hannah's hairbrush and deftly comb out the tangles. My fingers work swiftly as I make two tight French braids that curl around her ears to rest on her chest. It's taken me three years of practice to be able to create perfect plaits on a wriggly child. As soon as the second hair tie is in place she skips off to her room.

"Have you brushed your teeth?" I call to her. I hear a frustrated groan from the depths of her bedroom. She re-emerges and stomps to the bathroom.

I find Jackson still in his pyjamas playing with his toy cars in his bedroom. I have to physically, wrangle him from his toys so I can undress him and put his little cowboy outfit on. He has the day off kindergarten to attend the festivities today. I already know that we will spend a long time watching him bounce on the bouncy castle.... Well Steve will. I will be working today.

Twenty minutes later, all four of us plus Hannah's lamb, Bessie, pile into the car and we turn onto the country road that leads to school. Even though we're early, the carpark is almost full. We're lucky that the neighbours to the school allow visitors access to park in their paddock today. Grateful to be a closer walk, we take one of the last remaining school carparks and turn off the ignition. I turn around to face the kids. They are squirming and itching to get out to see how the school has been transformed.

"Come on Mum, let us out!" Hannah bellows from her seat as she tries to open her door from the inside. She throws me a reproachful glance as she realises I've turned the child locks on in my courtesy car.

Swivelling in my seat, I stare down at my two fidgeting children with my best no-nonsense face.

"Now before we go in, I'm going to lay down the rules." I speak clearly with all the strict 'mum' persona I can muster.

The kids groan.

"Jackson. You must be able to see Daddy at

all times. You must not run off. In fact, I'm imposing a two-meter rule. So if you cannot reach Daddy's outstretched hand, you are too far away. Got it?"

Jackson looks out the window, purposefully not answering.

"Jackson, answer me. What are your rules? We're not going in until you repeat them back to me."

Jackson reluctantly answers. "I must be able to see Daddy and be able to reach his hand."

"Good." I turn to Hannah. "Hannah, this is your school. You will have roll call three times today, make sure you are there. I recommend that you stay with Dad until you've seen everything first. After that you can run around with your friends."

"Yes Mum." She says it quickly with one hand on the door handle. She's learned that the quicker she answers me, the quicker she can do what she wants.

Steve takes my hand and squeezes it. "I will be here all day. Call me if you need anything." He gives me a meaningful stare and Lily's name passes silently between us. A loud bleat comes from the boot. Bessie has been brushed and adorned with a pale blue ribbon. As we all pile out of the car, Hannah attaches her leash to her lamb.

Hannah and Jackson lead Bessie to the animal holding area with Steve in close pursuit. I gather the last few things I need from the car and make my way to the teacher staff room for the morning briefing. I already know what my role is today. I'm the treasurer but I look forward to getting a copy of the final schedule and list of jobs and volunteers.

As I approach the main office building, I feel apprehensive, like I'm going to war. After two weeks of anxiety and processing, I have done a complete 180 and I'm ready to go into battle.

I enter the staff room and put down my box of petty cash paraphernalia on a nearby table. A few teachers and mums are milling about making coffee so I join them. As I approach, the conversation is hushed by a cold blanket of silence. Expecting this reaction, I combat it by wearing my biggest smile.

"Good morning!" I beam at everyone. I see Sandra shift uncomfortably as she eyes me warily. I start making myself coffee and ignore Sandra's disconcerted shared glances with Tracy and Jennifer. I attempt to strike up a conversation with them anyway.

"How were your kids this morning? Mine were up at the crack of dawn! Little Hannah was already dressed when she came into me this morning. It's a miracle!" I flash them my straight white teeth and project through my eyes that I'm a mum, just like them. I finish making my coffee and turn towards the ladies, expectantly awaiting their responses. Jennifer glances sideways at the others but returns a small smile.

"Yes, Charlie and Mackenzie got up before dawn. This is my third coffee and it's only

8:30!" She chuckles and I'm relieved. Her sharing has broken the awkwardness and the other mums start sharing their morning battle stories. I sip my coffee and listen attentively. Agreeing when necessary and shaking my head in feigned disbelief of some of the shenanigans their kids got up to.

A loud "Ahem!" breaks through our conversation.

"Everyone take a seat please! Let's get this briefing started."

Stacey's loud voice echoes over the hum of idle chit-chat and the room is hushed almost instantly. Everyone files into place and takes a seat. Stacey hands out clipboards with the schedule attached then runs through all the jobs and responsibilities of the day.

My job is roaming and collecting the cash from the market stalls and games, then counting them out in the small back-office room at intervals throughout the day.

"Right, the most important part of today is to make sure the kids have fun! This is what we're here for so let's make as much money for them as we can!" Stacey shares a rare smile with us all and words of "Yes!" and "Hear! Hear!" erupt from the group.

As the group disperses, Stacey beckons me to her and hands me a heavy bag of coins and cash. "You brought the cash boxes?" I nod. "Right, floats of $50 need to go into each one." Stacey's tone is brusque, but her eyes shine a friendly warmth I'm slowly getting used to.

Pulling out my petty cash boxes, I start

making up the floats. I hear the teachers and parents chatting animatedly, comparing where they will be stationed and when their breaks will be. It's a nice happy hum and the fear I have felt over the past few weeks starts to ebb away.

Floats complete, I beckon for the stall holders to take their assigned boxes. The rest of the adults assemble their relative bits and pieces and head out to their assigned stations for the day. I start studying the map to familiarise myself with my rounds. Once everyone is settled in, I'll do a reconnaissance of the area myself.

I sense someone coming towards me and glance up from my map.

"May I sit?"

Stacey holds a clipboard and I assume she wants to discuss something else about the day. I nod, still feeling slightly uncomfortable by her newly found kindness. She takes the seat next to me and ruffles through some paperwork, making it look like she will change something on my schedule.

"Pretend we're discussing today's event." She whispers conspirationally. She darts a 'there are people watching us' sweep with her eyes. I nod my understanding, wondering where this conversation is going.

"I've heard the rumours, Evie. They're not good."

I open my mouth to refute her, but she cuts me off.

"I know we're not exactly friends, but I

also don't believe what is being said in the schoolyard." She points to something on her clipboard, and I make myself pretend that I'm looking closer.

Under my breath I mutter "I'm not the problem. The police have just issued a restraining order on..."

"Lily?" She asks quietly.

"Yes!" I sit back in my seat, surprised. I thought Lily had been carefully discreet in her rumour mongering.

"You don't work in a lawyers office without picking up a few sleuthing skills along the way." She winks. "We'll have to talk in more detail at another time." She relays in hushed tones. Then louder and sardonically she adds. "You'd better walk your route Evie, so you know what you're doing today." Even though her words bite she flashes me a covert smile and for the first time I see her as an ally. She stands up and walks away without looking back.

New questions swarm my pondering mind as I watch her depart the room.

What other details have I missed?

What new rumours are circulating?

Oh god... has Simone heard them yet?

I pray to whatever powers that be that she has listened to my voicemail. Well, maybe not all of it...

I take another moment to study my map before heading outside to walk the loop and get my bearings. The school is not huge, just 450 students attend between the ages of five and thirteen, so it takes me twenty minutes to place where the stalls are in the courtyard, tennis courts and the sports field. The bell rings for 9am and all the kids rush to their meeting point for roll call. I meander down to the sports field to listen to the deputy principal explain the rules, then rally the kids into excitement. I see Steve and join him for a moment before the chaos of free roaming kids erupt around us. Steve puts one arm around me in a supportive squeeze. I lean forward to smile at Jackson who is behaving surprisingly well and is holding Steve's opposite hand.

"Any sign of Lily? Or Simone?" He whispers into my ear.

I shake my head and a nervous jitter jumps into my chest at their names. Jackson is starting to pull on Steve's hand.

"Daaad. You said we could go on the bouncy castle." Jackson whines.

I smile at him. "Sure thing Jackson, let's all go now before the queues get too long." Jackson jumps for joy and skips along next to the two of us as we make our way to the tennis courts where they have been set up. I have a chuckle to myself as I watch Jackson's eyes bulge in excitement at the size of the under-six castle. It's bright yellow and has inflated pineapples and coconut trees on the front. There's a large slide which ends in a ball pit on the side. The whole thing has mesh safety walls and probably spans twelve metres wide. We join the queue and it's not long until Jackson has removed his shoes and is bouncing happily. Hannah runs up to us with Katie and my breath hitches. If Katie is here, Simone will be too. I pull out my purse and pay for the two girls to join Jackson on the bouncy castle. After a brief "thanks!" they rip their shoes and socks off and giggle in delight as they climb aboard the fake tropical inflated garden.

Discreetly, I scan through the throngs of people to see if I can spot her. I see a flash of curly hair, but when they turn around, I disappointedly realise it's someone else. Disheartened I return my gaze to the kids. Happy shrieks erupt amongst the sound of the noisy inflatable fan and the thud of little feet on the PVC fabric. Steve squeezes my hand and motions my attention across the court. I look up and feel my heart stop cold in my chest.

Lily is talking to Simone.

I am too far away to make out what they are saying. They are standing slightly away from the throngs of people and Lily is leaning in too close for my liking. Her hair is brushing against Simone's shoulder and her mouth is close to Simone's delicate ear. A sensation ripples through me that I've never known before. Red hot rage and green-eyed jealousy mix together inside me. Fiery butterflies swarm my insides, threatening to erupt out of my stomach and shoot their deathly venom at Lily.

I can feel myself start to tremble with bubbling wrath and Steve murmurs in my ear,

"Don't cause a scene Evie."

I can't drag my eyes away from the scene unfolding before me. Then, as if Lily is a mind reader, she turns and glances my way. A sly grin is etched on her face as she takes in my angry glare from across the courtyard. Simone follows her gaze and our eyes lock for the first time in three weeks. My breath catches in my throat and I can feel the blood drain from my face. Simone's expression is guarded, I have no idea what she is thinking. I attempt to project the message: *"I'm sorry and don't trust Lily!"* across the court, but Simone turns away from me. I watch as she touches Lily's arm and excuses herself.

She's leaving!

Turning to Steve, I plead silently into his eyes that he will understand what I'm about to do next.

Dropping his hand I rush after Simone.

I hope he will forgive me.

Twenty-Eight

Evie and Ag Day Part Two

My mind clears to a single thought as I stride across the court.

Simone.

I ensure she is front and centre as I follow her through the throngs of people. Staying in hot pursuit, I observe as she emerges from the crowd. She'll be able to see me if she turns around now. My eyes dart wildly, searching for a safe haven where we can talk. By sheer luck, she heads up the path alongside a row of empty classrooms. I seize my chance. I lunge forward, grabbing her elbow and pull her through an open door on my right.

"What the fff..." Simone says in surprise.

"It's just me Simone. I need to talk to you." I sound calm but my heart is hammering inside my chest.

"I really don't want to hear it, Evie."

I can tell by her tone that she's not going to make this easy for me. She glares at me and tries to exit the classroom, but I block the door and push it closed behind me. The loud hum of the crowd outside muffles as silence stretches out between us. Like all the other mums I've seen recently, she can't look me in the eye. A knife twists in my heart as I realise she has also fallen victim to the sordid rumours.

Not my sweet Simone.

"Did you get my voicemail?" I manoeuvre my face so I can look deep into her eyes, pleading that she has with every inch of my being.

"I saw it come in, but no, I haven't listened to it." Her eyes flick to mine but dart away again.

"I don't know what Lily has told you, but it's not true. She's been harassing me and there is now a restraining order on her. She's not allowed within 50 metres of me."

"What?" Simone looks up at me, confused, like something is not adding up.

I see her confusion as an opening to continue talking. "She keyed my car and has been tracking me with a GPS device she planted under my door."

Simone shakes her head. "No. You've been stalking Lily. She put a restraining order on *you*. She wants me to file a report too.... I... I saw the messages."

"What messages?" I say incredulously. "These messages?" I pull out my phone and show them to Simone, relieved I hadn't deleted them just yet.

I watch her eyes rapidly scan over them.

Her mouth drops open slightly as she starts to come to terms that I might be telling the truth.

She frowns, still not quite convinced. "But I saw…" She pauses, then locks eyes on me quizzically. "Then why would she do this?"

"Because I told her I didn't want to sleep with her again."

"*Again?* What the fuck Evie?" I watch her mind whirr behind her eyes. "So, did you sleep with Rachael too? Is that true?" Her eyes narrow as she tries to separate the rumours from the truth.

I put my hands up in a symbol of 'hear me out' but I can see the doors closing behind her eyes.

"I never slept with Rachael. That's a lie. But yes, two months after you and I slept together the first time, Lily came onto me at a party. We had a casual fling, and I am seriously regretting it." I watch Simone wince as I tell her the truth. I feel so ashamed and wish that I had never done it. I should have waited for Simone to be ready.

"I only wanted you, Simone. But you wouldn't talk to me. I didn't realise what you were going through. As soon as you told me, I ended it with Lily." I reach out and take her hand in mine. I circle my thumb on the back of her hand to remind her of our moments together, but she pulls her hand away and takes a step back.

"You know what Evie, I don't know what's real anymore." She shakes her head and her voice sounds defeated, drained.

I don't know what to say, so I wait for her to continue. I wasn't prepared for what came next.

Simone's eyes dart from side to side, sorting out the puzzle pieces in her mind. "Who's to say that it wasn't the other way around? That Lily *was* the victim...I can't believe you slept with her… I thought what *we* had was special." Her voice is barely above a whisper, but I still hear it crack. I watch the tears form in her eyes and it breaks my heart that I've hurt her.

Indignantly I grab her hand again. I need her to believe me when I say "it *was* special Simone! I… I've fallen in love with you!"

"Love?" She spits back as she rips her hand from mine. "That's a real nice way to show it Evie. While I was having an existential crisis over the fact I'm attracted to you, as well as coming to terms that we cheated on your husband together, you ran off and had an affair with *Lily*!"

I stand there watching her get angry and I know I deserve *all of it*.

"I'm sorry." I say meekly.

Her eyes dart wildly and I can see she's overwhelmed. Suddenly, she squares her shoulders and stares me down with a look so cold I stumble backwards.

"You know what? Sorry is just not good enough." She pushes past me and storms out of the classroom slamming the door behind her.

The silence that follows is deep and

hollow.

I feel like I'm suffocating.

Like all the air in the room departed as she left me. The darkness of a life without Simone engulfs my broken heart. Hyperventilating, I collapse to the floor, wishing the pain in my chest was a true cardiac arrest and not just a stupid panic attack. I don't know how long I lay there, curled in a ball on the floor of the classroom. All I know is that *Simone doesn't believe me.*

Lily has won.

The weight of Simone's pain and anger crush my heart and I start to wonder if it will be me going to prison for two years.

My phone alarm chimes and pulls me from my tortured thoughts.

Shit. I still need to collect the money.

I don't know if I can stand, let alone act normal as I collect the surplus cash. The happy sounds of children slowly enter the periphery of my consciousness.

My children are out there.

The thought of my beautiful, innocent children pulls my rational mind out from my depressed, black abyss. I wipe at the tears on my face and take some deep, steadying breaths. I remind myself of the truth:

1. *Lily planted a tracking device.*
2. *They have her messages that are traced to her phone.*
3. *There is a restraining order on her, not me.*

I say the facts several times over before I can pull myself off the floor. I pull out some wet wipes that are meant for sticky fingers from my purse and a compact mirror. I attempt to clean myself up as best I can. I end up removing all my make up as the mascara has smeared everywhere. I don't look like a *hot mess*… I am just simply *a mess.*

My face is blotchy, my eyes red and puffy, but I don't care anymore. I open the door to the classroom and complete my rounds as quickly as I can. A few mums look taken aback by my distressed appearance, but not a soul asks if I'm OK. Each interaction is transactional and now that my money bag is full, I make my way to the small room in the back of the office to count up.

It's a relief to be away from the crowds. In my solitude I allow more tears to fall down my cheeks. I have to recount several times as my vision keeps blurring. My mind tortures me by replaying Simone's smarting words over, and over again.

Recounting the money for the final time, I place rubber bands around the notes and ready the coin bags. The clatter of money swiping off the desk and the gentle clink, clink of it landing in the bag has me so deep in a trance that I don't hear the door open quietly behind me.

"Alone at last Evie."

I spin around in my swivel chair and find myself looking up at the last person I wanted… or expected to see.

"Lily, you can't be here. You're in breach of the restraining order." The strained high pitch in my voice betrays the strength I was hoping to convey.

"Ohhh am I Evie? What if *you* are in breach of the restraining order I placed on you?" She flashes me a vindictive smile. "Not to mention the one that Simone will place after I explained earlier how much of a *predator* you are."

Her words strike me dumb and for a moment my worst fears of losing Simone, my husband and my children engulf my mind.

She closes the distance between us and pins both my wrists onto the arms of my chair. Her fingernails bite into my wrists and her face hovers inches from mine. She inhales slowly.

"Oh Evie, it's so nice to be close to you again."

I struggle against her hands, but she has me in a vice-like grip.

How is she so strong?

My skin breaks under her nails and a warm trickle of blood escapes down my wrist.

"Lily, you're hurting me. Please." I beg, searching her eyes for the Lily I used to know. The Lily that used to laugh so hard about the chaos of raising kids.

But that Lily is not there.

Her eyes are vacant, and I realise that the Lily I thought I knew is well and truly, long gone.

A manic laugh escapes her as she leans in and tries to kiss me.

I turn my head and say as forcefully as I can.

"NO! I don't want this."

"Yes you do, darling." She releases one wrist and deftly pulls a cable tie from a bag I didn't notice before. She skilfully cable ties the hand still secure in her fist to the arm of my chair. I struggle against her with my newly free hand and push her off balance. The bag of cable ties drops to the floor. I try to stand but I can't manoeuvre out of the room. I awkwardly twist away but the chair I'm cable tied to holds me back.

Frantically, Lily searches for something to subdue me with. I watch in horror as she grabs the nearest thing to her, an industrial sized stapler and smacks me in the face with it. A searing pain cuts across my cheek and stars dance in front of my eyes. In a daze I hear the stapler drop to the ground and I feel Lily's hand in my hair forcing me back into the seat. She sits on my legs with her back to me as she reaches for the fallen cable ties. I buck my legs trying to throw her off, but she wraps her legs around mine and pins them together with thighs of steel. Triumphantly she secures my free hand to the other arm of the chair.

She releases my legs and spins quickly to kneel on top of them so that she can face me.

"Now why did it have to come to that Evie?" She says breathing hard. "Look at your beautiful face."

She trails a hand across my cheek and I feel my blood spill from an open wound onto her hand. I realise that a protruding staple must have caught me just under my eye. Lily looks me up and down and admires me appraisingly as she pushes her legs down into my thighs. I can now feel the warm drips trickle from my cheek, to my chin, to my chest.

"That might scar." Her syrupy voice is dangerously soft.

This woman is a psychopath.

I search around my surroundings wondering how on earth I'm going to get out of this. The squeals and laughs of approximately 800 children and adults outside hum around us. I wonder if anyone would hear me if I cried for help.

"I like seeing you bound. I always hoped we'd get into a bit of BDSM Evie." She undresses me with her eyes and it makes me feel sick.

"I was so disappointed when you cut me off. Sex with you is quite the drug. I don't think you realised what you were doing when you said no to me."

I say nothing and stare at the wall. She leans down trying to kiss me again. I clench my mouth shut, jerking my head away. Lily raises her hand and strikes me hard again, searing pain explodes in my temple and there's a strange ringing in my ears, like I'm underwater in a swimming pool.

The words "Behave Evie!" filters through the fog in my brain and I wonder if I should do as she says just to get this over with. Lily pulls my tank top down, exposing my bra then leans her breasts into my face as she rummages in the draw of the desk behind us.

"Aha. Just what I was hoping to find."

Lily sits back and holds the scissors in front of me while tapping her lip with her finger. My eyes widen in fear.

Jesus, what will she do with those?

I remain completely still as I feel the sharp tip of the scissors touch the base of my neck. She trails them down my chest towards my exposed bra, then she snips the join and it pops open. She places the scissors on the table behind me and I release the breath I was holding. Lily rakes her darkened eyes over my vulnerably laid bare breasts. She moves in closer but I don't want to see anymore. I clench my eyes closed as I feel her lips and tongue flick at my nipples. I am *so* ashamed that my own body betrays me as I unwillingly respond to her touch.

"See Evie, you do want this." She murmurs up from my chest.

She continues to work relentlessly on my nipples and I realise her hands are snaking down to my denim shorts.

No. I don't want this.

With the scissors safely behind me, my eyes snap open and I buck, trying to dislodge her from my lap. The movement startles her and as she slips off me I take my chance. At the top of my lungs I scream: "NO LILY! HELP! HELP! HELP! Somebody PLEASE!"

I feel her fingernails scratch my bare thighs as she pins them down so she can re-straddle my lap. Laughing, she says "scream all you want Evie… it's just like our first time. Isn't it wonderful that no one will hear *you*?"

Her words are like ice rolling down my spine.

How did she know I would be here?

How did she know the crowd would be so loud?

It suddenly dawns on me that I am possibly... *no, probably*... not her first victim. The thought makes bile come up into my mouth and I choke it back down.

"Now I'm going to make you come, Evie, and you're going to like it. Be a good girl and let me in."

Lily tries again to unbutton my shorts and I attempt to wriggle my hips away from her grasp. She leans her weight heavily on me, her feet tuck under my knees pinning them widely apart. My top button snaps open and I close my eyes willing this to be over.

Suddenly I hear a startled gasp escape from Lily's mouth and my lap feels light as I feel her ripped off of me. I snap my eyes open to see Lily being pulled away from me, by Stacey.

Stacey struggles with Lily's arms as she tries to pin them behind her back. Lily rears and violently pushes herself back so that Stacey hits the wall behind her.

"Get the fuck off me!" Lily yells.

Stacey is stunned but she holds Lily tight.

"Steve! Help me!" Stacey calls and my husband appears in the doorway. His face pales as he sees me bleeding, exposed and strapped to the chair. The look on his face is one I'll never forget.

Fear, protectiveness, then a deep rage darkens his face all in the blink of an eye.

Steve wastes no time. He grabs Lily and his male strength is enough to hold her still. Stacey spies the bag of cable ties Lily had dropped on the floor and quickly secures her wrists behind her back.

Lily rants and resists with all her might. "You will regret this! Let me go!" Steve pushes her into a spare chair against the wall.

"You're not going anywhere." Stacey stares Lily down with so much contempt that even I shrink back in my chair. "It's over Lily. You're not getting away with this."

Stacey pulls out her phone and says "I'm so sorry Evie, but I have to do this." She snaps a few photos of me strapped to the chair, of my injuries and torn clothing. When she is done, she calls the police.

"This is Stacey Briggs. I have a situation at Clayburn Primary School. I've caught a sex offender in the act and we have her restrained. Her victim, Evie Monroe, is bound to a chair and injured. She requires medical attention."

She pauses as she listens to her instructions. I look at her, wondering how she could have known that this was happening.

Did she hear me?

Stacey nods and says "Yes. Her name is Lily Burke." Stacey puts her phone on speaker and places it on the desk beside me. I hear the female dispatch officer say "Please stay on the line. The police and an ambulance are on the way."

I look from Stacey to Steve with such relief and gratitude.

They are my heroes.

Steve continues to hold the squirming Lily in place while we wait for the police.

I can't look Lily in the eye, but I feel her eyes still on me. I sense her looking at my exposed breasts and pulled open shorts. I feel my cheeks flush and I hear her giggle at my embarrassment.

"Oh Evie, don't go all shy now. You know you liked it." She grins up at Steve, challenging him, encouraging him to lose his temper.

Anger flashes in his eyes and I see him clench his fist.

"No Steve!" Stacey puts her hand on his shoulder. "She's trying to get you to hit her so that it looks like she's the victim."

Steve scowls. "I can't believe you did this to *my wife*." His voice is low and dangerous. "I hope you rot in prison."

Lily throws her head back and laughs. "No, I'm not going to prison. I'm going to a cushy psych unit where I'll get out early when my *temporary insanity* is cured."

"I have that on record." The dispatch officer's disembodied voice calls out of Stacey's phone and for the first time I see Lily's smile falter.

In the distance I hear sirens approaching the school and I know this will all be over soon. Lily hears them too and the colour drains from her face. As the sirens get louder and closer, Lily attempts a final escape.

"Agghhhh" she stands up and shoves her shoulder into Steve's chest, throwing him off guard. She manages to escape through the open door, but she doesn't get far.

The sound of Lily fumbling with the main door floats back to us in the count out room. Suddenly she screams "HELP ME!"

I can't see what is happening from my bound position, but she must be unable to open the door with her hands cable tied behind her back.

Stacey runs after her and I hear "Stop her! She's the predator!"

The main office door is wrenched open, followed by the commanding voice of Officer Dan Jones.

"Tilly Blackmore, you are under arrest." I hear the clink of hand cuffs being applied. "We've been searching for you for three years."

Wait, did he just say Tilly Blackmore?

My mind whirrs and I wonder what that even means.

The sound of heavy booted footsteps of additional police pound on the office steps.

I hear the murmurs of a growing crowd.

Disembodied orders of 'move out of the way so the paramedics can get through' float down the hall.

Suddenly a policewoman bursts through the doorway, followed by two paramedics.

"I'm constable Murphy. Can you please wait outside and one of my colleagues will take your statement shortly." I realise she's talking to Steve who is standing by my side, reluctant to move.

"I'm her husband." He replies and stands firm.

Constable Murphy's eyes soften, but her voice remains sharp. "This is a crime scene sir, and the paramedics need space to look after your wife." Gently she adds, "please." She motions to the door and Steve squeezes my shoulder.

"I'll be right outside." He doesn't take his eyes off me until the door is closed in his face.

I'm startled slightly by the flash of a professional camera.

"Stacey's photos aren't good enough. I need to take photographs of your injuries Evie. If you're OK for just another few minutes I'll make this quick."

I lower my chin in a nod, then look away as the flash continues to assault my eyes. True to her word it only takes a moment. She snaps a few more photos of the room then she steps back and motions for the paramedics to get to work. In a daze, relief washes over me as gentle hands cut the cable ties from my wrists. A blanket is finally draped over me and I pull it tightly under my chin, grateful to have my aching wrists free and my naked breasts covered. I feel monitors being attached to my body under the blanket and lights are shined into my eyes.

Questions are fired at me:

Do I know my name?

Do I know what day it is?

Do I know what happened?

Where does it hurt the most?

I answer them as best I can. Special glue is rubbed into the gash under my eye. Saline is applied liberally to gauze pads as they clean away the blood. Gloved hands search my body for wounds to ensure nothing is missed.

My mind takes me away, the beeps from the monitor and the murmur of voices fade into the background. I close my eyes, trying to pretend that I'm not even here.

That none of this happened.

That any moment I'm going to wake up and find that this has all been just a horrible *nightmare.*

But strong hands help me to stand. In my periphery I see Constable Murphy placing the dreaded stapler, scissors, and cable ties into evidence bags. The door is opened and I'm escorted to a waiting stretcher. I am smoothly assisted onto the soft bed and blankets are tucked around me. I hear the loud snap as the side bars are pulled up to ensure my safety.

I take in my surroundings. I'm lying on a stretcher in the middle of the school reception. Police are interviewing Stacey and Steve. Lily is nowhere to be seen so I can only assume that she was escorted to a police vehicle outside. I hear the drone of the growing crowd gathered in the courtyard.

"Steve!" I suddenly call. "Where are our kids?"

He is by my side in an instant. "It's OK

Evie, they're with Hannah's teacher, Mrs Fuller."

His words do not settle me. I can't see them, and my heart anxiously races inside my chest. My body trembles and my mouth feels dry.

I think I'm going to be sick.

The monitors I'm still attached to start making unfriendly beeps and whirrs and I hear the words:

"She's going into shock."

The head of my bed is dropped flat while I feel rolled towels being shoved under my legs. All I can see is the ceiling of the reception and uniformed bodies working around me. My vision turns dark and cloudy, I know I'm about to faint. Just before my body submits me to sleep, I hear my name.

"Evie!"

I must be dreaming because it sounds like Simone.

"Evie!"

There it is again.

I feel nauseous and my head feels heavy, but I force myself up to see around the paramedics.

I can't believe my eyes.

Simone is trying to get through the door, but officer Dan blocks her way. I hear him say, "I'm sorry miss you can't go in there."

"You don't understand. I need to see Evie!"

I watch as Steve strides up to Officer Dan.

"It's alright officer. Please let her through."

Officer Dan nods and steps aside. Simone

looks at Steve gratefully and a mutual respect passes between them. Simone rushes to my side, her hand over her mouth in shock as she takes in my appearance. She takes my hand and I feel the familiar gentle circles of her thumb on the back of my hand. The sensation is so soothing that I close my eyes and the beeps return to a steady rhythm.

With my vitals stable and my near-fainting episode over, the paramedics give us some space.

"I'm so sorry Evie." I hear her whisper.

I don't open my eyes, fearing she's just an apparition.

The paramedics and Officer Dan are discussing a plan to get me to the hospital, but I hear only the odd word. I focus all my energy on the sensation of Simone's hand in mine.

Dazed and with eyes firmly shut I feel the paramedics wheel me out of the office and bump me down the steps. Shocked parents gasp and the sound of scared children murmuring questions surrounds me from all sides.

The softness of a female hand in mine is still there. I force my eye open a crack to check its Simone and not the hands of the paramedic.

There she is.

Simone, jogging beside me.

I feel a rough squeeze of my opposite hand and I look up to see Steve is right there too.

The paramedics lift the gurney into the back of the ambulance and through the buzz of over a hundred hushed conversations around me, I hear my children.

"Mummy!" They scream.

My eyes snap onto them quickly and I watch them break free from Mrs Fuller's grip. They run towards the ambulance and Simone picks up Jackson and Steve sweeps up Hannah. They bring them to me in the back of the ambulance and I hug them tight in each arm.

I cry into their hair and they cry onto my chest.

"It's OK" I whisper to them.

I kiss their tears away and through my own misty eyes I lock on Simone, then Steve.

"It's all going to be OK."

Twenty-Nine

Evie and the Visitor

Slowly my eyes open and blurrily take in the room. The décor is cream on white. A grey light shines around the edges of faded mint green curtains. The steady pitter-patter of rain beats against the glass window. A monitor beside me beeps rhythmically and the soft shuffle of comfortable shoes can be heard coming from the hallway. Bright artificial light casts a strip on the grey linoleum floor under the door to my room. On the wall above me there are tubes and medical instruments ready to be used in case of an emergency. The blankets are warm and not as scratchy as I expected. The truth of my surroundings dawns on me.

I'm in a hospital room.

My head throbs with the onslaught of the worst headache of my life. I wince as the memories of yesterday's events flow foggily to the surface of my mind.

The fight with Simone.

Lily binding me to a chair… a stapler to my face.

I reach up and gingerly touch my cheek. A soft dressing is in place and with gentle pressure, I feel stitches moving tenderly underneath. I wince.

Ouch!

I feel the need to use the facilities and I am relieved that this room has its own ensuite. Pulling myself out of bed I realise everything hurts.

I feel like I've been hit by a truck.

As I wash my hands afterwards, I glance at my reflection in the mirror. My eye and temple above the dressing is so swollen I can barely see out of it, my surrounding skin has turned an unsightly shade of purple. I cringe.

What a sight.

I dry my hands and shuffle back to the bed. My legs ache and the memory of Lily sitting on my lap rushes back.

A gentle knock on the door interrupts my unwanted thoughts and a kind looking nurse pops her head in.

"Oh good, you're awake. Would you like something to eat?"

I nod. "Please… Is there coffee?" I ask hopefully.

She laughs. "Yes, but it's not great. I'll be right back."

She disappears for a few moments. While I wait, I adjust myself on the bed. My wrists ache as I pull over the squeaky-wheeled bedside table and position it over my lap. I notice they also have dressings and some purplish bruises peeking out from the sides.

The nurse returns, placing a plastic tray holding my breakfast along with a black coffee on the table. She walks around my bed and opens the curtains, natural grey light fills the room. I recoil from the brightness and squeeze my eyes closed as my headache rises a notch.

"I didn't know how you liked it, love, but there's sugar and a little milk in the jug." She says as she motions to the tray.

"Thank you" I murmur. Looking out the window I realise I have no idea what the time is.

"Excuse me, do you know what time it is?"

She glances at her nurse's watch pinned to her uniform. "8:30 in the morning. You'll be allowed visitors from nine."

"Thanks."

"You've got a headache haven't you?"

I nod.

She departs the room swiftly and returns with a cup of water and two paracetamol tablets.

"Take these before you drink that coffee."

I take the tablets gratefully and swallow them down, finishing all the water in the cup for good measure. Satisfied, the nurse nods then offers me one last caring glance before exiting the room. I realise all the staff must have been told what happened to me.

I go about making the coffee how I like it. It tastes bad, but I need the caffeine to shake off the drug induced sleep they put me in last night. I pick at the hospital food.

It's not bad, but not great either.

I wish I had something fresh, like a piece of fruit. After a few minutes I push the food aside and just sit, sipping my coffee.

I dislike hospitals.

I see a remote next to me and I realise there's a TV on the opposite wall. Picking it up, I flick through the channels trying to find something to help me not think for a while. I settle on some reality garden landscaping show and lean back into my pillows to watch, the pain medication thankfully taking the edge off the pounding in my head. Twenty minutes into the show I hear a firm *rat-a-tat-tat* on the door.

I switch off the TV and clear my throat, nervously I say "come in."

The door swings open and Officer Dan stands there in uniform with Constable Murphy whom I remembered from yesterday.

"May we come in?" He asks as he stands awkwardly in the doorway.

I nod and they enter. I feel slightly embarrassed in my hospital gown, so I pull the covers a little higher up my chest in an effort to show a semblance of decorum.

"Good morning, Evie, how are you feeling?" Constable Murphy asks kindly as they each pull up a chair.

"Oh, you know… like I've been hit in the face with a stapler." I laugh, but it feels unnaturally hollow.

They offer sympathetic smiles.

Officer Dan continues. "We won't take up too much of your time. We just wanted to come down and tell you in person that you'll be pleased to know that Tilly Blackmore is in prison and is being held without bail."

I hold up my hand to make him pause. "Wait… who is Tilly Blackmore?"

"Lily Burke was an alias. When we ran the prints on that tracker you gave us we realised who we were dealing with. We were just creating our plan to arrest her when Stacy's call came through dispatch. Tilly has a history of sexual assault charges across multiple districts and has been eluding authorities for three years. Unfortunately, her earlier victims didn't come forward until after she had already fled the area. Now we have her, she'll go through the system and you can rest assured she'll be behind bars for a long time."

"Oh... right." I mumble, overwhelmed by the new information. Something niggles at the back of my mind.

"What happened to Willow? Where's Lily's… I mean… Tilly's husband?"

"Willow has been reunited with her father. She will be protected by the system and go through trauma counselling. Tilly was never married to Cameron Drake. He has been searching for Willow for the past three years. He is very grateful to you for speaking up and he sends his condolences for what happened."

I shake my head as the puzzle pieces lock into place. "That's why her husband was always out. He was *never* there!" The realisation strikes me as so obvious. I want to kick myself for not connecting the dots earlier.

We never made it to the bedroom.

"I knew something was off right from the beginning. I just couldn't put my finger on it." I can hear the frustration in my voice and my heart skips a beat.

Constable Murphy reaches out and holds my hand. "You couldn't have known Evie. Tilly is an intelligent, calculating and manipulative sexual predator. You're not the first to have gone through this, but if we have anything to do with it, you will be her last. You stood up Evie. You said no and you told the authorities so that we can do something about it."

She squeezes my hand and my eyes sting with tears.

"You're going to be OK Evie. We will provide you and anyone who you think needs it, with trauma counselling. You are a survivor." She smiles at me warmly.

The door to my room opens slowly and Steve stands half in the room, half out. He's holding flowers but he looks disconcerted by the presence of the police officers.

Officer Dan stands up and shakes Steve's hand. "Steve" he nods. "We were just finishing up. Murphy, come on, let's give them some privacy."

Officer Murphy stands up. "We'll be in touch Evie, but please reach out if you have any questions."

"I will." I attempt a smile, but my lips

betray me by trembling.

Steve doesn't miss a thing. He stands aside so that the officers can exit the room and as soon as the door is closed, he rushes to my side, placing the flowers on the bedside table.

"Oh Evie, look what that *bitch* has done to you." He holds my hands protectively as he searches my eyes to see how I'm really doing.

Compassion and love for me shine through his periwinkle blue eyes and I feel so blessed to have this man in my life. Tired and overwhelmed, I allow my tears to roll down my cheeks unchecked, and he embraces me tightly. I sob into his shoulder, feeling so much safer with him here.

He pulls away slightly and hands me a box of nearby tissues. I wipe at my eyes and my dripping nose gratefully.

"What did the police have to say?" Steve implores gently.

"Oh, just filling me in on Tilly's history and what happens now. Can you believe that she'd kidnapped her own daughter Steve? Her ex has been searching for Willow for three years.... What that poor man must have gone through... Poor Willow..." I break off, not knowing what else to say. As a mum, my heart swells for Willow and wish I could help in some way.

"That poor child." Steve's face is etched with concern and he stares at the bed for a moment before his gaze settles on me.

"And poor you Evie. None of this was your fault, you know that right?" He brings my hand to his lips and kisses it gently. "I should have never encouraged this..." he trails off and his gaze lowers.

I tug on his hand so that his eyes meet mine again.

"This wasn't your fault either. I got swept away in the lust of it all. I said yes to her Steve. I wish I'd never done it..."

My mind flicks to Simone and how devastated she was when she found out.

"I feel terrible about how Simone got mixed up in all of this, she must really hate me."

"She doesn't hate you, Evie. The look on her face when she saw you on that stretcher told me that."

I say nothing, staring out the window at the falling rain.

He didn't see her face in the classroom.

We sit in comfortable silence and after a while a nurse comes in to check on me. She quietly changes all my dressings, cleaning each wound in turn. It suddenly occurs to me that apart from my now dull headache, my wounds are superficial, and I could probably have the dressing changed at my local doctors.

"Umm excuse me nurse, but when can I go home? I don't need to be here, do I?" The thought of my own bed fills me with so much longing.

"You've had two decent knocks to the head, concussion symptoms can be delayed. The doctor will do another full examination, just to check nothing has been missed. Plus she wants you to meet our resident psychologist. Together they will ensure a plan is in place for when you're ready to be discharged."

"Oh… right." I feel a bit deflated.

"But she might be able to come home today?" Steve asks hopefully.

"Maybe today, but probably tomorrow." She puts the finishing touches on the last dressing. "That wound looks a little red around the edges. I'll recommend that the doctor takes a look, you might need antibiotics."

She makes some notes on a clipboard and throws all the rubbish in the bio-hazard bin. With a curt, proficient nod she departs the room.

"Another night!" I groan.

"I know Evie, but if that's what they recommend we should follow their advice… Shall I nip home and get you some more underwear and clothes? I should have thought to bring you supplies, but I thought you'd be coming home this morning."

"Thanks Steve. Let's wait and see what the doctor says. Hopefully I can go home tonight." I look out the window again. Suddenly I remember that there is a café on the ground floor near the entrance.

"Hey Steve, I'd love a real coffee."

"Say no more." He stands up and kisses me on the forehead. He opens the door to leave and a startled *"oh, hello"* piques my interest.

I look up to see Steve standing face to face with Simone. My heart flutters in my chest and

I frantically finger brush my hair.

I must look a sight!

Steve looks from Simone to me, a grin spreading across his face as he watches me attempt to groom myself. He chuckles and shakes his head.

"I'm going to get coffee, want one Simone?"

"Sure, thanks Steve. Flat white." She gives him an awkward smile as they sidestep each other to swap places in the doorway. Over Simone's shoulder I watch Steve give me a wink before he closes the door.

Simone walks over to me and instead of sitting in the vacant chair, she perches herself on the side of my bed. Her hand finds mine and the familiar circles made with her thumb soothe me, but the overwhelming guilt swirling inside propels me to make amends.

"Simone, I'm so sorry."

"Shh. Stop Evie. It's OK."

"No! It's not OK! I feel terrible for hurting you. I can't believe you're even here after what I did." Tears form in my eyes, and I look away, feeling ashamed.

"Evie, shhhh. It wasn't your fault and I'm sorry I didn't believe you. Watching Lily being led to the police car in handcuffs certainly put things into perspective… And after you left in the ambulance, Rachael and Stacey found me and we had a big chat. They told me everything they knew, and afterwards, I finally listened to your voice message."

Her eyes bore into mine, then she

impulsively pulls me into a tight hug. Her soft, clean, floral scent wafts over me as I breathe her in. This is the closest I've physically been to her in three weeks. Her proximity makes me feel giddy. Simone pulls back but doesn't let me go.

"What she did to you was unspeakable..."

Her hand reaches up and gently strokes my face. I lean my cheek into her warm hand and it feels so nice on my skin. Simone's eyes glisten, her gaze dips to my mouth as she trails her hand down to brush her thumb over my bottom lip. I reach up to hold her hand there, a fire blazing inside me as I remember the first time I did that to her. Tears well in my eyes as I kiss her palm before pulling her hand down to my side. Simone leans in closer and rests her forehead against mine, our noses touching.

"You've been through so much Evie." She whispers.

"You too." I return. "Lily had you in her clutches with those awful rumours. It drove me insanely jealous seeing her so close to you on the tennis court yesterday." I confess softly.

"You never have to be jealous Evie, there will never be another woman for me." Her words are barely audible. Her confession soaks into every pore of my existence.

"Simone, I love you." I breathe the words out and she breathes them in. I barely hear a "you too" before her lips are pressed against mine. The emotions between us dance on our lips. The intensity is intoxicating. We kiss each other like we are starved and insatiable. Our hands are in each other's hair and our faces become wet with each other's tears.

For the moment I don't care what our future does or doesn't hold. This is *real* and I lose myself in the beauty of all that this *is*.

A soft knock on the door interrupts us and Steve's friendly face pops around the door, catching us in the act; "Coffee delivery!"

Reluctantly, we separate as Steve enters the room. A wolfish grin plastered on his face. He's never actually seen me kiss another woman. I wipe my face with another tissue and offer one to Simone.

"Jesus, are you both crying? I thought kissing made you happy?!" A smirk rests on his lips as he hands us each a coffee. Simone and I laugh as we dab at our faces.

"It's been a big couple of days." Simone ventures.

"Days? It's been a big few weeks!" I chuckle as I say it, but the memories of how painful life has been without Simone still sting.

"Thanks" I murmur to Steve as I sip my latte. It's not as good as the one from the café Rachael and I visited, but it's better than the one the nurse gave me.

Simone murmurs "thanks" as well, and a silence drifts between the three of us as we quietly sip our hot drinks.

I don't know who to look at; my sweet Simone who had her delectable velvet tongue inside my mouth mere moments ago; or my amazingly cool-headed husband who just walked in on me kissing someone who wasn't *him*.

I know I should say something, but I don't know what, or where to start.

A loud knock at the door makes all three of us jump and we look up to see the doctor in the doorway.

"Ahhh yes the café coffee is better than the crap they would have given you with breakfast." She breezily beams at us.

We all offer small uncomfortable laughs and Simone stands up from the bed. I cast her a furtive glance as I don't want her to leave, then I flick my eyes to Steve who takes in my every move.

The doctor, oblivious to the small, shared glances between us all carries on like there is nothing unusual about our dynamic.

"Right, I do apologise to you both, but I need to examine Evie, then I have someone I'd like her to meet."

Steve and Simone nod and they both reach over and take turns giving my hand a squeeze.

"We'll just be in the waiting room." Steve says as he leans in to peck me on the lips.

I glance up to see if Simone has taken this exchange in, but she already has her back to us and is walking out the door. Steve follows and I watch the door shut behind them.

After a few cognitive and physical tests, the doctor is happy with my neurological responses. She is confident that my headaches and other injuries will improve in time with rest. She agreed with the nurse about antibiotic coverage and she also ordered a tetanus shot as my last booster had recently lapsed. She introduced me to the clinical psychologist, Jane, who is lovely. I'm grateful that we've set up several home appointments and check-ins over the coming weeks. She has also given me her mobile number so I can text in emergencies or if I need to reschedule.

I can go home tomorrow! One more night for concussion watch and I'll have my dressings changed in the morning. After that, my GP can take over.

I can't wait to see my children and my parents, who I know are anxiously waiting at our house for news…

Jesus…what did Steve tell them?

Thirty

Evie Comes Home

The day I came back from the hospital blew my mind. There were flowers and cards all over the kitchen table from teachers and parents. I'm sure a few of them were sent out of guilt, but nonetheless I was pleasantly surprised by all their kindness.

The kids were so wonderful and had made gorgeous drawings of me lying in bed with a plaster on my face, the words: 'get well soon mummy' scrawled above. It's the little hearts that always get me. The way they're slightly misshapen with disproportionate sides. The way the colour is slightly outside the lines. I can picture their little looks of concentration as they would have done it. Jackson pokes his tongue out when he concentrates. I'm waiting for the day in which he accidentally bites that tongue of his. Hannah gets the cutest little furrow between her eyebrows when she draws.

It's so good to be *home.*

My parents were appalled that I'd been assaulted. They couldn't understand why another mum would do that, let alone hit me with a stapler… I probably should have given them more of the back story, but I just didn't want to deal with their condescension… or give them a heart attack from *impropriety*. They *still* don't know that I like women as well as men.

Maybe when things settle down a bit, I might be brave enough to finally tell them.

Three weeks have now passed and I am relieved that my headaches and concussion symptoms are finally gone. My days are a little different, but life is moving along. I'm getting used to talking to the psychologist. I see her twice a week and she's helping me get through a few things. Steve is being amazingly understanding. I've shut up shop so the only action he's getting is the odd kiss, and they're not the hot and heavy ones he's used to. We both know this will take a little bit of time.

I talk to Simone every day, but I only see her for fleeting visits. My mum has been visiting me daily and I get the impression Simone feels awkward in her presence. Mainly because I haven't told her about our special friendship. I thought I'd get tired of my mother being at my house every day, but I'm quietly relieved. She has inadvertently become a welcome buffer as I'm not ready to be completely alone with Simone just yet. I still don't know what that means but I'm putting it into the same camp as my newfound reluctance to leave my house. My psychologist keeps reminding me that it will take time for me to regain my confidence in myself and the world again. I asked her about my new fear of intimacy in our last session. She said it's a normal response and we're working through it.

One good thing is that I no longer need dressing changes and the stitches were removed last week. Nearly a third of my face is still bruised, but it has progressed to a sickly green-purple blotchy-blend. I can see the doctor did a great job of stitching me back together, there will definitely be a scar, but it will be thin. Once the redness is gone, I should be able to reduce its appearance with some form of miracle oil or moisturiser.

Work has been so supportive too. I don't have to go back for another week as they gave me a month off. They said I can work from home as long as I feel I need to. It's so nice to not have the pressure of facing colleagues with a black eye.

Rachael pops in every few days with a real coffee for me and a treat from the bakery. It's amazing to have a good friend who can take my mind off things for a bit.

Friday has rolled around again, the third one since that awful day and the kids are finally asleep for the night. Steve and I are having a lovely glass of wine on the couch and I'm scrolling through Netflix. My app has been getting a serious hammering as I prefer to stay indoors like a hermit while my face heals. Another hour of escapism and absent-mindedness is just what I need. I suggest a few titles to Steve, but he's not really interested. I look up to see him lost in thought.

"Steve? Are you OK?"

"Hmm?" He responds non-committal.

"Do you want to pick tonight?" I offer. He's been pretty good at watching all my choices lately, maybe it really is his turn to choose.

"No, no you pick something you want. I was just thinking…"

Alarm bells ring inside me and I'm suddenly very anxious.

"What about Steve? You're making me nervous."

"Oh no it's nothing bad. I just don't know when a good time would be."

Now I'm really confused.

"A good time for what?"

"Well, I know you talk to Simone every day… and I was just wondering if the three of us should go out for dinner… you know to talk about things…"

"Oh… umm what are you wanting to achieve from a dinner with the three of us?" I shift in my seat awkwardly. I know Simone and I are talking, but I'm not up for anything more right now and if Steve is itching for a threesome, it's really *too soon.*

"Evie, I love you and I know you love me. We have a wonderful life together… but I've seen how you are with Simone. I know you love her too and if a special friendship with Simone is going to continue, we all need to talk and get onto the same page. Discover expectations… set some boundaries… parameters etc."

Oh.

My heart swells for the man in front of me. I don't think I could have won a better husband lottery. In all honesty, I do wonder what Simone's expectations are.

"That's not a bad idea Steve. But are you sure you really want to open up our marriage? Would you truly be happy sharing me?"

"Well, we don't know what Simone wants either. So, let's be adults and talk about it… over a nice dinner with expensive wine." A toothy grin swathes his face.

He makes it sound so logical, so *normal.*

"OK. Let's do this." I return his smile and open my chat app. I punch out a quick message to Simone.

'Hi Simone, how are you? Just wondering if you would like to go out for dinner with Steve and I?'

The three dots cycle for a moment then Simone sends a quick reply.

'Sounds great. When? I won't have Katie tomorrow night if that works?'

"She wants to go out tomorrow night as Katie will be with Jonathan. Is that too soon?" I look into Steve's eyes, nervousness etched on my face.

"Tomorrow works for me, but does that work for you? If it's too soon, we can postpone." He reaches over and squeezes my knee.

I love how thoughtful he is.

Is this too soon?

I reach up and touch my face. It's still bumpy, and sensitive to touch but a bit of concealer might help. Then another question strikes me.

Am I ready to know what Simone truly wants?

Cogs crank over in my head and the answer resonates in my mind.

Yes, and I pray she wants the same as me.

I nod at Steve and punch out my reply.

'Yes, tomorrow night is great. 7pm? I'll make a reservation at that little French restaurant in town.'

'Perfect, see you then. Xx'

I love how Simone ends her messages with kisses. I find it fascinating that two little markings can stir so much sentiment and cause me to melt inside.

"7pm at La Maison D'Or. Would you mind booking?" I ask Steve.

"No problem." He replies as he stands up and heads to the kitchen to make the call.

I send one last message to Simone.

'Really looking forward to seeing you. xx'

I turn Netflix back on and scroll again for a TV show. I settle for something light that I've already seen as I know I won't be able to concentrate.

I'll be seeing Simone tomorrow, *without* kids in tow.

My heart and body hum with the thought of another opportunity to be close to her, even if it will be in public.... with Steve. I feel a familiar pull below my navel, something that I haven't felt since before that awful day three weeks ago. The sensation gives me hope that I will have great sex again one day…

Not this week.

But I might be willing to try soon, to see how it feels.

Steve returns with cups of tea to replace our wine as he settles on the couch next to me.

"Dinner is booked and my parents can watch the kids."

I take the tea and smile gratefully. "Thanks Steve, you're wonderful."

"I know." He grins.

Thirty-One

Evie and the Dinner Date

Saturday is filled with anticipation for the dinner date with Simone. It feels a little different, knowing that the three of us will be sharing a meal. I play out the scenarios in my mind for how the conversations might go. Then change them repeatedly to see how I'd feel if the outcomes were different.

I don't know why I'm torturing myself to be honest. The closer we get to departure time, I've come full circle and just want to see Simone and take things from there.

Steve's mum is putting the kids to bed and I'm deliberating over my chosen outfit. Even though I know there will be no sex tonight, I've chosen a racy bra and panty set. I want to test myself to see if I can feel sexy again. I catch a glimpse of the scar and bruise on my cheek in the mirror.

They do not make me feel like myself.

I focus on shimmying into an 'above the knee' floral print dress. It's feminine and secretly I hope Simone will like it. The weather has been warmer and I look forward to the full heat of summer when it arrives in another month or so. I don't normally wear a full face of make-up, but tonight I reach for my foundation. I work on applying it lightly and I'm pleased that it actually covers the bruise as well as the little spots either side of the thin line. You can still see the scar, but I arrange my hair so it covers part of that side of my face. With the addition of eye shadow and mascara, I am satisfied with the result.

Exiting the bathroom I find Steve buttoning up a crisp pale blue shirt in our bedroom. It has a faint embossed pinstripe, and it accentuates his muscular frame. I watch him tuck it into his slacks, doing up his zip and belt. Again, I feel a stirring inside me as I eye up his crotch.

Well, at least my body is recovering.

I sidle up to him and wrap my arms around his waist, a question burning in my mind.

"Steve, what do *you* want to get out of tonight?" I raise my eyebrow in curiosity.

"I want to keep my wife happy."

His eyes smoulder into mine and he leans down and kisses me tenderly, albeit briefly. As he pulls away, I find myself lingering with my mouth upturned to his.

"Come on, let's go." He wears a saucy smile, knowing he's left me wanting.

I pop into each kid's bedroom and kiss my children. Hannah is bouncing around her room, happy that her Nana is here. I get the briefest of hugs and a "byeeee" from her, but saying goodnight to Jackson is emotionally challenging. In the calm of his room, he wraps his arms around me and holds me tight.

"Don't go mummy, what if you get hurt again?" My heart swells and my eyes sting. My children have been through this just as much as I have.

"No one is going to hurt me again Jackson, I promise you that. Plus, I have your amazing Daddy to protect me." Jackson squeezes me again, then reluctantly lets go. I kiss his forehead and murmur "I love you".

Steve and I drive in silence to La Maison D'Or but the anticipation makes me nervous. I fidget with my dress and check my make-up repeatedly. Steve reaches over and brings my restless hand to his lips.

"Everything is going to be fine." He soothes.

Pulling into the carpark, my heart increases speed. I feel slightly light-headed and start to wonder if this is all *too soon*.

Taking a deep breath with Steve squeezing my hand for support, we walk into the restaurant.

Steve talks to the maître-d and I scan the restaurant with my eyes. It's just as I remember. Soft lighting and private velvet booths with privacy screens in between each set. There are beautiful fleur-de-lis on the walls and every edge, every detail is painted a brilliant gold.

The maître-d leads us to a small U-shaped booth in the corner where I find my Simone. She stands to greet me, wearing a gorgeous navy V-neck dress. She hugs me tight and a soft kiss is brushed over my cheek. She nods to Steve and gestures for me to climb into the booth and take the seat at the back. Simone and Steve sit either side of me and suddenly, I feel like I've been put in the corner like Baby from Dirty Dancing.

We're handed wine menus to peruse but I already know what I'd like. I put the menu down.

"I'll have the Loire Valley chardonnay please" I ask politely.

"I'll have what she's having." Simone nods in my direction.

"A bottle for the table please… and I'll have the Chablis." Steve smiles at us, then up at the maître-d as she takes our orders. She excuses herself to give us time to read the menu.

I feel nervous sitting here between Steve and Simone, it still feels awkward having them in the same room together. As I fidget with my napkin on my lap, a soft hand slinks its way into mine *under* the table. Simone flashes me a stunning smile.

Returning her smile, I glance at Steve who is surprisingly relaxed. He reaches over and takes my other hand that is resting, in plain sight *on top* of the table. My heart thrashes in my chest as I feel both my loves' hands in mine.

Elegant wine glasses are placed in front of us, and the wine is poured. Our bottle is left on the table.

Steve raises his glass to make a toast and we follow suit.

"To good friendships and great loves." He wears a wolfish grin, but his eyes are sincere.

I remove my hand from his and we all clink our glasses and sip.

Damn this wine is good.

We peruse the menus for a moment, deciding what's good and whether we should share appetizers.

The maître-d returns and Steve orders for the table. We will start with chicken parfait and le pain du jour. Then he relays our mains choices.

I beam appreciation at his ability to take control in these situations, he makes me feel loved that he knows what I like. After the maître-d departs I glance from Simone to Steve, wondering if I should be the one to start the conversation.

Simone cuts into my thoughts.

"How are you, Evie?" Simone's eyes are shining with concern and she gives my hand a squeeze under the table.

"I'm getting there. One day at a time." I squeeze her hand back and trace a small circle with my thumb as I like to do.

Steve clears his throat.

"Ladies, it's so lovely to see the two of you together."

Simone and I smile coquettishly at each

other, eyebrows raised awaiting Steve to lead the conversation that we know we're all here for.

"This is why we're having dinner. I don't want there to be any awkwardness between the three of us."

Simone and I nod in agreement.

"So, let's get everything onto the table shall we. How are we going to move forward together? I am very much in love with Evie and I want to support her in every way I can. I do not want our family dynamic to change, but I... we..." Steve takes my hand. "Wanted to know how you feel Simone. Do you think you could be alright with sharing her with me?"

Simone looks from me to Steve, I can see the thoughts racing behind her eyes.

"Well... Steve... to be honest, I didn't know what to expect from tonight. I might need some more information. Are you suggesting we become a thrupple? Because I need to be honest Steve, you don't really do it for me."

I watch Steve's face as he takes the rebuke. The light behind his eyes flickers but he wears a serene smile which soothes the hammering in my chest.

"That's completely OK Simone. What I hoped to achieve from tonight is to discover everyone's ideal and see if we can set some clear boundaries so we're all on the same page."

Simone lets out a whoosh of air. "Thank

goodness for that Steve! I thought you were itching for a threesome!"

Steve shrugs. "Well… I'd be lying if I said the thought hadn't crossed my mind." He flashes a cheeky grin. "But I'm a gentleman, I will never expect either of you to do anything you don't want to. I believe in consent."

"Good, because that's not going to happen." Simone's voice is firm, but I notice a sparkle of amusement in her eye.

"The thought of the two of you together is enough for me." He looks from me to Simone with a sexy look in his eye. "…and maybe you'd let me watch sometime?"

His question hangs in the air and none of us speak for a moment.

Too soon Steve.

I send the thought through my eyes which he catches and puts his hands up to placate.

"Again, consent, I'm a gentleman."

Turning to Simone I take the plunge. "So, what do *you* want Simone? This is not a conventional relationship. Do you want to keep seeing me? Have sleep overs? Would you be OK having me only part-time? …Or is this all too hard? Tell me if you want to call it and… we'll just remain friends."

The thought of never being intimate with Simone again makes my heart feel heavy, but I need her to know that there are options. I am not going to pressure her into anything she doesn't want.

Simone furrows her brow as she considers my questions. She takes my hand above the table. It's symbolic as this is the first time she has ever held my hand in view of others. It feels so significant that my heart flutters as she speaks directly to me. Steve and the hum of the restaurant fades into the background as I focus on her every word and facial expression.

"I would have preferred it to be just us… but then it never would really be, would it? We both have children, and I don't want to uproot either of our families. We have responsibilities, mortgages… but do I want to keep seeing you? Do I want you to sleep over again?" Her eyes flutter down demurely for just a moment, then flick up to smoulder into mine. "Well, the answer is… *yes* Evie, *I do*."

A content, soft sigh escapes me. I can't break eye contact with her. So much emotion flows between us unspoken as she strokes my hand in plain sight.

From my left I hear Steve roar enthusiastically, "this is great!"

The ice breaks between the three of us as we all laugh at his fervour. I feel myself sag comfortably into my seat and I sip my wine again. Simone folds her arms across her chest, she leans forward towards Steve and for the first time I see the business side of her.

It's quite sexy.

"Right Steve, so how does this work? Do we have set weekends? Do we tell our kids?" She pauses a moment then casts me a sideways grin. "It's like Evie's our time-share…"

I suddenly feel apprehensive sitting here

like I'm not part of the conversation. I realise I'm not in the driver's seat and it feels odd. Simone doesn't miss a beat and a wrinkle of concern appears between her eyebrows as she realises that she may be objectifying me.

"Are you OK with that?" she asks me earnestly.

Am I OK with that?

I look from Simone to Steve and I can't think of a better solution.

"Yes, I am definitely OK with that."

I raise my glass in a toast, "To love and new adventures!"

Epilogue

The sounds of waves crashing on the shore rouse me from my peaceful slumber. The tent is still dark, but I can hear the first twitters of native birds as they start to welcome the morning. It's early, but the air is warm with the promise of another spectacular summer's day. Quietly, I climb out from under our blankets, doing my best to not make the air mattress squeak as I shift my weight. Steve stirs and gives me a sleepy "hey". I lean back over the camp bed and kiss him tenderly.

"Are you alright with the kids for an hour?"

"Of course." He gives me a knowing smile.

Unzipping the door of our tent compartment, I hear the buzz of another zip opposite me. I smile sleepily as Simone steps into the main room to greet me, a couple of towels tucked under her arm.

As quietly as we can, we unzip the main door and head outside. The sky is brightening on the horizon but there are still stars above us. The air is balmy and the ocean smells fresh. I can't wait to lay my eyes on it. Simone and I walk hand in hand with our fingers entwined, along the deserted road.

The houses and holiday sections come to an end and a large park reserve stretches out before us with a winding concrete path. We follow it towards a thicket of trees, content in each other's company, not needing to speak. The hard concrete soon turns into a refreshing mixture of cool sand and earth beneath our bare feet. Beautiful summer flowering trees now frame the path and embrace us with their subtle morning scent.

"Mmm. I love the smell of frangipani in the morning." Simone sighs beside me.

I snuggle into her as we turn the final corner into the small private bay. Large rocks flank us on both sides and ancient trees with their gnarled and twisted trunks cling to their crags. Their branches dancing upwards to find the sun from their secluded space. The tide is high and there's only a small crescent of white sand before it fades under the blue sea. I scan the bay with my eyes, searching every tree and outcrop of rocks. There's not another soul in sight. Satisfied, I pull my top quickly up and over my head and drop my shorts and panties onto the sand.

"Last one in's a rotten egg!" I call gleefully as I run towards the water.

My hair bounces on my back and water splashes up my legs as I hit the sea. It's colder than expected and I slow down, suddenly unsure if I can dive in as quickly as I thought I would. I pause for just a moment as I stand thigh deep in the cold water.

"Ahhhhhhh" Simone hysterically yells as she tackles me.

We both fall hard into the sea, a tangle of naked bodies. I suck air into my lungs before the icy water swallows me, then jump up quickly to escape from the chill that presses in on all sides. Panting, Simone grabs my arm as she hoists herself back up out of the water.

"Jesus it's cold!" She laughs between breaths.

I rest my hands on my knees joining in the laughter from our sudden plunge. Salt is in my hair and cool water drips down my back. I pull Simone to me and hug her for warmth.

"You know the best treatment for hypothermia is to cuddle naked right?" I raise one eyebrow and grin up at her.

Simone's lips twitch into a lopsided grin. Our breasts press against each other and Simone's gaze darkens. A fire glows in her deep brown eyes, showing me her want, her *need* for me.

I'll never grow tired of her looking at me like that.

She leans down and claims me with a kiss. We mould into each other, our tongues in sync, dancing rhythmically. I hear more birds join the dawn chorus, their voices announcing that the sun will be rising soon. I pull back slightly, tugging Simone further out, our bodies now adjusted to the cool temperature.

The water swishes in ripples around us and feels delicious against my skin as we bob in the calm sea. Glistening droplets drip down Simone's neck and they call to me. Mesmerised, I entwine my fingers in her wet hair as she tilts her chin to the sky. I place feathery kisses along her jaw until a contented moan escapes her lips. A familiar pull dances below my navel as the sound spurs me on. My spare hand wraps around her waist pulling her close, creating a delectable friction between our bodies.

Simone's hands devour my body as she strokes every inch of skin she can find. I feel her push away from me slightly, our breasts causing a hilarious sucking sound as our bodies' part in the water. We giggle heartily and our mirth sounds loud against the calm of the bay.

Our eyes lock again as our laughter subsides. Simone gently tucks a stray lock of wet hair behind my ear.

"I love you, Evie."

"I love you too."

Without another word we collide into another passionate kiss. The intensity of our kisses feels as natural as breathing. We are each other's oxygen; nothing could ever douse these flames between us.

Simone nibbles at my lower lip with her teeth as she runs her hand down my body. She scrapes her fingers over my thighs with the most delicious pressure that I can't help but space my feet wider in the sand below, inviting her closer.

Our kisses turn frantic as she circles her fingertips around to squeeze my bum. I know she's making me wait just a little and it leaves me so hot under the collar. I wonder if I could warm the bay with the heat radiating from between my legs.

She breaks the kiss and bends her head to my chest, paying exquisite attention to my breasts as her fingers finally snake between my thighs. She strokes the outside of my folds tantalisingly slow. All this build up makes me impatient, so I cup her hand with mine and guide her fingers inside me. Her gasp mirrors mine as she realises just how ready I am.

I will always be ready for her.

The thought surprises me, but as it crosses my mind, I know it to be true. My eyes close to savour the delectable sensation of her hand moving deftly underneath mine, my cold fingers on hers adding to the rapturous sensation.

Our breasts bump against each other and I clutch her to me with my spare hand. She knows I'm close, so she does the move she knows I love. I splay my fingers over hers, stroking my inner thighs while she pushes me over the edge. She circles my clit so expertly as my pleasure swells beneath our entwined touch. Suddenly, she nips my neck and I am temporarily blinded by the lightening hot release. I slump into her as I pulse underneath our hands, my forehead resting on her shoulder.

While I catch my breath and wait for my heart to stop pounding in my chest, Simone kisses my forehead tenderly. She gently spins me around and hugs me from behind, her hard nipples deliciously pressing into my back.

"Look. The sun's coming up." She murmurs as she nuzzles my neck.

I watch as the bright orange ball crests over the horizon. Its' golden V of light sends a myriad of sparkling diamonds across the rippling water towards us.

It's magical.

The water dances around us as we hold each other in the glow. Through my back I feel Simone's heart beating rhythmically, her hands resting on my hips.

I could stay like this forever.

But we don't have all day.

Turning, I slowly walk Simone towards the shore until her thighs are above sea level. As the sun rises, it casts her glistening skin in gold. Her eyes bore into mine and I note a shiver run through her. I run my hands up and down her body, warming her with my touch. Slowly, I trail kisses between her breasts, over her navel and down to the apex of her thighs. Kneeling in the water, my bare back is warmed by the rising sun.

I lay gentle kisses on her skin as I edge closer to her sacred spot. My hands reach around, softly squeezing, as I pull her hips towards me. Darting my tongue inside, I taste her heady cocktail of sea salt and musk. Simone gently shifts her weight, allowing me in. I enjoy every taste, every flick as her excitement intensifies underneath my agile caresses. Voraciously I pleasure her while my fingers trace along her entrance beneath my chin. Her desire burns hot on my fingertips before she tightens around me, drawing me in. Her hips tilt upwards as I work my magic, her moans low and rolling.

I know she is close.

I glance up to take in the scenery.

Simone stands gilded, her head tilted back, eyes closed, and lips parted as if she is drinking in the glorious peach sky.

Smiling, I return to my task. With closed eyes, I sync my mouth and hands in a rhythmic symphony of delight. Simone's breathing quickens and her body stiffens under my lips. Her orgasm explodes around me, her sanctified knot throbbing on my tongue as she lets out the most exquisite sound of rapturous pleasure. Holding my mouth and hand in place while she rides the waves, I peek up to witness her exquisite carnal abandon.

This is my Simone, her beautiful body arched towards the sun, completely lost in the moment, with *me*.

For Drew

Taken before your time.
Like a lotus flower, you were beautiful inside and out. Underneath each petal was another glowing aspect of your soul.

When we met I was still healing from a head injury. Learning new things was increasingly difficult but your enthusiastic, infectious encouragement helped me to achieve finishing this book.

I dedicate my first pubished novel to you, Drew.

Without your consistent support and unwavering belief in me, this story would be just three pages. Thank-you for seeing my potential and for helping me realise it.

Your final words to me were:
"Goodnight you amazing author!"

Thank-you.
You will be forever in my heart.

Trigger Warnings

This story touches on the following topics that some readers may find disturbing:

- Dubious / non consent
- Assault
- Sexual non-concordance
- Stalker behaviour
- Manipulation
- Gossip / Social ostracism
- Explicit language

If any of these topics invoke trauma, or you realise you are in a similar situation in real life, please seek help from the police, your regional victim support groups and a professional therapist.

Never be afraid to ask for help.

All my love,
E.P. Stuart

www.ingramcontent.com/pod-product-compliance
Ingram Content Group UK Ltd.
Pitfield, Milton Keynes, MK11 3LW, UK
UKHW012251290726
14090UKWH00016B/594

9 781067 020408